PARKER

RODNEY WETZEL

ARCHWAY
PUBLISHING

Archway Publishing books may be ordered
through booksellers or by contacting:

Archway Publishing
1663 Liberty Drive
Bloomington, IN 47403
www.archwaypublishing.com
844-669-3957

ISBN: 978-1-4808-9484-6 (sc)
ISBN: 978-1-4808-9485-3 (e)

Library of Congress Control Number: 2020916057

Print information available on the last page.

Archway Publishing rev. date: 09/16/2020

For my kids: Judi, Jesse, and Betty.
You make my life complete.

PART ONE

CHAPTER I

COLD AS HELL

December 9th, 1998

At the end of what she considered the perfect day, Shannon White drove her little blue Volkswagen Bug down the narrow back streets on her way home. In another twenty minutes, she would be telling her mother and father the good news. Mike Shelly had finally done it, asked her to marry him, and she had said yes. She knew her parents would be very pleased; they thought the world of Mike and they had known his family for years. As for his parents, she knew that they would be very overjoyed indeed. They treasured Shannon, of that she was certain. Even Mike's sister was closer to her than she ever was to him. It was the perfect fit.

Just wait until mom sees this rock, Shannon thought, holding up her hand for another look. He had a good job, but still; this must have set him back a lot of coinage. After waiting for so long for him to pop the question, Shannon started questioning if he was truly in love with her. After all, they had been together for five years now and never once had he brought up the subject of marriage. At one point, she even thought of ending the relationship. But that, she knew, was nothing more than a brief flash of insecurity. She knew he was the man for her; she loved him with every inch of her being.

As the snow started picking up, she turned up her wipers. She hoped she would make it home before it got too bad. She loved her V.W. Beetle, but it was not the best in snow, even with the sandbags her father placed in her trunk. Her dad had tried to talk her into a truck last winter, telling her that it would be safer, but she refused. It was a long way to the town where she worked, and she could barely afford gas for the Bug as it was, let alone a pickup. Maybe after she and Mike were married awhile, she would think about a new ride. But for now, the bug would have to do.

She would wear her mother's wedding dress and, of course, her grandmother's saltwater pearls. The bridesmaid dresses would be her favorite color, light pink, and nothing too outlandish, something they could wear more than once. For her bouquet, she wanted beautiful white roses with angel's breath. She had it all worked out.

As Shannon was coming over a slight hill, a white object appeared out of nowhere, just to the side of the road. She struck it at full speed, never getting the chance to brake before impact. Shannon heard a loud thud as the car struck whatever it was. Then came the feeling of the front tire as it lifted and fell. Whatever was in the road she had hit, she had managed to run over it as well. Quickly she applied the brake, but her small car started to swerve. She was able to steer successfully against the slides until she came to a complete stop along the side of the road. Her heart was beating so hard and so fast that she thought it would burst. *What the hell just happened?* She thought, while trying desperately to calm herself down. Whatever it was that she hit, it succeeded in taking out her front passenger side headlight. Only the driver's side light now shown in the darkness.

"Shit!" she yelled and hit her hands on the steering wheel. This was not how this day was supposed to end. Her first thought was a deer, and she had been fortunate in that department. Almost everyone in her family had hit one at some point. Still, in that momentary flash of the headlights before impact, the object seemed far too small for a deer. Shannon turned and looked back up the road, the red glow of her tail lights reaching all the way to the crest of the hill. The figure lying along the roadside resembled that of a little child. Now, terror filled her whole being. *Had she just killed someone's kid?* she thought. With a burst of adrenaline, she flew out of her car into the bitter night air and started to run back up the hill to where the child laid. The figure did not move, just lying there with its face turned in the opposite direction. It was a girl clad only in a white night dress, no shoes, no hat, no coat. Shannon had been along this road a million times. There were few, if any, houses along this stretch of road. That is why she always came this way. There was no traffic at all.

A million thoughts were racing through Shannon's mind as she rushed forward. *Why would a little girl be dressed like that on such a cold night? Why would she be walking along the road?* And most important: *Was she still alive? Did I just kill an innocent little girl?* Shannon dropped to her knees when she reached the girl. Then, with a deep breath, she ever so gently turned her over to see her face. She was as cold as ice to the touch.

Shannon jumped back as she gazed down at the form in front of her. Even in the limited light, she could see this child had been dead for some time. Her face was not blue with cold but greenish brown from some bizarre form of decomposition. Shannon's mind was now in overload. *Had someone thrown a dead body at her car?*

That is when the little girl opened her eyes and sat straight up, glaring out into the darkness. Shannon froze, fear immersing her to the point she could not move. Every instinct was telling her to run, but she couldn't move a muscle. Gradually, the girl turned her gaze towards Shannon, her long-deceased eyes fixed on hers. Then the adolescent gave Shannon a very unnerving grin. That's when

Shannon felt a hand reach for her from behind and grab her by the throat.

*

Sheriff Malcom Wiseman of Phelton, Michigan walked into his office and stomped the snow off his boots. Ice had formed on his bushy mustache and oversized eyebrows. Elma, his wife and only office staff, greeted him with a smile as he ambled through the front door. He didn't know how much longer he was going to be able to deal with this frigid weather. He was past retirement age, and both he and Elma had talked for years about pulling up stakes and finding a nice little piece of land in Arizona. Malcom's only son, Luke, who was also his longest- serving deputy, would make a great sheriff, even if he was far too liberal for Malcom. If he did retire, he recognized that the town would be in good hands.

"Mr. and Mrs. White are in your office. I put them in there because it's warmer than sitting in the breezeway," said Elma, pointing to the two folding chairs next to the front door. This was their unofficial waiting area. The front of the office consisted of a very small room with two chairs and a front counter. "I put the space heater on."

"Did they say what they wanted?" asked Malcom, putting his coat and hat on the standing coat rack behind the counter.

"No, just that they had to see you," responded

Elma, moving her petite, thin body from behind the counter. "I'll bring in your coffee."

"We got any of those donuts left?"

"No, Luke finished those off last night. But there are still some of those bite-sized banana bread muffins you like."

To the left of the counter was a steel door going to the back of the office. Down a narrow hall there were two offices off to the right, before opening to a large break area in the back. This back room also held the only cell for detaining individuals, and a bathroom. Malcom halted in the doorway and leaned in to give Elma a kiss.

"Now I know why I keep you."

"Old man, you got it wrong. I am the one who keeps you," said Elma as the door closed between them.

Malcom marched down the small hallway to the second door. This was his office, a little bigger than the first one, but still a tight fit when there were more than a couple of people in the room. Most of his time was spent at the kitchen table in the break room, where Elma would leave his coffee and muffins.

"Sheriff," said David White, rising to shake Malcom's hand. "Sorry to bother you so early in the morning."

Malcom could feel the tension in the man's voice and in the trembling grip of his hand. "David," he replied, and then looked over at his wife sitting in front of his desk. Malcom observed she was still in a pair of bedroom slippers, and her nightgown was visible below her full-length coat. "Cindy, so glad to see you both. What brings you down here on such a bitter morning?"

"It's our daughter, Shannon, she never came home last night," said David, still standing.

"David, please have a seat and let's talk about this," said Malcom, pointing to the chair next to Cindy. While David was in the process of taking his seat, Malcom made his way around the desk.

"She still driving all that way up to Jonesville for work?"

"Yes, but she was not coming from work. She was meeting her boyfriend at eight for dinner," said Cindy.

"We called her boyfriend first thing this morning. He said she left the restaurant about nine thirty," added David.

"What restaurant?" asked Malcom.

"Some pizza place in Hillsdale," said Cindy, "Mike drove up there to meet her after he got off work..." She turned her head and started to sob.

"Look, Sheriff, I know we sound a little paranoid. But it is not like Shannon to just not come home, no phone call, nothing," said David.

"No, no, believe me. I don't think you are at all paranoid. I would be beside myself as well. By Mike, I presume you mean Mike Shelly," asked Malcom

"Yes, sir," said David.

"Did he say anything about any other stops she mentioned making before she came home?"

"No, Mike said she was in a hurry to get home and tell us something important," responded David, rubbing the palms of his hands together.

"And what was that?"

"He told us he had proposed to her, and she said yes," said Cindy, who was now openly weeping. "There is no way she would not have come home to tell us that, no way."

After giving Cindy ample time to compose herself, Malcom continued.

"Ok, well, I will drive some of those roads up that way. We can't file a missing persons report for twenty-four hours, but at least I can start looking. If she happens to turn up," he said while standing up. "And let's hope she does sooner than later. Just give me a call. She still drives that little German car?"

"Yes, a blue Volkswagen," said David, rising once again to shake Malcom's hand.

"Thank you, Sheriff, I can't tell you what this means to us," said Cindy. She held back tears as she and David left the room.

Malcom followed them out of his office and turned right into the break room. There was his coffee and muffins waiting for him, along with his morning paper. Elma, after escorting the Whites out of the front door, returned to the break room and poured herself a cup of coffee. She took a seat on the opposite side of the table.

"White girl is missing, "said Malcom, looking up from his paper.

"Shannon? When?"

Malcom grabbed his coffee, ignoring the muffins. "Yea, seems she never came home last night."

"Oh, she is such a sweetheart, I hope she is ok," responded a now-concerned Elma.

"I'm sure she's fine, but can you call that son of yours and tell him I need him here this morning? I want him to take a drive with me," said Malcom.

"Funny, usually he's only my son when you're pissed at him."

"Yea, well, I haven't made up my mind yet this morning if I like him or not."

"Malcom, you are so full of stuff, your eyes are brown." With that, Elma got up and walked toward the front of the building carrying her coffee. "You love him as much as I do, you mean old son of a B."

Malcom just smiled.

*

Just as Malcom was stomping off his boots in Phelton, Captain Hazel Cowan of the Jackson Police Department was walking into her office. In front of her were three men. Sam Helmen, the medical examiner, and her chief detective Vinnie Moretti, both sat in chairs by her front door. Standing on the opposite wall was Professor Franky Lake. As she entered, Vinnie and Sam stood and started clamoring about why they were there.

"No, no, no, I want you both to be quiet. I love you both dearly, but I will send you out of this office in a heartbeat if it comes to it," said Hazel. She took off her coat and put it over the back of the chair behind her desk. Then, she glanced directly at Franky. "I only want you to speak., I have a few questions I want answered before we go any further. I know your friend, Parker, is missing. I saw the missing persons report some time ago."

Slowly, she took her seat behind the desk and leaned in closer to Franky. "Am I right in presuming you are requesting assistance to locate him?"

"Look...," started Vinnie.

"Stop," said Hazel, turning to Vinnie. "If you want this meeting to happen... then shut it." Then, turning back to Franky, she continued, "Am I correct in my assumption?" Hazel could see the anxiety in Franky's eyes, but he did not hesitate.

"Yes, that's correct. We have tried everything we know and have not uncovered even a clue." He looked Hazel directly in the eyes.

Hazel leaned back in her chair, putting her cupped hands behind her head. "I am open to helping you. But first, I want answers. And this time the truth, and nothing but the truth. Do I make myself clear, Professor Lake?"

"Now, wait a minute, Franky. You...," said Sam, getting to his feet.

"No, no. It's ok, Sam," said Franky, motioning for Sam to sit. "If she is going to help, she needs to know everything."

Hazel, still leaned back in her chair, took a good long look at Franky. He wasn't a boy anymore. In truth, she was only a few years older than he was, but to her, he had always been the wise-ass college kid who knew how to avoid her questions about the murder of her mentor, Captain Kip Gillmore. She knew in her heart she had never gotten the truth out of him about that night. After a brief pause, she asked in a well-controlled tone. "Did you see the murder of Kip Gillmore?"

Once again Sam raised to his feet, but before he could say a word, Franky waved him off and answered. "Yes."

"Who killed him?" asked Hazel, again trying to remain as calm as she possibly could. She had not expected his honest response.

"Not who," said Franky, leaning in on her desk, "but what. Kip died trying to put an end to something unnatural that was terrorizing Parksville."

"And what was it that was terrorizing Parksville, Mr. Lake?" asked Hazel, almost sarcastically.

Franky looked at Sam and Vinnie for a second for reassurance, but both looked shocked he had gone this far so quickly. Turning back to Hazel he blurted, "A witch. A witch by the name of Fritz. He killed the priest, my mother, my cousin, the girl I was in love with, and yes, he killed Kip. I saw him choke him to death in front of my eyes. Phillip tried to help him, but he couldn't stop it."

Franky now looked down at his shoes, avoiding Hazel's glare.

"If that was the case, why did you lie about it for all these years?" asked Hazel, in disbelief

Franky now squatted down so that he was face-to-face with Hazel. "Look, it's not easy knowing the truth and not being able to tell it. Sam and Vinnie have told me a little about your encounter with the supernatural. Did you tell everything you knew when all was said and done?"

Hazel saw Vinnie and Sam glance at each other. She knew that they had talked, something they had sworn they would not do. But instead of being angry she felt a sense of liberation, knowing they were not the only ones to endure forces beyond their control.

"Yes, I know what you mean Professor Lake. I think we have a lot in common and I would like to hear the whole story when there is time. Maybe I can tell you mine someday as well; you might find it fascinating." Throwing a scowl in the direction of Sam and Vinnie, she continued. "At least the parts that have not been told already."

Both men diverted their eyes from Hazel.

"I would like nothing more," said Franky. "I have been praying that you would help us. We have investigators looking but we can't really tell them what we are looking for, other than two people who went missing in Florida." Then Franky looked away, overtaken with emotion. Hazel could see tears welling up in his eyes.

"I'm not even sure what we are looking for."

"How can we help you, Mr. Lake?" asked Hazel.

"Well, I would like you, Sam, and Vinnie to come to my house tonight for dinner. There, we can fill all of you in on everything that's happened. I have a friend flying in from L.A. this morning who can collaborate my story."

After a few moments, Hazel smacked her hands on the top of her desk.

"Fine," she said, standing to shake Franky's hand, "just give these two goons the details and I will be there."

Both Vinnie and Sam got up as well.

"Hold on, I'm not done with you two yet," said Hazel.

Franky simply grinned, gave them both a sympathy look, and left the room.

*

As Malcom was consuming his morning coffee, waiting for his son to arrive, and Hazel chewed off Sam's and Vinnie's ears, Marge McMurphy was showing up for work at The Wooden Spoon, next-door to the Sheriff's office. She was running late, sure that her new boss would not be impressed. The small restaurant's patriarch, Barbara Townsend, had passed away just over a month ago. Now, her new boss was a snot-nosed thirty-something grandson from Pontiac. Barbara had left the restaurant and the upstairs apartment to him in her will. Wouldn't you know that would be the morning she lost power and her electric alarm clock never rang.

As she walked in, she was stunned to see the changes the young man had made. The restaurant looked brighter; he had put a new coat of paint on all the walls. All the tables had nice new tablecloths made of real fabric, and all the tables were preset with plates, silverware, and real cloth napkins. All the old pictures of the town that were spread out through the restaurant were now hung neatly on one wall in a time collage. The portrait of his grandmother that once hung over her fireplace now occupied the uncluttered wall to the left of the front door, with a beautifully decorated two-foot Christmas tree setting on the floor beneath.

"Marge, is that you?" came a voice from the kitchen.

Shit, thought Marge, *he will be all over me for being an hour late on his first day, and this is the new grand opening.*

"Yea, sorry I'm late."

"No problem, I heard half the town lost power last night. It's that damn wind."

With that Howard Townsend came strolling through the double doors of the kitchen wiping his hands on his apron.

"Well the grand opening could be better; we haven't had a soul in here yet."

Marge walked past him and put her things in

the seat of the last booth. "There will be; everyone in town will want to check you out. I'd better get the coffee going."

"No need, I ran two pots when I came in, then remade them when no one showed up. Can't serve old coffee on my first day."

He turned and walked back into the kitchen. "I wrote the specials on the white board. Would you be kind enough to put it by the door, on that tripod?"

Marge glanced up above the dining room counter and, sure enough, the white board was not there. But a new one sat on the countertop all made out. *He wants it by the door when they walk in... It will take a while for our regulars to get used to that,* she thought.

"The menus are new, too. You might want to give them a look over," said Howard.

This is what she feared most. The specials looked okay, but what did he change on the menus? Placing the white board on the tripod, she walked over and grabbed a menu. They were indeed new, done in bright colors and laminated, of all things, but the food and prices were the same as they always were. Marge let out a sigh of relief. The locals would not be happy if he had come in and changed everything.

Coming out of the kitchen, Howard sat down at the counter. "My grandmother loved this place; I hope I make her proud."

Marge walked over and sat next to him. "Your grandmother was one of the best people I ever knew. It broke her heart when your dad moved away and took you away from her."

Just then, the bell on the front door rang and in came Dale Harris, the town's official undesirable. He drank too often, washed too little, and never left a tip.

"Dale, what can I get you?" asked Marge, getting to her feet.

"Coffee and toast," said Dale, not bothering to even look up. "Don't forget the extra jelly."

"Damn it, Dale, you order the same thing every morning. Why not shake it up a little and order an egg to go with your toast?" said Marge, only half joking.

"Nope, just the toast, buttered."

Marge smiled and sauntered back to give the order to Howard, who had already moved back into the kitchen. "Your first big order," she said with a grin.

"If this keeps up, I will need to franchise," he replied.

Dale had inadvertently unlocked the floodgates, as the small diner was at capacity for the rest of the morning. Marge had not seen it this busy in years. Every time she cleaned a table, someone new would occupy it. She was worried at first that Howard would have a tough time keeping up, but she had never seen food come from the kitchen that fast, and without mistake. Not one order did she have to send back.

She was glad when the dishwasher, Joey Carson, showed up for his shift at eleven. It wasn't until after the lunch crowd left that she eventually got a chance to sit down. The diner, open for breakfast and lunch only, closed at two-thirty in the afternoon. That gave her a half hour to fill her jellies, sugar containers, salt and pepper shakers, and arrange the tables for tomorrow's guests. Still, she needed a few moments off her feet. Howard and Joey were busy cleaning in the kitchen. Marge thought they would be in there for quite some time, but to her amazement, Howard came out and sat at the counter next to her.

"Joey, come out here and have a seat for a few!" Howard yelled back at the kitchen. "Good kid; works hard," he added in Marge's direction.

"Yea, you did a good job picking that one," said Marge. The old dishwasher they had was now off to college in Indiana.

"Yea, I wish I could give him more hours. You hungry? You never got a chance to eat." he asked.

"Sure, but I will fix something when I get done with my prep-work," she responded, just as Joey walked in.

"All the dishes are caught up and I bleached the screens above the grill like you said," relayed Joey taking a seat. "I will sweep out here after we close."

"No honey; that's part of my job. And here are a few dollars for bussing and setting my tables when you got a chance. That means a lot," said Marge, pulling out her tips and giving a ten spot to Joey.

Howard got up. "I am going to fix all of us a cheeseburger and chili fries."

"That sounds great," said Joey.

"Works for me," confirmed Marge.

Just as Howard made his way to the kitchen, the bell on the front door rang. Marge turned to see Elma Wiseman coming through the front door. "Marge, it looks great in here."

"Yea, he did a great job getting it ready didn't he?" asked Marge

"I love it," said Elma. She took a seat at the counter. "I came for a to-go order for Helen. She is still in a bad way and you know she can't cook anything for herself. I will be glad when that damn arm of hers heals. Can I get a cup of soup and a nice BLT? I know she will eat that. I will bring her supper later tonight, I got Mondays and Tuesdays. Tomorrow Ms. Hastings is going to feed her."

"Sure thing, I will put the order in right now, "she said, getting up, "Man, we were packed today."

The bell rang again. It was Dale coming back for lunch.

"I want a bowl of chili," ordered Dale before he made it halfway to the counter.

"Damn it, Dale! Do you have to bark your order at me? Just sit down and I will help you in a second," sighed Marge, putting in Elma's order.

*

As Franky Lake pulled up to the terminal at Detroit Metro, he saw Shawn standing with his luggage on the curb. He was blowing desperately into his hands for warmth. Dressed only in a light jacket, without gloves or a hat, it was obvious to Franky that Shawn had no sense of how unsympathetic December in Michigan could be. As soon as Shawn recognized that the car approaching was Franky, he made a mad dash for the car, hurriedly threw his luggage in the back seat, and hopped in the passenger seat.

"Fuck, it's cold. I think my balls are in my stomach."

"And you are thinking about taking the job in New York?" asked Franky with a huge grin painted on his face. You know it's just as cold there."

"I already took the job. Now, will you turn up the fucking heat so I can feel my fingers again?"

"Really, you got it?" That's great!" exclaimed Franky, reaching over to turn up the heat to full blast. "Did you tell your parents yet?"

Shawn, still rubbing his hands together, looked over at Franky and gave him a shit-eating grin.

"What did they say?" continued Franky.

"My dad said I was a fool and my mother could have cared less."

"So, pretty much what you thought."

"Pretty much," responded Shawn, "So I gave them both a big wet kiss and told them I loved them and would see them soon. You would have thought I just rubbed acid on their cheeks the way they pulled away."

Franky started to chuckle. "Well good for you. Being the bigger man."

"Have you heard from Benjamin or Josette lately? Are they coming for the holidays?"

"No, talked to Benjamin last night. He and Josette are still planning on going to the Banthom House before they come."

"Too bad. Hopefully I am here long enough to see them. What about Ethel and Brandy?" queried Shawn.

Franky's face showed a hint of disappointment, "No, they can't make it either. Mrs. Cartwright said that she and Ethel had to go to New Orleans. Something about Ethel's family."

"Man, too bad. I was so looking forward to seeing them as well. So, I guess it's just the two of us."

"Well," said Franky, pulling out of the airport, "I hate to spring this on you at the last minute, but we are having dinner guests tonight."

*

Malcom and Luke were finishing up their extensive day of searching for Shannon White. They had driven every road they could think of, from Hillsdale to Phelton, that she may have used to get home. Conversation had stuck to sports, hunting, and police work. They both knew better than to touch politics, the news, or religion. Malcom personally felt that Bill Clinton was the spawn of Satan, leading the county to total and utter destruction. Luke, on the other hand, was a borderline socialist who was convinced the only problem the country had was the growing separation between the haves and have-nots. After having a few too many beers one late Saturday afternoon, the two had had a heated argument at the dining room table. But it was Elma with the final word, telling them both they were not allowed to discuss politics in front of her. Since that day, they avoided any subject that would lead to a political debate.

They were just ten miles from the White's house on a seldom-used country backroad when Luke exclaimed, "There, up there! Off to the right!"

"Shit," cried Malcom, pulling the Sheriff's truck to a stop. There on the side of the road was a blue VW Bug. Its driver's-side door was open. Luke, standing six foot five inches and topping off at a hearty, muscular two-twenty, jumped out of the truck and ran up to the vehicle. Malcom, not as young or limber, took his time. The road was slick, and he knew that a fall would put him out of commission for a long time.

"No sign of her in the car. Her purse is still in the front seat and the key is in the ignition," offered Luke.

"Yep, and just enough snow fell last night so you can't see which way she headed off. Try the key and see if the little bastard starts."

"I doubt it. The lights were left on."

Malcom walked up and examined the back seat, then popped the trunk. Nothing. There did not appear to Malcom to be any signs of a struggle.

"There's some damage to the front; she might have hit a deer or something," said Luke, coming around to the side door where his father stood.

"We will need to walk the perimeter and see if we can pick up her trail. As cold as it was last night, she may have started walking and, well…"

"Ok Dad, I will start canvasing the perimeter. You go back to the truck and call Mom. We might need a few more bodies on this. I mean, if she did get lost and, you know, then that would be a lot of ground to cover. Especially not knowing which way she headed."

"Well, before we call in a search party, we need to finish following this road. If she took off, chances are, she took the road. No one in their right mind would be walking through open fields in this weather. You start looking, I will come back for you. If neither of us finds anything, then we will call your mom. She will need to call the Whites and give them an update."

"They are going to lose their minds," said Luke sympathetically.

"You better pull down your face mask. It's colder than shit and it will take me awhile to get back."

"Ok, Dad. God, I hope she is alright."

"Well, let's just hope the right people picked her up and she's okay," said Malcom, climbing into his Ford Ranger. As he looked on, Luke made his way around the car, searching for clues to the young girl's direction. He knew it would not be

easy. There was just enough snow to cover the
ground, but the wind last night had been brutal.
If the snow had been deeper, deeper footprints
would have been left, easier to track. But with
the little snow they had, it would be damn near
impossible. Still, if anyone would find the track it
would be Luke; the boy was part bloodhound.

*

Vinnie was the first to arrive for dinner. He was
wearing the same clothes from earlier in the
day, so Franky figured he came straight from
the station. Franky had grown close to Vinnie
at the YMCA, where they both worked out.
Though Franky preferred the pool and Vinnie the
basketball courts, both ended their nights with a
run. They had many-a-long conversation while on
the elevated indoor track that encircled the main
gym. From there, they would both walk down to
the locker room where their lockers were in the
same row, shower, get dressed, and walk together
to their cars. Franky recalled how it became their
"thing." And they'd agreed that when the other did
not show on the track at the end of the day, the run
was canceled. It didn't seem right to either one of
them to run alone.

"How are you holding up?" asked Vinnie at the
front door "You ready for a meeting with Hazel?"

"I know I said too much this morning, but
damn it. I just want to find Phillip and Mary,"

replied Franky. "I have a terrible feeling that they may be suffering, and that just drives me nuts. Maybe they are both dead, who knows. But I need answers."

"I know you do, and I'm glad you laid it all on the line with Hazel. She is a good person, Franky, and she has a heart of gold. It's just, well, up until our little run-in with the devil child, she had always seen things black and white. Now she is a little more open, if you know what I mean."

"Trust me, I know you couldn't have convinced me that witches and demons existed, not until I seen it myself," said Franky

Just then, Shawn came bounding out of the bathroom, with nothing on but a towel around his waist and a giant smile. "Sorry, I didn't know we had company yet. Let me throw on some threads and I will be right out to meet you."

"Why, is the dinner formal?" joked Vinnie.

Shawn smiled and walked into the spare bedroom. "I want to make a good first impression and not expose my shortcomings," he yelled back over his shoulder, just before closing the door.

"I like him already," said Vinnie

"Shawn is a great guy. When we tell our whole story, I hope that Hazel will offer some help," responded Franky. "But enough about that. How have you been? It's been awhile."

"Well, I still go to the Y at least three times a week. I missed it when you stopped coming."

"Sorry, man, I miss it as well. Maybe when this

is all said and done, some normalcy will come back into my life. I spend all my non-working hours looking for answers."

"Have you found any yet?" asked Vinnie.

"None that I like."

"Well, now you have some help looking," said Vinnie, just as Shawn was making his way back into the living room. "Well the naked man comes forth in casual attire."

Shawn reached out his hand. "You must be Vinnie. Franky has told me a lot about you."

"Well I hope he didn't tell you everything," said Vinnie, giving Franky a questioning look

Just as Shawn and Vinnie finished introducing themselves, Sam showed up at the front door. As Franky opened it to let him in, he noticed Sam had taken the time to shower and change clothes, but he still looked like he was ready for a day in the office. *Typical Sam*, thought Franky.

"Is this where the party's at?" sneered Sam holding up a bottle of wine as he walked through the door.

*

With all the excitement of putting together volunteers to search for the White girl, Elma had almost forgotten about taking supper to Helen. The old woman had fallen and broken her arm in two places the week prior, and the church was taking turns providing her with meals.

Poor old woman is probably starving, thought Elma. She rummaged through her refrigerator for leftovers. *Meatloaf from last Sunday's dinner would have to do*, she thought, grabbing the leftover green beans to complete the meal. She would microwave the plate at Helen's house. Elma didn't have anything to keep it warm in the cold night air.

As she left her house, she took the turn to the right, down Main Street towards Helen's house. She had always loved seeing the streetlights with their lit Christmas lights and wired forms of wreaths, stockings, and Santas. *Thank goodness she lived so close*, thought Elma. Thoughts of the missing White girl weighed heavy on her mind as she strolled the ice-covered sidewalk. Malcom was beside himself when he called. They had found the car, but no Shannon. He had told her he had driven all the way to the White's house with not a single sign of the girl. Luke had done a search near the car and turned up nothing. The group of volunteers would start their search in the morning. There were a total of twenty men and woman who responded to Elma's request.

The toughest part, of course, was her call to Cindy and David. Elma could barely understand their words as they wept openly into the other end of the phone. She could sense the distress and panic in their voices. All she understood, for certain, is they were going to meet the volunteers near Shannon's deserted car at first light.

At the front door of Helen's house, Elma rang

the bell. Usually Helen was there in a heartbeat, but this time she did not come to the door. Elma rang the bell again. Then, knowing Helen never locked her door, she simply walked in. The television was on in the living room, but there were no other lights on in the house. It seemed eerie, as if something had changed. It didn't seem right somehow. Helen was not in her recliner or any other chair in the living room.

"Helen, you in the bathroom?" yelled Elma in that direction. "I got your dinner here. Sorry I am so late. I'll warm it up in your kitchen, is that ok?"

No response came from the bathroom or anywhere else in the house.

"Helen, you here?" yelled Elma. Her first thought was that Helen had fallen again and couldn't answer. Elma put the dinner plate on the kitchen table, then headed upstairs to the bedrooms. The upstairs was completely dark when Elma reached the top of the steps. Being the wife of a police officer for so long, she knew better than to investigate on her own, but she was so afraid of Helen laying on the floor somewhere, needing help, that she pushed the idea out of her head. Turning on the hall light, she cautiously advanced room to room, but still there was no Helen.

"Her car was in the driveway," said Elma to the open air. Her concern for Helen grew as she crept back down the steps and started searching the back porch, the laundry room, and the dining room. Elma finally came to the realization that

Helen was gone. She was not laying somewhere suffering, but that did not ease Elma's troubled mind. Elma knew Helen never left the house after dark, even when she was in top form. Something was just not right.

*

The dinner with Franky Lake was nothing like Hazel had imagined. Besides setting a formal dining room table, he had served homemade beef tips and noodles with a brown gravy that was to die for. Even though he was a single man living alone, the house was spotless, even with the addition of a guest staying there.

The story that he and his house guest, Shawn, had communicated was astonishing... the things that they had seen, the evil they had faced. The part about hunting and killing flesh- eating witches made her cringe. Sam was there to confirm much of the Fritz story and the stranger, Shawn, filled her in with Banthom. There was no doubt in her mind that what they said took place, just as they said it did. Her heart sank when they wrapped up their tale with the disappearance of Mary and Phillip. *She had been so rough on Phillip for so long. If only she knew the truth years ago*, she thought to herself. But, like Franky explained, she wouldn't have believed then. Only now, after being shaken to the very core, would she have believed such an outlandish claim.

It was Vinnie who insisted they tell their own tale of terror as a show of good faith. After all, it took a lot of courage for the other two men to spill their guts the way they did. It seemed funny to Hazel that, as she told the tale of Bobby and Richie, she could not help but think that they would never believe it, even after the others had relayed the most bizarre story she had ever heard. But both men listened intently, clinging on her every word. They seemed to believe every occurrence she related without even a moment's hesitation.

The one thing that Hazel had not counted on, at all, was her new attraction to Franky. He was so sweet, so understanding of Hazel's questions about the death of her good friend, Kip Gilmore. He took great pains to inform her over and over again that Kip's death was swift and painless, even reaching over and taking her hand when he talked about it. Hazel felt bad about her continued questioning, even when he talked about the death of Franky's mother. She did not mean anything bad; it was just in her nature to find answers. Even when the guy had been close to tears, she did not know how to comfort him. To have gone through so much and still have his shit together was more than inspiring to her. She felt something intense stirring in her, something she had never felt with any man. *You fool, what man would want a pregnant woman,* she thought. *Besides, this is not the time or place for a new romance. It's only been a couple of months since you saw your baby's father explode in your living room, for goodness' sake.*

One thing she did know with some certainty was there was a battle imminent. Franky's fight against evil was not concluded. Hazel only hoped that it would happen somewhere other than Jackson, or even Parksville, for that matter.

*

Mickey Harris knew all the back trails from the Cadet Bar to home like the back of his hand. It was a long way from Concord to Pulaski by snowmobile, but he had made this trip a million times. The roads were clear of snow, so he knew the trails were his only option. He was drunk, horny, and very cranky. Instead of hooking up with Vickey Smothers, an easy blow job after a few drinks, he spent half of his paycheck on some college girl from Parksville University. Beer after beer, shot after shot, she poured down her pretty little throat, shaking her nice firm tits in his face. An hour before closing, she left with some other guy while Mickey was taking a dump in the bathroom. *Stupid cunt played me like a violin*, he thought. *Got me all excited, got me to spend my money, and had no intention of putting out. Bitch.*

As he approached the other side of Concord's only golf course, which, of course, was off limits to snowmobilers, and about to enter the woods on the other side, he noticed something odd. An enormous mass seemed to be stirring just beyond the tree line. To Mickey, it seemed far too big for a dog or cat, maybe even too big for a deer.

"Fuck me! What the hell is that?" he said aloud. Instead of proceeding forward, he stopped and waited. He was not sure what was out there, but he didn't like it.

After what seemed to be hours, Mickey started off slowly, staring deep into the forest, waiting for another glimpse of whatever it was. *Screw this, I will just follow the tree line to the road*, thought Mickey. But it was not to be. From behind him, he heard something enormous approaching on a dead run. It circled him in the darkness, its huge feet slapping the ground as it advanced. Mickey didn't take the time to turn to look. He gunned his sled and headed towards the woods. Seeing the trail ahead of him, Mickey knew it was mostly straight for the first half-mile or so before the terrain turned into huge hills with sharp turns. He knew if he didn't lose it by then, whatever it was, it would surely outrun him. He felt the first blow just as he approached the tree line. The snowmobile soared in one direction and Mickey the other. His sled collided with a big elm tree with a loud crash of bending metal and splintering wood. Mickey, on the other hand, landed on the edge of the ninth fairway. As he hit the ground, he tumbled, stopping face down in the snow. Before he could even raise his head, he felt the next blow that sent his helmet sailing. His ears rung, but not loud enough to cover the sound of the creature's breath... it was on top of him. It had to be a fucking bear. Even though bears were unheard of in these parts, he knew there was no other explanation. Mickey put his head down and covered it with both hands, like he'd once heard his Uncle Louie explain. Louie lived out in Montana and talked about playing dead when a bear attacked. He never thought it was true, but what other option did he have? As he laid there, he could hear the monster circle him, gauging him. Fear took over, his thoughts were no longer clear, and the ringing in his ears was relentless.

Then it came, the third and final blow. His decapitated head rolled across the frozen ground and stopped by his sled, and for a second, he saw the beast feasting on his now-headless body.

*

Tom Phillips made his way around the back of the Wilson house. He was afraid he would be late for his nightly viewing. He quickly did a three-sixty, making sure he was not seen before hopping the back fence. Sneaking to the very far side of the backyard, he pulled out his binoculars and nonchalantly took his seat on the steps of the Wilson's shed. Debbie Wilson worked second shift every night and returned home just before midnight. From his vantage point he could see directly into her bedroom window. Every night she would come in, undress, and head to her bathroom for her nightly shower. About ten to fifteen minutes later she would appear in the window once more, where she would drop her towel and put on the flannel nightgown laid out on her bed.

Tom had been making this trip every Monday through Friday for the past month and would continue to sit and watch undetected as long as she was willing to put on the show. Her husband Brad worked third shift, leaving just before Debbie's arrival home. He wasn't scared of that pussy, anyway. The man worked as a nurse for piss sake! And as far as Tom knew, the man did no hunting or fishing, didn't work on his own car, and never once came to the bar for a beer with the boys. No, that sissy didn't scare him, but Malcom did. When Malcom caught him in the boy's bathroom standing on the back of the toilet in the furthest stall, looking through the vent into the girls' locker room at the high school, Malcom made it very clear that the next time he would be behind bars, and for a very long time. The vent was closed off after that; otherwise it would have been just a matter of time before Tom went back. Then the Wilsons moved in and it was not by accident that Tom found his new obsession. He watched the house for months, watching the couple's daily routine. Finally, he got up the nerve and sneaked into their backyard, only to see Debbie's young, flawless breasts pointing at him from her bedroom window. He had never seen tits so rounded and firm, with pink little nips stiff enough to cut glass. The next night, he got to witness her bare ass as she bent over to retrieve her panties from the bottom drawer, and the next night she turned just enough to expose her well-trimmed bush. It was like hitting a home run at every turn to bat.

As he sat waiting for the bedroom light to come on, Tom took out one of the beers he had stashed in his pocket and popped it open. The show only lasted a half hour, at most, but it was enough time for a couple of beers and a chew.

CHAPTER II

BANTHOM REVISITED

Josette pulled up to the Burk Estate in the limousine that Benjamin had sent to fetch from the airport. She was astonished at the Christmas decorations illuminating the main house. In every window a candle was lit, showing the way home to those who had left for foreign shores. The house was outlined in white twinkly lights, from the very tip top of the roof and across the house to ground level. In between, every window and doorway completely encircled with the same display. It was quite beautiful despite the out-of-place Neptune fountain that stood in the middle of the circular driveway. Here, Benjamin and his staff had placed a red Santa cap on the Roman god's head and encircled him with even more twinkling white lights. *Benjamin does have his own weird sense of humor,* though Josette.

As the car neared the front door, Josette could see Benjamin standing there, a large smile overwhelming his face. He came running out to meet the car, even before it had come to a complete stop. Following close behind him came a young man dressed conservatively in a waistcoat, grey-striped trousers, and a white shirt with a black tie.

"Josette, I am so glad you are here," said Benjamin, opening her car door. Reaching in to grab her hand, Josette caught Benjamin gazing at her stomach. "You are so big."

"That's the surprise I wanted to tell you about," she said, lifting herself up out of the car. "Twins! Twin boys to be exact."

"Wow, twins! That's awesome," exclaimed Benjamin. "Carl, get Ms. Bradley's luggage out of the car and take it to her room, please."

"Right away, sir," said Carl, strolling around to the back of the car.

They walked hand-in-hand into the house. Josette, amazed by the outdoor decorations, was even more taken aback by the inside. From every banister wrapped in ivy, to the beautifully ornamented oversized Christmas tree that stood twelve feet in the middle of the foyer, the house was the embodiment of the holiday season. This, coupled with staff darting throughout the house, gave Josette the impression she was in the wrong place. Last time she had been here, it was far less welcoming. There had been no staff and all the happiness had seemed to be drained from its very walls. Now, the house resembled something out of a Christmas time fairytale.

"Are you hungry?" asked Benjamin. "I know it's too early for dinner, but I could have the chef prepare something for you," he said.

Josette just looked at him and offered a smile. "What, just because I am pregnant you think I'm always hungry?"

"Yes, that's exactly what I think," chuckled Benjamin.

"Well, I would hate to disappoint," sighed Josette.

"Great, I will have something set up in the dining room."

"Oh no, please, I will just sit in the kitchen. I don't want to sit at that long table all alone."

"Fine, I will have the cook fix us something and we can get caught up," said Benjamin, walking toward the kitchen.

"Angela, will you show Ms. Barley to her room so that she can freshen up a bit?"

Suddenly, a hefty woman in a white apron appeared from the kitchen. "Right this way, please," she said gleefully and headed towards the stairs. "We have your room all ready."

*

Father Arno Kumalo was glad for the chance to get out of Rome, even though this trip was anything but a vacation. He had hoped his next trip would have been back to South Africa since he had not seen his family in a such long time, but when the bishop sent a message telling him to travel to

Dublin, he made his plans accordingly. It was not until Cardinal Vanzetti met with him in private, just before his departure, that he had learned the true nature of his trip. Father Arno was one of the Church's top authorities on ancient and medieval folklore, with an emphasis on demonology and witchcraft. When Vanzetti told him a guardian of the Church was in need of assistance to investigate an issue of some importance, he was, at first, very hesitant. *Another wild goose chase*, he had thought to himself. Then, when the Cardinal got to the part about it being a Burk seeking help, the same Burk that had returned two of the Grand Grimoires, Father Arno became elated. From the moment the books arrived, he had become obsessed with learning more about them. They were, of course, safe behind lock-and-key, but Arno had been given access for the purpose of praying over and blessing the books daily to keep their power contained.

Looking out the window of the plane, he felt both excited to be back in the field and, to be totally honest, a little frightened. He had encountered many cultures that had their own beliefs about the Grand Grimoires, each different, but each agreeing on a single point: No one needed to have *that* kind of power. Even when doing his routine blessings of the books, he could feel their darkness, their desire to be used, and their longing for the devastation that would follow.

"Attention, passengers, we are preparing for our descent into Dublin," came a voice over the intercom. "Please make sure all your seats have been returned to their upright positions and..."

Father Arno paid no attention to the announcement; his thoughts were on the Banthom House and what they might find there. According to Vanzetti, the witch, Banthom not only had possession of one of the books, but may have also used it. *If a stone has been thrown in the lake, there would be ripples,* he thought. *There was no way the book had been used without dangerous consequences.* Still, he knew his part in this adventure was minimal. A couple of days and he would be back on the plane to Rome.

*

Josette waddled into the kitchen and Benjamin could not help but notice her radiance. *It's true what they say about pregnant women,* he thought as she made her way to the table. No sooner had she taken her seat, the chef arrived with a large bowl of stew and soda bread. Placing it on the table in front of her, Josette gave the chef a smile and nodded her head.

"Please give us some privacy, Lori. We will give you a yell when we are done," said Benjamin.

"Yes Mr. Burk," the chef said. She nodded in return and left the room, closing the kitchen door behind her.

"You look absolutely lovely, my dear," said Benjamin, turning to Josette.

"Yea right," responded Josette, eyeing her stew, "This looks wonderful. I'm starving, eating for three here."

"No, I mean it. Your face is glowing."

Josette took the napkin from the table, placed it in her lap, then looked up at Benjamin, blushing, "Thank you, Ben."

Benjamin took a moment and collected his thoughts. He wasn't sure how Josette was going to respond to what he had to say next. "I asked Rome for help with our situation and they're sending someone to meet us at the Banthom House in the morning."

Josette looked back, puzzled. "By Rome, do you mean the Vatican? You know people in the Vatican?"

"Well," started Benjamin, not knowing exactly how to respond, "Let's just say I have some friends there."

"Well, thank God!" exclaimed Josette, attacking the stew, "The thoughts of going back into the house gives me the creeps. I don't care if you did have it cleansed; houses have history and that one, I fear, has the worst kind."

Benjamin had never thought about anything still being tied to the house, but was now glad he had asked the Church for help deciphering whatever the paper parchment might contain. If something malicious remained, at least they would have a priest to intervene. Since the day Josette had disclosed the presence of a hidden scroll in the

Banthom House to the group in Tampa, and that it would aid them in their quest to find Phillip and Mary, Benjamin had given a lot of thought about what it may contain. He figured that, whatever it was, would not be in English. After all, Banthom was really the gypsy Gunari Danior. The script could be in some form of Romani, Latin, or even some obscure Germanic language long forgotten.

Looking up from her stew Josette asked, "Do you know who they are sending? Not that a good COE girl like me would have a clue."

"COE?" questioned Benjamin.

"Church of England, dear Ben."

Ben smiled, "I have no idea; they did not say. Only that he was a priest with a strong background in this kind of thing, and that he would be meeting us at the house in the morning."

Josette soaked up the remainder of her soup using the soda bread. "The answer has to be in that house. Kip told me, and he is the only spirit guide I have ever had that I trust so completely. He wouldn't lie to me."

Benjamin offered yet another smile. "I am sure he is right, otherwise I wouldn't have called in my favor with the Church. Have you spoken to him lately?"

This time, Josette put down her spoon and bread. Avoiding Benjamin's gaze, she said timidly, "No, not for a long time. I am afraid that his time in this plane has come to an end. Once you pass over it is hard to come back into this world. It takes a lot of will to punch a hole to enter, and even more will to stay. I feel it's safe to say I will not be getting any more visits from him. The last thing he told me was there is a staunch darkness encircling Phillip and Mary, and that he could not see beyond it. He doesn't know any more than we do at this point."

Benjamin felt that, for the first time since they met, Josette was holding something back. He had never known her to look away in a conversation. If there was a reason why she was not telling everything she knew, there must be a damn good reason. Instead of pressing further, he merely gave her a smile and words of encouragement.

"That's okay, I am sure we will find the answers we need in the morning."

"Do you miss her?" asked Josette, keeping her eyes down on her bowl. "I know for me it's been unbearable. The first few weeks when I returned home, I did nothing but cry."

"I miss them both," replied Benjamin.

"Yes, but I know you were falling in love with Mary. I could tell by the way you lit up whenever she was in the room."

Benjamin hung his head to avoid eye contact.

"Yes, I was in love with her, as you were with Phillip." Not another word was spoken as they finished their meal. Benjamin could not help but think what life would have been like with Mary at his side. She was so full of life. And even though she would have denied it, she desired someone to love as much as he did.

The chef returned and retrieved their bowls and cutlery. "Now that you finished your meal, I would very much like it if you would join me in the dungeon. We still have so much to catch up on."

"The dungeon?" questioned Josette.

"Trust me, it's changed a little since you were here last," said Benjamin with a smirk. He assisted her from her chair and walked to the door leading to the dungeon.

As they made their way down the stairs Josette questioned, "Doesn't this place still bother you? I mean, after all you went through down here and…"

Benjamin's motion sensor turned on the light. The room was engulfed in a fluorescent glow. "I made a few changes," he said. "All the torture devices I donated to the National Museum of Ireland, right here in Dublin. I can tell you they were more than overjoyed to receive them, and I even more elated to be rid of them."

Gone were the stone walls, which were now covered in drywall and natural wood. Every corner had racks filled with expensive bottles of wine. The old cells were now made over to look like nothing more than extra wine storage.

"Wow! You turned your medieval dungeon into a fucking wine cellar! Now that's what I call class," said Josette in disbelief. "I mean, talk about night and day."

"Yes, I love it. I feel like I washed away a lot of bad memories. Not just mine, but that of generations of Burks. You like?"

"Are you kidding? I love it. I could tell from the moment I walked through the front door of this house that the climate had changed. It feels more like home, safe and comforting. I think this change had a lot to do with that."

"I do, too," agreed Benjamin. "When I first returned from Florida I went back to my flat in the city, but it just didn't seem right. I was letting that bastard Banthom win, so I came home and decided to get all that shit out of here. I know I gave away a fortune in antiques, but it was worth it. The moment those torture devices were out of this house, it felt like home again."

"The problem with keeping items from days gone by is they often keep an imprint, a memory of sorts. God only knows if they were used, but if they were, think of the suffering surrounding them. I mean, can you imagine the pain they would have caused?"

Josette shivered.

"Well, they're gone now. Thank goodness."

Josette smiled and rubbed Benjamin's back.

"You made the right choice, Ben. Besides, they belong in a museum, not in some personal collection. People need to be reminded of their past, so they don't make the same mistakes again."

"Trust me, having a cage on my head and sharing that cage with an immensely starved rat woke me up. It's hard to believe one man could do that to another, but they did. And Banthom did, on me."

The night that he was held captive raced before him with the force of a locomotive. He remembered every detail as if it was yesterday. He could still feel Banthom touching his skin, the vulgar smell of the creature circling him, and, most of all, the rat tearing at his ear. If it had not been for Phillip, Josette, and Franky, there was little doubt more torture would have followed. Then, a horrifying thought came to him. "Do you think he tortured them? Phillip and Mary, I mean?"

Josette gave him a long embrace. "I don't know, and I don't want to know. I just want to find them and bring them home," she said at last. She let him go, and with tears forming in her eyes, gave him one more pat on the shoulder and walked back toward the stairs.

Benjamin stood there for a moment lost in thought, then turned and followed.

*

Josette was just starting to fall asleep when she heard the soft sound of footsteps at the foot of her bed. At first, she was a little disoriented with waking up somewhere other than her own bedroom. Getting her wits about her, she looked in the direction of the sound. There, standing at the foot of her bed, stood a girl not more than ten. She was covered in dried blood, from her matted hair to her once-white nightgown. Her left cheek had been ripped from her face, bone and muscle exposed in the dim light. Josette knew anyone else waking up to such a vision would have went screaming to the door, but this was not the worst Josette had encountered in the middle of the night. For years, she had dealt with the departed seeking her assistance, each carrying their own open wounds that resulted in their death.

"Can I help you, dear?" Josette offered softly.

The little girl had deep, murky, sunken eyes that clashed with the paleness of her face. She did not utter a word as she sauntered around the oversized bed. Silent as the grave, she moved until she was standing inches away from Josette. It was apparent by her attire that, whoever she was, her death had been ancient history.

"Why are you here?" asked Josette, pulling herself up so she was sitting straight. "Are you looking for me to help you cross over?

The child stood there, silently.

"If you don't speak to me, I will not be able to help you," said Josette, somewhat intimidated.

This girl was not like most of the other spirits she had dealt with. For one thing, she did not seem to understand what Josette was saying. As Josette spoke, the apparition only stared blankly at her, as if confused. Then, without any warning, the girl reached out both hands and placed one on each of Josette's cheeks. Josette screamed and felt herself tumbling.

Down and down she went, farther and farther into a seemingly endless black abyss. Just when

Josette thought she could take no more, the blackness faded into the darkness of night. Standing under indistinct moonlight, she found herself standing in the middle of a narrow dirt street in the middle of an insignificant village, contrived of nothing more than tiny wicker and plaster houses with thatched roofs and livestock fencing. There were no paved roads, no streetlamps, no signs of the modern world.

On the ground at her feet crawled the mutilated girl, gasping for breath, barely clinging to life. She was not alone; there were others laying on the street. Josette saw one elderly woman with her broken and twisted body still twitching, her head lying flat on the back of her neck. One rather large man lay dead in front of a church at the end of the street, his chest wrenched wide open. Everywhere she looked, there were people shrieking, writhing in pain and agony. To her left she saw a small boy missing his leg, and another boy laid next to him missing both arms, blood forming in puddles on the ground beneath them. The entire village had been massacred; she doubted any had escaped the onslaught. Dread filled Josette's body. Were the culprits still there, was her life, and those of her unborn sons, endangered? The moaning, weeping, and cries of agony would not end. She wished those still alive would just die, not only to put them out of their misery, but hers. Men, women, and children. There was no discrimination. Every single person was either dead or dying. Then came a sound, a sound like nothing she had ever heard before. It was the sound of heavy breathing, like the panting of a bear breathing down her neck.

Josette turned, but there was no enormous beast waiting to strike a blow. There was only a middle-aged woman wearing a lengthy black frock, with a sleeveless tunic and a black wimple covering her hair. On her face she bore the hideous grin of glee, pleasure, and revenge. Josette started to scream, but before a sound left her lips, she heard the comforting sound of Kip Gillmore's voice from a far-off place

"Fear not, Josette. It was I who sent the girl. Heed the warning." With that, she felt herself a waken, as if from a dream. Josette found herself sitting up once more in the bed. The girl was gone. At least, Josette hoped she was. But also gone was Kip.

*

It was Benjamin who first spotted Father Aron as they pulled up to the Banthom House. He stood just outside of his car staring up at it as if it were Windsor Castle. As Benjamin and Josette neared, he turned and offered a wave. Although a black priest was not unheard of in Ireland, Benjamin could admit this was the first time he'd ever seen one outfitted in robe and collar. On the drive over, Josette had filled Benjamin in about her nighttime specter visit and, again, he was thankful for the

Church's assistance. If what Josette saw was real, then the warning meant that a lot of innocent people could possibly be in danger. How this was all tied to Phillip and Mary he was not sure, but Josette asserted that she would be leaving for the states as soon as she could make the arrangements.

"I have to get there. Whatever it was Kip wanted me to know, I know it affects Phillip. I am afraid if we do not resolve this soon, his life will be in danger, as well as many others. Kip would not have shown me these things if he wasn't alive. I've got to get to him."

Benjamin simply responded, "We need to find him first."

As they got closer to the house, he could see the apprehension in her face. Maybe seeing a priest standing in the drive would help alleviate some of her tension. He knew it did his.

"Hello, hello," said the priest, walking towards the door. As Benjamin and Josette entered, a cold blast of air took them all by surprise.

Benjamin reached out his hand in greeting. "Benjamin Burk. I own this house."

The priest grinned. "I know of you Mr. Burk; your name is well-known in Rome. And who is this beauty?" he asked. Josette made her way around the car.

"Hi, my name is Josette," she said. She reached out her hand, but the priest did not shake it. Instead, he took her hand in his, bent over slightly, and kissed it.

"Charmed, my fair lady," the priest responded.

"Shall we?" asked Benjamin. He waved towards the front door. "Let's get out of this chill." He could tell Josette was uneasy at the priest's seemingly forward gesture and thought it best to get right down to work. "Josette is a very famous medium."

"Oh, no disrespect, but I don't believe in mediums. You see, I don't believe in ghosts so I cannot believe there are those who can see or speak to them. When you die, you go to either Heaven, Hell, or Purgatory. There is no option of staying in this world. I do, however, believe in demons, and they often trick the living into believing they were once human."

Benjamin looked at Josette, unsure how she would respond. She seemed to take no heed. She spent her life dealing with doubters.

"The first thing I need to find, Benjamin, is something that is original in the house, something that might have some lingering memories of Banthom, something personal, if you get what I mean," said Josette, ignoring the priest and talking directly to Benjamin.

"Oh, Josette. You are talking a couple hundred years. I doubt we will find anything like that here," said Benjamin, unlocking the front door. "I mean, this place has gone through a lot of people since he lived here."

Walking through the front door, Benjamin noticed the bloodstain on the floor where Hoffman had met his demise. He had paid a local company to clean the stain, but obviously, they had done a piss-poor job.

"It is my understanding that you want me to decipher some kind of transcript or written material left by this Banthom fellow. Is that correct?" asked Father Aron. He closed the front door behind them.

"That's correct," replied Benjamin.

"And where is this parchment? I can start working on it immediately," the priest remarked.

"Well, that's just it, Father," said Josette sarcastically. "I need to find it first, and all I know is it's behind one of these walls."

"And who provided you with this information, if you don't mind me asking?" asked the priest.

Benjamin started to say something, but Josette interjected. "A very dear friend of mine and Benjamin's... that we trust completely. If he says it is here, then it is here."

"And where is this good friend, and why did he not tell you where to find it?"

Benjamin could tell that the priest was irritating Josette, so when he started again, Benjamin circled between the two.

"Father, would you come with me for just a moment? I want you to tell me more about Rome and what they are saying about me. Why don't we just step back into the dining room and have a seat, let Josette do her thing, and we can sit down and chat?"

"Ok, very well," the priest agreed, reluctantly.

Walking back into the dining room, Benjamin could hear the sigh of relief escape Josette's lips. "Tell me. Why do they know of me in Rome?"

"Well," said the priest, sitting down at the table, "the Grand Grimoires, of course. You are the one that brought them to Rome, are you not?"

Benjamin worried that the books had become common knowledge. "Well, yes I am. But how do you know about them?"

The priest smiled knowingly. "Because, my dear man, I am the one who prays over them, who keeps their darkness at bay. Trust me, there are a very select few who know they are there. I assure you. I know your family had been charged with their protection for centuries, but I tell you, I don't know how you kept them out of the hands of those who would do evil."

As Father Aron spoke, Benjamin kept an eye on Josette as she walked from room to room on the ground floor. The first place she looked was the same pantry they found the two children in.

"I was in hopes that whatever writing you found here would give us a clue to the location of the last book," continued the priest, not noticing Benjamin's distraction. "I mean, the thought of another one of those vile things out there... Well, to put it plainly, scares the shit out of me."

Josette was now in the living room area, blocked from view by the staircase. "I couldn't agree more, Father. The last one needs to be found," responded Benjamin, craning his neck to see Josette.

"Until the Church can find a way to destroy them all together, the only place they need to be is in Rome, under a watchful eye."

Josette emerged from the living room, ascended the stairs, and was out of sight again. This was not setting well with Benjamin, but it kept the priest at bay. "I quite agree, Father, but my family's liability was only to watch over the two. No one knows anything about the third book or where it might be located."

Benjamin could hear Josette's footsteps moving towards the back bedrooms upstairs. The priest droned on, but Benjamin was only half listening. The majority of his attention focused on Josette's movements. She was making her way from the front to the back of the house, along the back hall, and returning again along the left side of the house.

"That's why I think it is imperative that whatever is found in this house is returned to Rome..."

"Excuse me, Father. I hate to interrupt, but I want to check on Josette, if you don't mind. I will be back straight away so we can finish this conversation about the possibilities of the writings going back to Rome. But first, I want to make sure she is ok. You know, a woman in her condition."

"Sure, sure," said the priest. "Maybe I should go with you."

Benjamin jumped up. "No, no, it will only take but a minute." He dashed for the stairs. At the top, he saw Josette looking at the door leading to the attic.

"I get a strange feeling about what lays behind this door, Ben. Will you come up here with me?" she asked, turning the knob.

"Sure, I've been up there a few times. Not much to see up there."

"That's ok, I still think it is worth a look," said Josette. The door opened to a tiny space with a narrow set of steps going up the wall to the left. Benjamin knew at the top was another door that opened into the attic. It was dirty up there, and cobwebs were everywhere.

"Is there a light somewhere?" asked Josette.

"Here, let me go first. There is a light at the top of the stairs, but the string is hard to find."

He squeezed past her and made his way up to the door at the top step. Though it was still unlocked, it was stuck shut. Benjamin tugged on the doorknob to get the door open. Once inside, it took time pawing in the dark, above the door, before his hand found the string. He pulled on it, and the attic filled with light. "Ok, come on up!" he shouted to Josette.

The way Josette waddled up the steps reminded Benjamin of a duck and he couldn't help but chuckle.

"Yea sure, laugh at the pregnant lady. And I thought you were a gentleman," joked Josette.

"Sorry, but you remind me of a duck," said Benjamin, still chuckling.

"Well instead of laughing, you could at least help me with these last few steps."

Benjamin reached out his hand and assisted her the rest of the way. At the top, Benjamin watched as Josette stopped and looked around. After a few moments she asked, "Over there, under that small round window, what is that?"

Benjamin looked in the direction she was pointing but saw nothing. "What?"

"Right there against the wall. You can barely see it. It looks like the back of a picture frame."

Josette was right. Squinting as hard as he could, Benjamin could make out the back of what appeared to be a painting. Brushing cobwebs out of his way, Benjamin made his way across the attic and retrieved the item from its resting place.

"Bring it down here," said Josette, turning and descending the stairs once more.

Benjamin did as he was instructed and carried it down the steps, turning it sideways as the frame was wider than the stairs. At the bottom, Benjamin turned it over, but the front of the portrait was caked in dirt, concealing the image below. He took his hand and started brushing it away. Josette's eyes widened as more of the image became clear.

"Oh my God!" she exclaimed. "It's her. Oh my God, it's her."

Benjamin lifted the painting so he could see what Josette was talking about. He saw a woman dressed all in black, her face taut with discontentment.

"That's the woman I saw last night in my dream. It's the woman from the village."

"Are you sure?" asked Benjamin.

"Ben, I am going to touch this painting. Whatever you do, don't stop me until I am done. You understand. You have seen me in my trances before and you know how I get. Please, don't interrupt. I have a feeling that, after all these years, we are looking at the mother of Gunari Danior."

Benjamin watched as Josette reached out her hand and laid it on the painting. As soon as she came in contact with the portrait, her eyes rolled into the back of her head and her body began to quiver and shake. Benjamin knew she was no longer aware of the world around her. After a few moments Benjamin became worried. What if she didn't come out of it? What if she had been taken to a place where there was no return? He was about to grab her to try and shake her back when she let go of the object and opened her eyes. She gave no notice of Benjamin, but instead turned and made her way back to the first floor. Once at the bottom of the steps, with Benjamin trailing right behind her, she walked into the kitchen, reached into the bottom cabinet beneath the sink as if she had done it a thousand times before, pulled out a pipe wrench, and walked into the dining room. Father Aron glanced up as she walked by, but she took no notice of him. Josette swung the wrench into the wall, creating a gaping hole inches above the fireplace.

"What is going on? Has she gone mad!" yelled the priest.

Josette ignored Father Aron. She reached into the wall and pulled out a long, thin, wooden box. With her back towards the priest, she rebuked him.

"You say that there are no ghosts, that houses do not hold memories. Well, this house holds the memories of satanic rituals, orgies, rape, sodomy, pedophilia, bloodletting, vampirism, murder, sacrifice, necrophilism, and bestiality, and it all occurred right here, where the portrait of his fucking mother hung."

Turning to face the priest, Josette continued sarcastically. "Tell me, Father. Now do you believe I am what I say I am?" She slammed the box onto the table.

Benjamin was taken aback by this. He had never known Josette to act this rudely. "Josette, are you, alright?" asked Benjamin.

Father Aron sat there with his mouth agape, obviously unaccustomed to being spoken to in that manner.

"Oh, I am sorry, Father," Josette said apologetically. "It must be the hormones." She rubbed her belly. "I haven't quite been myself as of late."

"Completely understandable, my dear," said Father Aron. He appeared to still be in a state of confusion.

Benjamin walked over to the table to open the box's contents.

"Wait!" exclaimed Josette. "Maybe it is best we open this somewhere else; I don't feel comfortable opening it in this house."

"Agreed," said Benjamin. He knew there was more going on with Josette than just hormones, something she was not saying, something that had her on edge. Still, he knew this was not the time or place to dig any deeper.

"Agreed," said Father Aron to their surprise. Benjamin thought for sure he would want the task done right then and there.

CHAPTER III

NEW ORLEANS

N o one seemed to notice the boy as he strolled past the graves in the Saint Louis Cemetery. His white suit, white shoes and socks, and white fedora stood out against his black skin. He seemed to be enjoying his day, swinging a stick back forth in front of him as he walked. The sun was scorching and even though it was almost Christmas, there had been no cooling relief for the city of New Orleans. Yet not a single bead of sweat appeared on his forehead. A smile seemed to be permanently fixed on his young, yet dignified, face. The music was the best he had heard in a long time. The man who had died was a popular businessman in the community. He owned a barber shop on Dauphine Street, but everyone knew that not all his endeavors were legit. They say he loaned money to desperate people and then would threaten bodily harm if they failed to repay him, along with the large interest fees he imposed. Still, his turnout was like nothing he had seen for some time. He knew the crowd would eventually disperse and the consumption of alcohol would commence. That part did not interest him in the least. He would simply stay in the cemetery awhile, hang out at the grave, and say his own goodbyes when the time was right.

*

Ethel had insisted they drive from Tampa to the bayou and then on to New Orleans rather than fly and rent a car like Brandy had hoped. It was getting hard for her to sit that long, and even in the Cadillac she felt claustrophobic. The only thing they had seen for miles was woods, dirt roads, and swamps. Brandy had almost fallen out of her chair when Ethel stated she was going to visit her grandmother. Ethel explained that the woman was over a hundred years old and was living all by herself in the backwaters outside of New Orleans. Brandy knew that Ethel's mother and father were both gone... but who in the hell would have thought her grandmother was still kicking? It was near dark by the time they pulled up in front of a house that reminded Brandy more of an old woodshed than a home. The front porch was buckled with missing boards, but somehow a swing prevailed. *What the hell is holding up that damn thing*, thought Brandy as Ethel got out of the car.

"Come on, let's get this over with. This old bitch scares the hell out of me," said Ethel.

"Then why the hell are we here?" asked Brandy, following Ethel to the front door. There was candlelight coming from the only window in the front of the house.

"I told you. She may be able to help with finding Phillip and Mary. I know it sounds crazy, but you are just going to have to trust me on this one."

"Fine, fine. God knows you've talked me into worse things."

"Remember, she knows how to speak English, but she will act like she doesn't. She will be using French or Creole."

"Well she might as well be speaking Greek then, cause I don't understand either," said Brandy peeking in the window.

Before Ethel could knock on the front door, a voice came from inside: "Entrez!"

Ethel took a deep breath and opened the door. "Grandma, it's your little Ethel. I came with a friend."

An old lady, bent over with age, sat by a wood burner in the middle of the room, covered with a shawl. "Does your friend speak Creole?"

Brandy looked around. The inside was in no better shape than the outside. The only furniture adorning her one-room home was the bed, placed only feet away from an ancient, stove pipe wood-burning stove, a sink, a rocker setting directly across from the old woman on the other side of the wood burner, and a table with two chairs. There was shelving along three of its four walls, all of which was filled with jars and cans, books, and old collectable figurines.

"No, only English," said Ethel, putting her purse on the kitchen table.

The old lady looked up at Brandy, giving her a stern, long look. "This the same little girl you lived with in town, the one you ran a whore house with?"

Ethel was amazed she spoke English. She had never made the attempt before when Ethel would visit with friends.

"I told you it was a dance house, not a whore house," said Ethel. She approached the old woman and gave her a kiss on the cheek. "And yes, she is the same lady I lived with in New Orleans."

"I liked you back then, girl. Before you married that low-life hornblower," said the old woman. "I presume you're here because y'all need my help, right? I knows you ain't here just to visit. I'm old, girl. Not stupid. Toos bad y'all gave up on your studies. Maybes you could deal with this your own damn self."

"Now, Grandma, we've been through this a million times. You know I wanted to sing, not do what you do."

"Yea, your momma turned her back on me as well," the old woman said, turning her eyes to the opened door of the burner, watching the flames dance inside.

Brandy, who was perspiring, gazed at the woman in disbelief.

"How do you do, ma'am?" she asked, reaching out her hand. The old woman ignored her gesture.

"You want to find those two friends of yours. The ones taken by the witch," blurted the old woman.

Brandy, in shock by the old woman's knowledge of their plight, lowered her hand and sat in the old rocking chair directly across from her.

"Yes, Grandma. We do," said Ethel, unphased.

"Well I can't help ya. Y'all need to speak to someone who knows 'bout these things. I can't see 'em."

"And who is it we need to speak to, Grandma?" asked Ethel, putting her hand on the old woman's shoulder. "Please, Grandma. It's very important to us."

After a few minutes contemplating her response, the old woman simply replied, "Doctor John."

"Doctor John!" exclaimed Ethel. "You mean Bayou John? He died over a hundred years ago! Is there any way you can talk to him for us?"

Brandy fidgeted in the rocking chair. *Did Ethel really just ask her grandmother to speak to a dead man for them?*

"No, this is something you must do. Hand me that roll up there on the shelf," said the old woman. She pointed to the shelving above her kitchen table, at what appeared to be a map, rolled up and held tight with rubber bands. "That is the guide with the seven Gates, each point numbered, each marked with the offerings. If you don't follow it to the letter, well, girl... You know what will happen as well as I do."

"What is she talking about?" asked Brandy. A look of concern washed over her face.

"I will explain later," Ethel responded. She grabbed the map off the shelf.

"You get dragged to Hell," said the old, toothless woman, her face void of emotion.

"What?" exclaimed Brandy.

"I will explain in the car, ok? Sorry, Grandma, but we have to go. I love you. You know that, don't you?" asked Ethel. With the map under her arm, she waved Brandy toward the door.

"Even though this old bitch scares the shit out of you?" asked the old woman, not turning around to watch them leave.

"Yes," responded Ethel, opening the door with a big smile. "Even though you scare the shit out of me. I will come for a longer visit once this is over. I promise. Ok?" The old woman silently returned to the flames. Ethel turned to exit and closed the door behind her.

Back in the car, Brandy exploded with questions.

"What the hell does she mean 'dragged to Hell'? What seven gates? What does she mean by offerings?"

"Slow down, you old bat," said Ethel. She shifted the Cadillac into drive. "Let me turn this beast around so we can get the hell out of here."

Ethel began a U-turn in the middle of the road,

when her headlights caught a 15-foot gator. It was in no hurry to get out of their way.

"Why don't you get out and push it out of the way?" asked Brandy. The gator turned its head in their direction and snapped its jaw, showing them who, indeed, was king of the bayou.

Ethel backed up within inches of the front porch, then sharpened her turn towards the road. "Keep it up and you will be sharing a bed with my grandmother tonight. GIRL," said Ethel, doing her best impression of her grandmother.

Once back on the road, Brandy offered an ultimatum. "I am not doing anything else with you until you tell me what the hell is going on."

"She gave us the map to the Gates of Guinee. Everyone thinks they know where they are, but only my grandmother ever truly knew. It has been known in my family for years," Ethel replied. "It is believed in the Voodoo world that there are Seven Gates, each guarded by a different spirit, which keep those in Hell, in Hell, and everyone else out. The one person who can help us has passed over. But if I pass through the Seven Gates and make the correct offerings, and I get to Baron Samedi and if he finds favor with me, then I can speak, calling upon anyone I know who is, well, dead. He is the guardian of the dead and only he can grant permission to speak to the dead."

"And if this Baron Samedi does not grant you permission?" asked Brandy fearfully.

"If you anger Baron Samedi, or any of the

guardians, it said that they will drag you straight to hell without a judgement day," said Ethel. "This is well-known among my people."

"And you believe this?"

"Do we have any other options? I fear that Phillip's and Mary's time may be short. We have to do something. I know my grandmother believes, and you can see that she has knowledge like no one else."

"And you are willing to be dragged to Hell? I mean, really?" Brandy shook her head in disbelief.

"I don't think that really happens. Besides, don't worry. With the right offerings I think we can do this," said Ethel.

"You are one crazy bitch. You know that?" muttered Brandy. She stared into the darkness.

"Yes, I know it. And you know it, too. And you also know that if I'm riding on that crazy train, you're blowing the fucking whistle."

*

Walking into the bathroom and shutting the door, Ethel turned on the shower to warm. Pulling out her small toiletry case, Ethel proceeded to brush her teeth. When she looked in the mirror, she noticed how drawn her face looked. *I may think I'm twenty-one but all these lines on my face tell me something different*, she thought. She had dry skin and varicose veins, her back hurt, her neck hurt, and her feet were forever swelling. *This grand* *adventure was more than just finding Phillip and Mary,* she thought to herself. *This was about good versus evil, and somehow, she always knew she would play her part.*

She heard Brandy awake and shuffling around the room, and she knew it wouldn't be long before she would come through the door for her morning release. Ethel walked into the shower just as Brandy came knocking at the door.

"I gotta pee. You in the shower?" Brandy asked politely

"Yessum, I am," said Ethel.

"Thank God. I thought you might be on the pot," said Brandy, hurrying into the bathroom.

Ethel relaxed as the warm water massaged her neck and shoulders. *I will have to come up with some reason for Brandy not to come with me,* she thought. She took a deep breath in the hot steam. *There is no way I can let her come. I may be stupid enough to attempt this fate, but I will be damned if I endanger her as well.*

"We will need to make a list of items for the offerings. Some of them, I fear, will give us some trouble," came Brandy's voice beyond the curtain. "I mean, where in the hell are we going to find Cuban cigars?"

"Can you let me finish washing my ass before you start your questions, woman?" asked Ethel half-jokingly. "I need my coffee before you start running around at 90 miles an hour. We still have two whole days."

"Fine, fine," responded Brandy over the noise

of the flushing toilet. "I will call downstairs and have them bring up some coffee. Do you want anything to eat?"

"Just coffee," said Ethel. The door closed and Brandy was gone.

Maybe she would just sneak off when Brandy wasn't looking, or maybe she could tell her that something else needed to be done while she was walking the Gates. She knew Brandy would never take no for an answer. Brandy was as clever as they come... Whatever she came up with would have to pass her smell test.

*

Brandy walked out of the hotel and onto Bourbon Street, into a bright and humid morning. That's when it hit her: After all this time, she was back, standing in the middle of the French Quarter, where she and Ethel had called home for so many years. They were both young then, and they owned this town. They could walk into any bar on this strip and be welcomed by the owners, staff, and usually half the regulars. In all the time they ran their establishment, Brandy couldn't recall a single time she or Ethel paid for their own drinks.

There had always been tourists, but now it seemed that the sheer numbers changed the very fabric of the district. The streets were already packed, and it was just after ten in the morning.

Ethel followed. "I think we need to walk down here a ways," said Ethel, pointing in the direction of Esplanade Avenue. "There was a famous spirit store just past the LaLaurie House on Royal Street."

"Shit, I hate walking past that place. Gives me the creeps," replied Brandy.

Just at that moment, a little black boy, dressed elegantly in a white suit and dress shoes walked up behind them.

"That's because that place has evil living in its walls," he said. Both women jumped.

"Boy, what are you doing sneaking up behind someone like that?" asked Ethel. "You about scared me out of my wits."

The little boy, who could not have been more than 10, smiled.

"I heard you ladies say you were looking for a spirit shop. I know all the shops in the quarter, the ones for just the tourists and then ones for those who know better. Please let me be your guide."

"Ok kid, nice try. But I am not going to pay you to guide me around this town. I lived here for many years," snapped Ethel.

"Oh, come on, Ethel. Let's at least hear the boy's pitch. He's just so damn cute, and listen to how nicely he uses his words."

Brandy reached down and put her hand on the boy's shoulder.

"Fine," said Ethel, irritated at the delay.

"What's your name, boy?" asked Brandy with a comforting smile.

"They call me Sam," said the boy, extending his hand.

Brandy took it in hers and offered, "Well, Mr. Sam, it is an honor to meet you."

"It is an honor to meet you as well, Miss," replied the boy. He shook Brandy's hand.

"Ok, kid, how much you wanting?" asked Ethel.

"Oh, I want no money from such fine ladies. I only wish to help," said the boy. And he bowed.

"Oh, we have quite the young gentleman offering to escort us, Ethel. I say we take advantage of it."

Brandy put the boy's hand under her arm as if he were guiding her through the doors of the finest ball in town.

"Hold on," said Ethel. "If we are going to do this, we might as well do it right."

Ethel circled to the opposite side of the boy so he could take her arm as well. "Ok, Sam. Show us the best spirit shop in town."

The boy giggled as the three started down the street. "If you tell me what you are looking for, then I will know what shop to take you to first."

This surprised Brandy, for she thought for sure the boy was more than likely related to the owner of whatever shop he took them to. It was not uncommon, even in the old days, for shopkeepers to have their youngsters out trolling for potential customers.

"Well the first two things we need, little man, are a Cuban cigar and Barbancourt Rum."

The little boy stopped dead in his tracks.

"Those are the offerings for Baron Samedi, the Guardian of Guinee." Letting go of their arms and looking up at them with a look of grave concern on his face, the boy asked, "Are you wishing to pass the Seven Gates to speak to the dead? If you displease Baron Samedi, he will take you to Hell."

Brandy looked at Ethel as if to ask how to answer, but Ethel just shrugged her shoulders in uncertainty.

"Well, let's just say we have an interest and leave it at that, ok?" said Brandy.

The boy put his hand on his chin and thought about it. Finally, he reached a conclusion.

"I will take you to a shop I know. It is out of the way, but you can trust them to have what you need," he said, turning in the opposite direction. This time he walked ahead of them.

Brandy was hesitant at first, but once Ethel started behind the boy, she followed.

The threesome walked for twenty minutes. Then, the boy took a right turn down a less-traveled side street and a quick left down what appeared to Brandy to be more of an alley than a road. It was lined with many shops, but at the end of the street on the right-hand side, was a quaint pink establishment with large, white shutters and flower boxes.

"This is the best spirit shop in the city. If you can't find what you are looking for here, then you are out of luck," said the boy. Hanging outside was a sign that read, *"Ms. Rebecca's Spirit Shop."*

"Well, I don't think we would ever have found this without your help," said Brandy. "It is off the beaten path, that's for sure."

"Yes, thank you so much, young man," added Ethel. As she said this, the boy simply turned and started to walk away.

"You're not going in with us?"

"Nah, I have a lot of people I need to help today. You ladies have a great day," he called over his shoulder. "I hope you find what you need."

Brandy and Ethel stood there looking at each other. Finally, Brandy broke the silence. "What a strange, strange little boy."

"Well, let's just hope he knows what he's talking about. One-stop shopping is the way to go," said Ethel. She walked to the front stoop.

Brandy hesitated, watching the boy until he turned back at the end of the road. After he rounded the corner, Brandy walked into the shop. The shop smelled of incense. Along each wall hung what Brandy could only assume were African masks. They were beautiful yet chilling. There were shelves below the masks with a variety of jars, whose labels were printed in French. Not knowing a word of French, Brandy could only guess at their contents. One section of the store, which, at one time looked like a kitchen, was filled with long gowns, all different colors, hanging on portable garment racks.

"Lord almighty, I can't believe my eyes," came a woman's voice from the back of the store. "Ethel, is that you?"

Both Brandy and Ethel turned around to find a woman close to their age dressed in a long-tie-dyed dress with a Zulu Basket Hat. She stood at five feet tall and smiled from ear to ear.

"Rebecca, is that you?" asked Ethel.

"In the flesh, cousin. I have not seen you in over thirty years," the old woman said, running towards Ethel with her arms outstretched.

Brandy watched the two embrace.

"Oh, Rebecca, I am so glad to see you. I missed you so much," replied Ethel. Then, turning to Brandy, she added, "Rebecca, this is Brandy. Remember her? She ran the club with me years ago."

Brandy walked over and gave the woman a hug. "So nice to see you again."

"Club, my ass! You two ran a whore house... Everybody knows it," giggled Rebecca. "Just because you put on your show every night didn't mean it wasn't a whore house." The women started to laugh.

"Ok, Ok. Whore house, then," Ethel remitted.

"Grandma said you might be visiting. She called me last night," said Rebecca.

"That's weird. We didn't know we were coming to your shop. As a matter of fact, if it hadn't been for some little boy, we wouldn't have ever found this place," offered Brandy.

"What little boy?" asked Rebecca, with a puzzling look on her face.

"The little black boy dressed in a white suit," added Brandy.

Rebecca thought for a moment.

"I don't know any kids from the neighborhood, at least not anymore. Not since my kids were little, anyway. I just opened this place last summer so…"

"Well, what did my grandma tell you?" asked Ethel, impatiently.

"Nothing. Only that you might be stopping by for a visit. I worry about that old lady; she has been stuck in that bayou too long. I am afraid she is as crazy as a loon, but family is family."

"So, you kept up with the family tradition…," trailed Ethel. She picked up a jar that contained the plucked eyes of sheep.

"Well, yes and no. I have studied and studied, but I have no natural talent. Not like you."

Brandy gave Ethel a questioning look. In all the years they had known each other, they never really spoke about Voodoo or Ethel's family history around it.

"I keep the tourist shit out front. The real stuff is upstairs. You would be surprised how much of that shit I sell," continued Rebecca.

Ethel took a deep breath.

"I need the items on this list." She pulled out the rolled-up map that her grandmother had given her.

Brandy noticed the look of concern that suddenly replaced her smile. Rebecca unrolled the map in front of her. "Oh, God, Ethel. What the hell are you doing with this? Grandma should never have let this out of her house. If this falls in the wrong hands, God only knows the damage that could be done. I heard she had the only true guide, but I never really believed it. Don't tell me you're foolish enough to attempt the Gates."

"I have to," said Ethel. "I have friends that are great peril, and I fear they have been cursed by a black witch." She ignored Rebecca's warning.

Rolling up the map, Rebecca's hands shook.

"Well, if it was a voodoo curse, we can find a way. There is no reason to do this. Grandma is a Voodoo queen; she will take care of it."

"No, this was not voodoo. It was a satanic witch, a gypsy," responded Ethel.

"No good will come of this. It never does," said Rebecca. "Let's go upstairs. I will fill your order for the offerings. But Ethel, I wish you would reconsider. This is no game you are playing."

"Trust me, I know," said Ethel. "You know, it's funny. Somehow I always had this feeling deep down that someday I would be burdened with the Gates."

"So, I take it you are looking at Christmas day?" furthered Rebecca. She walked towards the back of the store and up the stairs.

"Why Christmas?" asked Brandy, still fuming about the date.

"You can only perform the Gates on a holiday, when the spirits are less likely to be angered," replied Rebecca. As they ascended the stairs, she added, "Ethel, have you told Brandy she cannot take part in this? You cannot take a white woman on this quest."

Ethel stopped on the stairs. Brandy could see a sense of relief on Ethel's face as she looked over at her.

"She's right. You cannot do the Gates with me. You weren't born into this culture and the spirits will know this. You would put both of us in danger."

Brandy realized that she never could have accompanied Ethel on this little adventure. She was not sure, but somehow, she got the feeling that Rebecca had just opened the door to a conversation that Ethel had been avoiding. Brandy did not say a word. This conversation would wait until they were alone.

CHAPTER IV

MISSING PERSONS

Hazel had given a lot of thought about what she would say when Sam, Vinnie, Shawn, and Franky finally showed up to her meeting. *It may be nothing,* she thought, *but it was the only lead they had gotten.* As the men piled into her small office, she closed the door and walked behind the desk.

"I received a call today from Elma Wiseman. Her husband is the sheriff down in Phelton." Sam and Vinnie took their seats. "She is requesting help from us. It seems a couple of their women have come up missing. I know you talked about this Banthom guy and how he hides his kills and, well, I thought maybe it might mean something."

Franky, who had taken up his spot standing next to her desk, asked, "They have no leads?"

"Apparently not. They asked if the city of Jackson could loan them a couple of officers to help in the search. I asked the mayor, and, of course, he said no. He's afraid he wouldn't get reimbursed for their time... The cheap bastard."

"Well, I'm off for the holidays. I could go and check it out," said Franky. He smiled at Hazel. "I will go down, throw some things together, and be down there this afternoon."

"Me too," said Shawn, leaning against the office door next to Sam.

Hazel was impressed with Franky's and Shawn's offers to dive right in, but Hazel knew it was not that easy.

"Well, I don't think that would be wise. I mean, a couple of strangers coming into town asking a lot of questions isn't going to bode well with Malcom, her husband. I know this guy and, well, he is pretty much a by-the-book kind of guy. I was thinking of sending Vinnie with you two.

"But I thought the mayor said no," countered Vinnie.

"Well, I thought about that as well, and ..."

Hazel hesitated for a few moments.

"Well what?" asked Vinnie.

Hazel paused for a moment then took a deep breath. "You're suspended for three weeks without pay," she blurted out.

"What? Suspended for what? What did I do?" balked Vinnie. He stood and approached Hazel's desk. "You can't just suspend me for no good reason."

Hazel reached into her bottom drawer and pulled out a magazine.

"I have been trying to decide for a while how to handle this."

Hazel threw the magazine on top of her desk. "Do you remember this?"

Vinnie was horrified.

"Sorry, but you didn't disclose the fact that you posed nude for a magazine before you were hired," continued Hazel. "Sorry, but I have to take corrective action."

"Nude! You have got to be shitting me," said Sam. "I got to see this."

He grabbed the magazine and flipped through the pages.

"It's not fair! I have worked here as long as you have and never once got a write-up. It's just not fair. Those pictures paid for my mother's medicine in the last year of her life. I did what I had to do."

"How did you find out about this?" asked Sam.

"One of my staff brought it to my attention," responded Hazel, lowering her eyes.

"Look, you can't do this to me Hazel. We have been friends for a long time, and…"

Sam defended Hazel. "Shut up, Vinnie. Can't you see she is doing this for you? She is putting her own career on the line here. We all have a good idea of who that officer might be, and let's just say she is not the best at keeping her mouth shut."

Finally reaching the centerfold, Sam gawked. He let out a loud, "Wow."

"Fuck you, Sam. I still don't understand why I am being suspended, and without pay."

"Because if this got out, you would lose your job. If she suspends you now, then you are off the hook and they can't punish you twice for the same offense. Hazel, on the other hand... She is not going through the proper channels. If anyone else found out she knew about this, she might be the one losing her job."

Vinnie looked over at Hazel, who was avoiding making eye contact. She didn't say a word. "Is this true?" he asked.

Now Hazel stood as well. "I know the mayor better than anyone. If he finds out, I will deal with him. For now, he doesn't need to know why you were suspended. Hell, he probably won't even know you're gone. This is still my department, and like it or not, I make the decisions on corrective actions."

"Shit," said Shawn, looking over Sam's shoulder. "That's impressive."

"Really, Sam. I am ever so happy you are taking the time to show my stuff to the world. Maybe you can just pass it around the room!"

"I'll pass," smirked Franky.

"Look, Vinnie. Take the punishment, let Hazel deal with the mayor if it ever comes out. This way, you can help Franky and Shawn. It's a win-win," said Sam.

Vinnie sat back down and thought for a moment.

"Fine, fine, I will take the suspension. I hate it going on my record, but what else can I do?"

"You can start by thanking Hazel. She could have just as easily canned your ass and kept her nose clean," said Sam.

For no apparent reason, Franky reached over and took Hazel's hand in his. The gesture sent a shock wave through her body; his hand was so warm and comforting. She looked over at him, but he was still looking at Vinnie.

"I know it sucks for you, Vinnie, but Hazel is trying to help. You're lucky to have a friend like her," said Franky.

"I know," said Vinnie sheepishly. "Thank you, Hazel. I know you are doing it to protect me."

Franky, letting go of her hand, turned and looked at Hazel. He smiled.

"But if Vinnie is suspended, how can he help us in Phelton?" asked Shawn.

"While everyone here will know he is suspended, I promise I will not disclose why. I can hide under HR policy on that one," said Hazel. She looked directly at Vinnie. "But if I forget to collect his badge, then I guess there is no reason for Malcom to know about it. He will just think the good people of Jackson are jumping in to help."

"And what about us?" questioned Franky. "How are we going to explain ourselves?"

"I am sure you will think of something. Anyway, Malcom, knowing Vinnie is a fellow officer of the law, will fill him in with all the details. I just hope I am not sending you on some wild goose chase. Worst-case scenario, you all help find some missing people."

*

Howard Townsend was getting ready for the lunch crowd. He'd finished making hamburger patties and filling the steam table with fresh homemade chicken soup, pork roast, beef roast, and chili, and was now moving on to cutting onions, tomatoes, and lettuce for the cold table. On his way to the refrigerator to grab his vegetables, his thoughts traveled to the two missing women. Being the new guy in town, he noticed people scrutinizing him. This he understood; he came at the same time the disappearances started. Still, it was somewhat uncomfortable knowing that people suspected him of doing something bad.

"Order up!" came Marge's voice from the window. She placed a ticket on the spindle.

Howard quickly retrieved the vegetables and walked back to the front of the kitchen. *Joey will be in shortly, thank goodness*, he thought. *Dishes are stacked everywhere, and Marge is still trying to buss tables from the breakfast rush.* Grabbing the order, he saw "BChili/GCh WW," a bowl of chili and a grilled cheese on whole wheat bread. When he looked through the window, he saw Dale sitting at the counter, the last customer left. He realized the order was for him.

"How are you doing today, Dale?" Howard yelled from the service window.

Dale turned and looked at the window. "Tired," was all he said.

"Damn it, Dale," said Marge. She wiped down a table just behind Dale.

"Why don't you tell Howard about the Woman of the Lake?"

"What's that?" questioned Howard. He served Dale's chili from the window, but Dale turned back to his cup of coffee.

"Dale lives in a small camper trailer on Pine Lake. Really, it's more of an oversized pond than a lake. But anyway, in the fifties, a woman was brutally raped and murdered there," said Marge.

"They say that sometimes the Woman of the Lake shows herself just before something bad is about to happen."

"Wow, that's scary stuff," said Howard. He buttered two slices of whole wheat bread and placed them on the grill. "But I don't get what that has to do with him being tired."

"Well, he says he saw her standing on the ice in the middle of the lake last night," continued Marge. "I guess it scared him so bad he couldn't sleep."

"I wasn't scared. I was watching, that's all. This wasn't the first time I saw her out there. Only this time her hair was the color of blood," snapped Dale.

Even though Howard was not a superstitious man, a chill ran down his spine."

Did anyone else see her?" he asked.

"Dale is the only one who lives on that lake," offered Marge, grabbing the buss tub from the counter. She made her way towards the kitchen. "As a matter of fact, he is the only one who lives within three miles of that place."

"She didn't look the same. She looks evil now," muttered Dale.

Howard was about to ask how she had changed when Elma walked through the front door. She looked even more worn out than Dale.

"Morning, Marge. I hate to do this to you, but we are having a meeting over at the Baptist church with all the volunteers from the search party, and Malcom wants to feed them all. Is there any way I can get a couple dozen hamburgers and fries to go?"

"Sure thing. What would you like on those?" asked Marge.

Howard knew how much Marge hated to-go orders since she was the one that had to wrap and bag them all. It was extra work for her for no tip.

"How is the search going? Any signs of the White girl or that other lady?"

"Hi, Howard. Sorry, I didn't see you in the window. No, nothing yet. We have been looking for days, but nothing so far. Jackson is sending a detective to help us out, so I hope it is someone good. It's just so bizarre. I mean, you can see a pretty little thing like Shannon, alone on a county back road, being attacked or kidnapped or whatever. But Helen is missing from her own home, and let's face it, she's older than dirt and was never really that attractive."

She sat down by Dale while waiting for her order.

"God, the weather has been somewhat better the last few days. But they say there's a big storm coming our way, and Malcom's afraid if he doesn't get a lead soon, he might have to suspend the search. That's what the meeting's about at the church."

"You want a cup of coffee while you wait, dear?" asked Marge, walking behind the counter.

"I would love one, thanks," said Elma.

"It's the Woman of the Lake," said Dale. "She is the one taking people."

"Dale, that's all a myth. Dolly Hurt was raped and murdered on your land over forty years ago, and the man who did it is rotting in jail, the sick son of a dog. Malcom made the arrest himself."

Elma was unimpressed with Dale's assessment of the situation.

Just then, Joey came bounding through the front door.

"Hi, everyone. Marge, there is a man standing outside. Said he wants to talk to you."

Marge looked outside and saw Tom Phillips standing on the sidewalk.

"Tom Phillips. What the hell does he want?"

"I don't know," replied Joey, walking past her towards the kitchen. "He just asked me to tell you he wanted to speak to you, is all."

"Go ahead, Marge," said Howard. "Joey and I will take care of these orders."

He watched as Marge stood up and walked outside. From his location in the kitchen, he could see them both through the front window. From the moment she walked outside, an argument ensued. Both were visibly angry and yelling at the other. Howard thought he might intervene when Marge came walking back in.

"What does the pervert want?" asked Elma, unconcerned whether Tom could hear her through the still-open door.

"Nothing, nothing. Just being Tom," sighed Marge.

*

Malcom was encouraged by the large crowd that showed up to the meeting. Over half the town was there, with David and Cindy White setting in the front row with Mike Shelly. Malcom had sectioned off the land around the White's home, and the group of volunteers had managed to canvas over half the ten-mile radius. Though they had searched every inch of land, there was no sign of Shannon anywhere. In town, he had another group walking door-to-door, looking for Helen McCallister. They searched people's backyards, sheds, and the only park in town, but still, there was nothing.

"Please, please. We need to get started!" yelled Malcom from the pulpit. "Elma has brought lunch for everyone, so the faster we get started, the sooner we can all eat."

As everyone made their way to a pew, Malcom pulled out his notes.

"Ok, Brad and Sherry Hollister found a pair of women's underwear near Robin Road. Though they looked like a pair that Shannon owned, it turns out that was not what she was wearing that day., Cindy found Shannon's pair in the laundry hamper. Mike and Brian found a woman's scarf on Huff Road, but that turned out to be Lilly John's scarf she lost last month. Behind the Wilson house, they found some footprints that the Wilsons swear they did not leave. We will have a detective keeping an eye out to see who's been jumping the fence... most likely kids."

Malcom turned to Luke. "Did I forget anything?"

Luke shook his head.

"What about that Howard guy. Did you question him yet?" exclaimed Tom Phillips.

Whispers rose from the crowd, creating a commotion.

"Funny, him showing... and the next thing you know, our people are missing!" Tom jumped to his feet.

The group grew louder. Malcom started yelling.

"Ok, Ok! I want you all to calm down. Calm down!" The roar died down. "I talked to Howard yesterday. He even showed me his apartment. There was nothing there."

"Maybe so, Malcom. But I still think he has something to do with this," said Tom. "For all we know, he is planning his next attack."

"Now Tom, I am not going to let you, or anyone else, start these kinds of rumors. You hear? It isn't going to help find Mike's fiancé or Mrs. McCallister," said Malcom.

Just then, Cindy White stood. "I say, we grab him and make him talk. His grandmother was a flake, and I don't trust him any farther than I can throw him."

"Cindy is right!" ranted Tom. "That little fucker needs to be locked up."

Luke walked over to Tom.

"Look, Tom. I haven't seen your ass out there looking, so why don't you just shut up and sit your ass down."

"Oh, I'm sorry, Mr. Tough Guy. Anytime you want to take this outside..." yelled Tom into Luke's face.

"Just let me know when, asshole. I'm ready," said Luke, taking another step forward.

"Stop it, both of you. You're only making things worse," said Malcom. "Cindy, I know you're upset, but inciting a lynch mob isn't going to help anything."

Malcom left the pulpit, walked over to Cindy, and put his hand on her shoulder. "Look, I know you want answers. We all do. But blaming an innocent man is not going to help us find your little girl."

The crowd groaned.

"Look, I called you all here because we have a blizzard coming this way. It could be here in just a few days, according to the news. If that's the case, we need to double our efforts. Once the storm hits, I will need to shut down the search," said Malcom sheepishly.

Another groan came from the crowd.

"You're calling off the search?" croaked Mike. "Are you crazy? We need to find Shannon. God only knows what's…"

Mike broke down in tears before he could finish his sentence.

"No, we are not calling off the search. We have a couple of days, and hopefully we can find some answers. I am meeting with a detective from Jackson over at the restaurant after this meeting," pleaded Malcom. "Now, please. We all need to work together on this. If we need to suspend the search to keep all of you safe, then I will. But only till the storm passes."

"My baby girl's body is laying out there somewhere, Malcom," sobbed David White from the pew. "Please help us find her."

Luke, who was still standing next to Tom in the back of the church, spoke up.

"We don't know she's gone yet, David. She could have just as easily been kidnapped and taken to an unknown location."

David turned to say something to Luke, but before he got the chance, Dale Dryer, who was sitting behind David, stood up.

"It's the Woman of the Lake. I tell you, she is real, and she took your daughter."

"Damn it, Dale. Now is not the time," said Luke.

"Yes, it is. It is time, time for all of you to realize what is really going on here." Dale grabbed his hat and headed for the door. "I keep my house safe; I suggest you all do the same."

"Get out of here, you old drunk," shouted Tom Phillips. "No one here wants to hear your old fairy tales. We've heard it our whole lives."

Dale said nothing more. He staggered out of the front door, which closed behind him with a loud bang.

"As I was saying, the weather calls for freezing rain, then snow. The last update was up to two feet. I just can't have people out in weather like that," finished Malcom. "We've got two days, then I will need to call off the search until the weather improves. Now, I want updates on the areas covered and areas still on the list."

*

It was close to two thirty in the afternoon when the three men pulled up to The Wooden Spoon. Vinnie, who had driven the whole way, was the first one out of the car.

"I really need to take a leak," he stated, not waiting for the others. He hurried into the restaurant. Once inside, he saw the signs for the restroom all the way in the back of the diner.

"Hi there, can we get a table for three?" he asked Marge as he walked by.

"We close in ten minutes. You have to make it fast!" she replied.

Vinnie didn't wait to answer. All the pop he had drunk on the way down there was coming back to haunt him. He was surprised how clean the men's room was. There was no writing on the wall, no pieces of toilet paper thrown on the floor, and, most of all, it smelled nice. *Strawberries,* he thought. *It smelled like fresh cut strawberries.*

When Vinnie was finished, he walked over to the sink to wash his hands. A large man in uniform came strolling in.

"Are you Malcom?" asked Vinnie, as the man made his way to the urinal.

"Sorry. I'm Luke, his son. You must be the detective from Jackson."

"Yea, that's me."

"Sorry, but I was expecting someone more…"

"I spend a lot of time undercover, that way I get away with the long hair and casual dress," said Vinnie. He flashed his badge.

"Well, thank God. We can use all the help we can get. We only have four deputies total, not counting my Dad. And to tell you the truth, we have all been putting in the hours." Turning towards the urinal, he unzipped his pants.

Vinnie dried his hands and walked back into the restaurant. Sitting at the counter was another man dressed in uniform. Vinnie wasted no time introducing himself.

"Sheriff, my name is Vinnie Moretti from the JPD."

Malcom stood and took Vinnie's hand. His handshake was firm.

"God, I'm glad to see you," he said with a smile. "I'm not going to lie; we are in desperate need of assistance."

Vinnie decided he liked this man. Malcom's smile was genuine, and he could tell from his handshake that he was a man he could trust. There were no games with him, unlike some of the sheriffs he had encountered in his past who were more worried about their image than upholding the law.

Vinnie saw Shawn and Franky seated at a table by the window, watching intensely as the two men talked. "I brought two friends of mine," he said, pointing to the front table. "We all go to the same Y.M.C.A., and both want to volunteer in the search if that's ok."

"Yes, yes, yes," said Malcom. "We need all the help we can get."

Luke joined them and they agreed to move to the large, round table occupied by Shawn and Franky.

Marge was annoyed that these people showed up at the last minute. Yet, she walked over with two mugs and a pot of coffee. She placed one mug in front of Malcom and one in front of Luke, then poured coffee into each.

"What can I get the rest of you all?" she asked politely.

Elma, who had just come in the front door, said, "Coffee for me, Marge. Thank you."

"Gentlemen, this is the real sheriff in town, my wife, Elma," said Malcom, standing as she approached.

"I didn't know we were getting three detectives," she said, taking a seat at the table next to them.

"This one is Vinnie Mor…" started Malcom.

"Moretti, ma'am," said Vinnie. He stood and shook her hand.

"Moretti, that's right. And these fine gentlemen we have not met yet. They came to volunteer," continued Malcom.

"How sweet of you both," replied Elma. "Where are you staying?"

"Well, we were hoping to stay at the Motel Six out by US 27," said Vinnie.

"That's almost a half hour away! No, you can stay with us. We have a big, empty house, and we don't even use the bedrooms upstairs."

"No, we can put you out like that," said Shawn.

"Yes, you can. And you will. So, when we are done here, you just pull that car of yours up to our house and unload your stuff. I am going to fix everyone dinner. I know Howard and Marge want to get out of here, anyway. Isn't that right, Marge?"

Marge looked at Howard, who had just come out of the kitchen. He smiled in agreement. "You know that's right," she said.

"Well, then, if it's ok with everyone, I would like for Luke and me to talk to Vinnie in my office," said Malcom. "Elma will show you which house is ours, and you can make yourselves comfortable."

"But..." started Franky.

"No buts. It is our pleasure," said Elma. She stood up, gesturing toward the front door. "This way, gentlemen."

Franky and Shawn sat looking at each other for a moment.

"Trust me. You're not going to win this one," suggested Luke. "You might as well grab your shit and follow. Once she makes up her mind, that's it."

Both men hesitantly stood and followed Elma outside.

"You might need these guys," said Vinnie. He tossed his keys to Shawn.

Malcom introduced Vinnie to Marge, Joey, and Howard. They seemed to welcome his arrival.

"Malcom, you want me to pour your coffee to go?" asked Marge, cleaning off her last table.

"No, that's ok, dear. I will make a pot at the office," offered Malcom. He got up and motioned for Luke and Vinnie to follow.

Once outside, Malcom pointed down the street to the fourth house on the left. Vinnie saw his car already parked in front of the Wiseman place. "That's our house right there. Knowing Elma, she is finding out all there is to know about your buddies. That woman is like an old mother hen, I swear."

"Mom just loves people," argued Luke. "She has always said to treat others like…"

"We know, we know," said Malcom. "God, that woman has drove me crazy with that saying through the years."

Malcom unlocked the back door at the station and the men filed into the breakroom, around the dining room table.

"Sheriff," started Vinnie.

"Malcom, please."

"Malcom, then," grinned Vinnie. "So, we have two missing persons, both female. Correct?"

"Straight to business, I like that," said Malcom.

"Yea, but it's hard to connect the two," said Luke. He took a seat directly across from Vinnie and his father. "One was a young girl snatched from the side of the road, and the other an old woman missing from her home."

"Yes, but that's just so far," interjected Malcom. He looked down at the back of his hand, noticing the darkening age spots. "I have a feeling they are not done yet. Unlike my son here, I think they are the same person. Granted he is right, the two women had nothing in common. But the last time someone disappeared in Phelton…"

Luke gave his father a sympathetic look. "My dad was a young man when he found the body of a local up at the lake. She had been brutally raped, and her head was bashed in with a crowbar. It took him over a year, but he found the perpetrator, a local farmer. The girl's father was good friends with Dad. Later that same year, he took a gun and shot himself in the head while standing on Main Street, right in the middle of town. Dad tried to stop him, but he couldn't."

Vinnie hung his head. "I know how he feels. I tried to stop a suicide not too long ago. A city commissioner shot his brains out right in front of me. I will never forget it."

"Well, let's talk about the case at hand, shall we? I think this son of a bitch will take someone else, and soon. Men like this don't stop until someone stops them." Malcom was curt.

"I will help as much as I can. Just tell me where you need me," said Vinnie.

Luke stood up and walked over to the coffee pot. "Both Dad and I were glad when Captain Cowan said she was going to send a detective. We only have four deputies besides me, and we cover an entire county. Now, with people missing, we are running extra patrols and trying to lead a bunch of volunteers that don't have a clue as to what they're doing. And all the while, trying to solve this case."

"What my son is trying to say in his roundabout way, is, we would like you to double check us, look at what we have already looked at, and make sure we are not missing something. Hazel said you were an outstanding investigator. If you could help us stop this from happening again, then we would be forever in your debt. A poor county like this has little in the way of resources, so any help you can give is welcomed."

"Well, if this guy is some serial killer, then most likely he will already be looking for his next target. A woman by herself, unprepared and unaware."

"So far, we have found nothing. And I mean nothing. No blood, no fingerprints, and no leads whatsoever to go on," added Luke.

*

Dale drove his tiny truck down the mile-long driveway to his trailer camper just as the last of the light was leaving the evening sky. He had not planned to be out this late, but with the meeting and everyone going over to the Watering Hole afterward for a few, time had simply slipped away from him. At the bar, Dale heard Tom Phillips spewing his theories about the murders, most of them directed at the new guy who bought The Wooden Spoon. *Fool*, thought Dale. *I told them all the truth, but they are all fucking morons.*

He put the truck in park a few yards away from his camper and grabbed his things to hurry inside. *Don't give a damn what they say,* he thought to himself. *The Lady of the Lake was real.* As a matter of fact, he had seen her not once, but three times now. Always, she was standing on the lake, her body covered in a ragged, old, white nightgown. Nothing more. *Bitch is going to kill me out here and no one will even know.*

As he turned and shut the car door, he noticed a little girl sitting on his front step, her head turned away from him. "What the hell?..."

He heard the sound of someone talking just beyond his drive in the woods.

"Do this in memory of me," came the eerie female voice.

Looking around, Dale could see no one near him. Then, out of the corner of his eye, a flash of white emerged from behind one large oak tree, only to disappear behind another one some twenty feet away. *It was her,* he thought. *It's the Lady of the Lake and she's finally coming for me.*

Forgetting about the little girl on his front steps, Dale made a mad dash towards the door, stopping short of the tiny figure. Now the little girl turned and looked straight at him. Never in his forty-eight years on this earth had he ever encountered anything as terrifying as the face on this child. Her stringy, black hair hung in mats, hiding her eyes from his view. *Her skin. For God's sake, her skin! It's was rotting from her skull!*

"You're a fucking corpse! You're not real!" screamed Dale. "Move away or I will kick you off my step."

But the little girl only responded with a grin.

The sound of someone running nearby caught his ear once more. He spun around in time to catch the glimpse of the white figure, only this time, it disappeared behind the opposite side of his truck. Ignoring the girl for a moment, Dale dropped to his knees and searched below the truck. He saw no feet, no legs, nothing on the other side.

"Do this in memory of him," came the voice once more. "The living God. Not the dead one."

Even though he saw nothing on the other side of the truck, he knew the voice had come from that direction. The little girl started to giggle, hiding her lips behind her joined hands. Doing his best to ignore her, Dale ran to the other side of the truck, but nothing was there. He completely circled the truck, and still, there was nothing. Looking back at his camper, the little girl was gone.

"Shit!" yelled Dale. "What do you want we from me?"

Nothing. *Should I jump back in the truck and take off, or make a dash for the door of the camper?* His mind raced. *The truck is right here, and the camper is a good twenty feet away., However, the camper is fortified to hold off the Lady, but not the truck...*

Dale never got the chance to decide. He felt two hands grab his feet from under his truck. One excessive yank knocked him over and he went down hard, face first into the snow. The blow made him dizzy and a little confused. He raised his head and took a deep breath, but as his head started to clear, he felt himself being dragged backwards. He could feel what he envisioned as talons digging deeper and deeper into the flesh of his calves, pulling him farther underneath the truck. Clawing at the ground, Dale screamed at the top of his lungs. But nobody was there to hear him.

CHAPTER V

OLD WORLD, NEW WORLD

Josette sat on the airplane pondering the past few days. Inside the box recovered from the wall of the Banthom House, they had found an aged and torn scroll. Father Arno Kumalo was able to translate only the first part that was written in Latin. The other parts of the scrolls were in an ancient form of Sanskrit, with a dialect that he could not follow.

The one section that was written in Latin read like a manifesto for the Danior family. Father Kumalo was clear that Danior was a common Romani name, and that this paper only applied to this one offshoot of the family name. The lineage of hundreds of Danior family members were listed in the narrative, going back centuries.

Josette could not remember the verbiage word for word, but the key points were well imprinted in her brain. The Danior family had one quest: to implement a savage revenge against the Catholic

Church. It droned on about the pain the Church had brought to their people throughout the years, the persecution and slavery they endured. Revenge was to be imposed regardless of the cost, and regardless of the consequences. Father Kumalo estimated that this portion of the script was most likely written in the early eighteenth century, when Banthom was still a young man. Though the family lineage did not include his name, Banthom, or Gunari, Josette had a strong feeling that he was the clan's next monarch.

Benjamin and Father Kumalo were on their way to the University of Bucharest to meet with a professor of Romani history. Father Kumalo assured them that he was the most reclaimed expert on gypsy culture, both Sinti and Roma. If all went well, they would be meeting up with everyone in the States within the next few days.

When they extended the invitation to her, Josette politely declined. She knew she was pressing her luck as it was. The doctor already told her she could not fly, that her preeclampsia could lead to serious complications. The doctor had even advised termination of the pregnancy early on, stating the risks were just too high. But there was no way Josette was going to give up her sons. They were a part of her now and a part of Phillip as well. Maybe the only part she would ever have of him. Though she felt in her heart Phillip was still alive, she wondered if he could be saved. Not knowing where he was, or what happened to him was sometimes more than she could bear, but she tried desperately to cling to hope. One thing was for sure, she would not go down without a fight. Josette made arrangements in case the worst was to happen. All the paperwork was complete. But damn it, the thoughts of having her family all together gave her strength, and no doctor or high blood pressure was going to keep her from it.

Benjamin, in all his kind ways, tried to get it out of her, tried to find out what was at the root of her ill temperament, but she kept silent. This alone was her cross to bear. She would not bother the others with this illness. She knew they would all try and convince her to stop, to spend the rest of her pregnancy on bedrest. This was not an option.

Josette had to find Phillip and her children needed to be born in the States so they would be U.S. citizens. Then they could all be together. She knew she was putting the health of her unborn children at risk, along with her own, but this is what she had waited for her whole life for. And nothing was going to keep her from it.

"We will be landing shortly at Detroit Metro..." the flight attendants voice said over the intercom.

This was it; she would finally see the house that Phillip called home. Though she had made a number of attempts to contact Franky, both at home and on his cell phone, she got no answer. *I guess this will be a surprise then*, she thought, double-checking her seat belt. She was so looking forward to the look on Franky's face when she showed up at his door, big belly and all.

*

While Josette was landing in Detroit, Benjamin and Father Kumalo were preparing for take-off. It was a four-hour flight to Bucharest, and Benjamin was having second thoughts about letting Josette travel to the States by herself. The last few days, she seemed withdrawn, only speaking when spoken to. He had pushed her more than once on her change in mood, but she just shrugged it off as hormones. Benjamin wasn't buying any of it.

She avoided all contact with the scroll they had found, but then again, after her experience with the portrait, it was easy to see why. The details of the carnage she described in her dream, along with the unsettling acts that she had seen take place at the Banthom House, made it clear to Benjamin that she wanted no part of the scroll or its contents. Josette seemed more than willing to leave all of that to Benjamin and the good priest.

As the flight crew rounded for cabin check, Benjamin leaned over to Father Kumalo. "This professor that we are going to go see... I take it you have worked with him before?"

"Oh yes. He has helped me more than once with my research. He is a good man."

"Did you ever get the meeting set with him? Did you give him any details?"

"Very little. I told him that a close confidant and I were researching an old manuscript and asked if he would help with the translation," The priest shifted in his seat. "He is indebted to the church. He will help us all that he can, I am sure." He took out a small pillow from his carry-on and placed it under his head before closing his eyes.

Benjamin took the hint and let the man rest. He had an uneasy feeling about the priest. Yes, he was a nice enough guy, but his motives for helping were somewhat muddy. At first, he was only to help with the translation, but now he seemed to have something else in mind. Benjamin remembered how quickly he had offered assistance in finding someone who could translate, despite Benjamin's insistence that he knew qualified translators right there in Ireland. The way he'd insisted going to *his* contact was a little unnerving. It was as if the priest had a hidden agenda, some unknown reason for wanting to tag along.

Benjamin remembered how the priest had opened up the night they found the scroll. Over dinner, he divulged that he had become a priest to escape the horror of apartheid, and how moving to Rome in his early twenties had changed his life forever. It was all fascinating, but when he got to the part of taking guardianship of the Grimoires, his demeanor seemed to change. The priest became serious in tone, as if the job terrified, yet captivated, him at the same time.

Benjamin hoped that he was truly there to help them and not just going through the motions to find clues to the last book's location. Still, Benjamin had hopes that he would see the whole thing through. He was sure it would be an asset to have a priest this time.

Any hopes of finding Phillip and Mary alive are becoming more and more dim, he thought to himself. *And let's face it, the light wasn't that bright to begin with.* Benjamin made up his mind that if he could find Mary, and if she was still alive, he was going to ask her to be his bride. He did not buy her claims that all she wanted to do was just party with no commitment. He knew her, and she wanted more. She wanted someone to love and Benjamin knew that someone could be him. Finding her had become the most important thing in his life. He recalled the first night they spent together, and that Dr. Hoffman had caught her slipping out of his bedroom the next morning. A smirk came to his face. *That woman has a lot of class*, he thought. *The way she carried herself that day said a lot about the kind of person she really is.* He liked that.

Another memory came unexpectedly. He saw her sliced body hanging from a hook. He remembered feeling for a pulse and telling Franky and Shawn she had passed. *She was dead*, he thought. *I know she was dead.* The memory haunted him daily. *Dead people don't just free themselves and walk out the door.* She was alive, and he would find her.

As the plane lifted into the air, Benjamin heard the priest snoring. It was going to be a long flight.

*

Doctor Tobar had not taught a class in years. He made income for the college through research. Scurrying his short, thin build around the expansive office, he took book after book off the shelves. His personal collection was extensive. Since he had received the call from Father Kumalo, he'd collected anything pertaining to Sanskrit. *Most people don't know that gypsies migrated from India, and that their nomadic ways led to many different variations of dialect.*, he thought as he searched. It was always a challenge, but he had never come across anything written in Sanskrit that he could not decipher. He also took the time to find some writings on the family name Danior. Danior was a popular Romani name, but if he could find their name mentioned in some text dating back to the early eighteenth century, the same as the section written in Latin, maybe it could be of some help.

Doctor Tabor did not mind helping the Church, even as a devout atheist. He believed in the search of knowledge regardless of a person's personal beliefs. It did not seem to bother the Church because they had used him on many occasions, and they often paid well for information. Facts were facts, and if they needed them, then he was willing to provide them. The thought of one being controlling the universe was a little beyond his scope of belief. If the wisdom he instilled gave them comfort, though, then who was he to judge? He had always been upfront about his views and somehow, he thought the Church appreciated the fact that his data was just that. Data, with no interpretation or perspective. *Just the facts, ma'am,* he thought with a grin. While the two men were flying in that evening, he assured them that it would take a couple of days to nail down the translation.

Even he had to admit that some of the things he found in the past made him give pause, but he had the uncanny ability to look beyond the lore and to the facts. Mankind created religion for the purpose of dealing with its own mortality and all the hoopla that went with it was just that, hoopla. History taught him that traditions could turn into religious conviction, fear and suspicion could be twisted into divine word, and, worst of all, faith turned into a means of control and loyalty. Whatever it was he would find in the scroll, he was sure it was nothing more than someone else's interpretation of the unknown.

*

Sally Smith returned home from work. She hated the winters. Most of all, she hated the early darkness. After her husband Bill was brutally murdered down by Briskey Lake, Sally had become somewhat of a recluse, choosing her socialization very closely. Yet, she hated being alone and hated being alone at night even more. Her only true friends remaining in Parksville had been the two professors who lived next door. Her attempted suicide was well known, but rather than spend time talking behind her back like the rest of town, they checked in on her, making sure that she was doing ok. When they lost power the winter before, it was the two professors who hooked up her generator for her, it was them who brought over supplies, and them who kept her from going over the deep end. Not her so-called friends and family. Sally could not remember all the times people from Parksville had tried to tell her she lived next to a couple weirdos, how it was unnatural for two men to be living together, how they had a strange father and son sexual relationship. Sally would just reply, "Gay or straight, they are the nicest people in town."

Then, there was the talk about their involvement in the Parksville murders. Rumors said they killed the mother and college student to cover up their deviant sexual desires. That's usually when Sally would flip a lid. She knew they had nothing to do with the murders. Professor Parker was one of the few people in town who would take time out of his day to sit and visit with Bill. He was his friend, and there was no way Professor Park was guilty of killing anyone.

So, when she walked up the steps to her front door and saw a figure moving around the house, she became alarmed. Just the other day, Franky asked her to keep an eye on the place and pick up his mail while he was out of town. She knew that Phillip had been gone for some time, and the car in the driveway was unfamiliar.

If Bill was still alive, she would have made him go over there and find out what was going on, but being alone since his death, she had developed an intense fear of strangers. Sally did the only thing she could think of: she called the police.

*

When Josette arrived at Phillip's house, she found it dark and empty. After multiple attempts to reach Franky on his cell phone, getting ready to hop back into her rental car, she remembered Phillip talking about break-ins. "I need to fix the back window. I think that is where they are coming in," she remembered him saying.

Out of pure desperation, she walked to the back of the house and onto the back porch. Sure enough, when she tugged on the laundry room window, it opened. She was afraid that the small window would not accommodate her oversized love bump, but she cleared it easily. Once inside, she turned on the lights, walked out to her rental, and carried in her luggage. She was sure that Franky would not mind; she only hoped he would be home soon.

After walking room to room to familiarize herself with the house, she placed her luggage in the small bedroom on the first floor. It was obvious that Shawn had already arrived because she saw his luggage and a pair of USC shorts in the same bedroom. They could figure out sleeping arrangements later. Finally, she made herself comfortable on the living room couch and turned on the TV set.

Two hours later, there came a knocking at the front door. Josette was surprised when she opened it to find a very attractive female wearing a business suit.

"Hi, my name is Captain Cowan with the City of Jackson Police Department," said the lady. "I am hoping that your name is Josette."

"Yes, I hear Franky and Phillip talk about you. But how did you know..." started Josette. Hazel stopped her.

"I know this is kind of unusual, but we got a call from one of Franky's neighbors. She knew he was out and saw someone in his house. Since I was close by, I thought I would come over myself. You see, I have been working with Franky, helping him find a lead on Phillip. When the call came in that someone was at his house, I was hoping it would be one of the people he had been telling me about."

Josette, coming to her senses moved out of the way.

"Please come in. Come in. I didn't know that Franky had even spoken to you yet. The last I talked to him, he said there was a possibility, but I didn't know he had done it." As Hazel made her way into the living room, Josette felt Hazel's belly inadvertently rub against her arm.

"Is that Irish gentlemen with you?"

"Ben? No, he has a few things to deal with and will be along later," answered Josette. She took Hazel's coat and hung it on the rack by the door. "Would you like a cup of tea? I just made a pot."

"That would be nice," said Hazel, taking a seat on the couch. "When did you get in?"

"I landed about five hours ago. Man, is it cold here," said Josette. She meandered into the kitchen. "How far along are you?"

"I'm sorry?" replied Hazel.

"Oh, have you not told people yet?" asked Josette.

"How did you know?" asked Hazel somewhat surprised. "I know Franky said you were a medium, but…"

"I just have a way of knowing things. You might say it's one of my gifts," responded Josette. She brought Hazel a steaming cup of tea. "Did you want any cream or sugar?"

"No, that's fine. And about my situation, can we, please, keep that between us?" said Hazel "I'm not ready to let everyone know quite yet."

"Sure, not a problem. I understand. Unfortunately, I think it's a little too late for me to hide the boys." Josette sat the teacup down on the coffee table then turned sideways to rub her enormous belly. "What do you think?"

Hazel smiled. "Yea, I would say the ship has sailed on that one."

"I like you, Hazel. I can usually tell about people, and I know you have a big heart." She sat down next to Hazel. "So, tell me, how far along are you?"

"Not quite three months, and you?"

"Six and half. I think Phillip got the job done on his first attempt, if you know what I mean. Man, I never thought it was going to happen to me." Josette smiled. "I thought I would go through my life alone, but Phillip is my guiding light. I never felt so comfortable with any man as I do when I am with him."

Again, Hazel offered a smile. "You know, I spent many-a-long year blaming him for something he didn't do. If I had known back then what I know now..."

"Look," said Josette, "Don't let the 'ifs and maybes' get you down. It keeps you looking backwards. Besides, I have a feeling you and I are going to be very dear friends. That is, if you don't mind being friends with a very pregnant woman who speaks to dead people."

"Well, let's just say a few months ago, I would have thought you a little crazy... but I recently talked to one myself," said Hazel, sipping her tea.

"Bobby. Yes, I know." Then taking a deep breath, she added, "Don't be frightened, but he is here in this room and he has been talking since the moment we touched by the door. He was the one who told me you were pregnant. I like him."

Hazel's eyes widened, "Bobby? Here?"

"Yes, he is standing right behind to you. He wants to make sure you are happy before he leaves for good. He cares a great deal for you."

A look of terror flickered across Hazel's face. "What about Richie? Is he here as well?"

"Relax. Bobby says that Richie has moved on and has no unfinished business here," said Josette. After a long pause, she stated, "Bobby wants you to tell Franky about the baby. Obviously, he is taken by him. I can understand why."

"Franky!" exclaimed Hazel. "Why in the world would I tell him about the baby? I barely know the man."

"I don't know. Bobby keeps saying something about him being the baby's father, but you two never, you know?"

"No!" yelled Hazel. She became defensive. "We haven't even been on a date, I swear."

"I believe you; I believe you," said Josette. She smirked. "Maybe he just thinks you two should hook up, then he could be the baby's stepfather or something. I don't know what he is talking about."

Hazel pondered this for a moment, then surprised Josette by saying, "I wish he was the father; he seems like such a sweet guy. I say this after years of trying to catch him in a lie."

"Look, I know and love Franky with all my heart. He is a gentleman, and those are hard to come by these days. By the way, where the hell are Franky and Shawn?"

"They are following up on a lead down in

Phelton. A couple of women have gone missing there, and since your last encounter with this Banthom guy started with missing people, I thought it might be worth looking into."

Josette stood up and started pacing. While staring into her cup of tea, she paused.

"I have got to get down there. God only knows what could be going on."

"Relax and set next to me for a minute," said Hazel, patting the cushion next to her. "I just talked to them last night. They have found nothing. They said they were staying with the Sheriff and his wife, so I am sure they are safe."

Josette, taking the seat next to Hazel, gave out a loud sigh. "I hope you're right."

Hazel smiled. "Look, they have my best detective with them. I am sure they are fine. Only just don't try and waste your time trying to call them. They have no cell phone service there. They have to call from a landline."

Josette sighed again. "I wish Kip was here to help."

"Who is Kip?" asked Hazel.

"Kip Gillmore, your old boss. He was my spirit guide," said Josette. She expected that would come as a shock to Hazel.

"Yes," said Hazel. Only now, it was she who stood and started. "Franky told me you talked to Kip. Is he here as well?"

"No, sorry. It is hard for a guide to poke a hole into this world and even harder for them to stay.

Kip was with us a long time so I doubt we will ever see him again. Still…"

"Still what?" questioned Hazel.

Josette could hear a hint of optimism in Hazel's tone. "He has visited me in my dreams. It's a little easier for a guide to do this when we are asleep, as we tend to glide through different states of consciousness. But unfortunately, I cannot converse with him and ask him the questions that need answered."

"What about Bobby? Is he my spirit guide?"

Josette reached out and took Hazel by the hand. She stopped pacing. "No, he is simply a kind spirit that is worried about someone he cares about. He's gone now, but he will be back, I'm sure."

"Look," said Hazel, "Why don't I come over tomorrow night and we will go out for dinner? Its Christmas Eve, you're all alone, and so am I. I don't know if the guys will be back yet, so let's have a party just the two of us. What do you say? I think you're right We are going to be very good friends."

CHAPTER VI

THE GATES OF GUINEE

Brandy Cartwright woke up to the sound of people laughing under her hotel window. The strangest feeling of Déjà vu engulfed her waking mind. It had been many years since she had lived in this city, with all its noises and people swarming around like ants, emerging from their underground nest, converging with the rest of the colony for food and drink. She still remembered falling asleep to the sounds of laughter, yelling, whooping, and chatter, only to be awakened by those familiar sounds at the break of each day. It was if she had never left. The town had changed, but not the sounds.

"Good, you're up," remarked Ethel, sitting on her bed.

Brandy looked over and saw Ethel wiping the sleep from her eyes. Ethel, too, had just risen. "It kind of takes you back, doesn't it?"

"What's that?" asked Ethel with a yawn.

"Waking up here in the city again. I mean, since we've been here, I've had the strangest feeling…"

"Like we never left, I know. I feel it, too." Ethel pulled herself to her feet. "Funny, but it's like we were always meant to return."

"I don't know about all that. I will just be glad to wake up in my own bed again."

"Agreed," said Ethel. She made her way to the bathroom.

Brandy sat up but made no attempt to get out of bed. She looked over at the bags of items stacked neatly on the small, round table. Everything was ready except for the flowers. Once she found out that the ritual needed to be completed on a holiday, they both agreed to wait until Christmas Eve to purchase them. *Don't want to piss off a spirit with wilted flowers, for goodness' sake*, thought Brandy.

She was already as nervous about this adventure as a dog squatting on a brier bush. She did not like the fact that Ethel would face this on her own. In some way, she knew the waiting would be worse than being a part of the action. It had been made clear to her numerous times that the souls resting in Guinee were of African descent who had endured years of slavery, lynching, beatings, and segregation. The last thing they would want to see is a white face. Yet, letting Ethel walk into danger alone, without her, was going to be the hardest thing she had ever done.

Maybe we'll just forget about this and find other ways to find Phillip and Mary. While the thought comforted her, she knew deep down that nothing on God's green earth would ever keep Ethel from doing this. This was more than just the search for two friends. To Ethel, it appeared as much a rite of passage.

"Will you call and have them bring up some fucking coffee?" came Ethel's voice from behind the bathroom door. "No breakfast for me. I just want coffee."

"Yes, dear, I will call for your coffee. Is there anything else you want? A massage, your car washed, maybe some of your clothes need mending?"

"Ok, you old bitch. I called yesterday and had it up here before you even poured your lily-white ass out of bed. If I want any shit from you, I'll squeeze your head."

"Ethel, always the lady." responded Brandy, "You want that on a silver platter?"

"That would be nice," said Ethel. The toilet flushed. "Think you can swing that, you old hag?"

"Sure," said Brandy. "I will just make sure it goes on your tab, princess."

Ethel came out of the bathroom. Rather than return to her own bed, she snuggled up next to Brandy. "I don't know what I would do without you. You know that, don't you?"

"Yea, I know. Probably you would just find another cracker to open up a whore house with, that's all. We all look the same to you, anyways."

"Not at all. Some white people are actually

good looking. Of course, I don't know any, but I've heard."

Brandy put her head on Ethel's shoulder. "Do you think we will see Sam again today?"

"Shit, that boy has followed us around every day since we got here. I don't know. I'm about ready to tell him to, 'Get lost.'"

"The little toad knows the city, though. We lived here all those years, and it's like we are seeing the city for the first time."

"I know, but he gives me the creeps. Young boys just don't act that sophisticated. I mean, he corrected my pronunciation of places I have visited for years, little butt sniffer."

Brandy paused. "You know, Ethel, I was thinking maybe we don't have to do this. I mean, we both want to find Mary and Phillip, but surely there are other ways. I'm scared, girl. I am scared for you. All this talk about spirits getting mad and causing trouble if you do anything wrong on the Gates, not to mention being dragged to Hell... I mean, it just doesn't set right, you know?"

Ethel smiled and looked Brandy straight in the eye. "You know, when I was a kid, I used to dream about the seven Gates. Sometimes I would have the worst nightmares, but other times it was like it was just a part of being who I am, at times almost comforting, the spirits knew me and wanted me there. I can't explain it, but I always felt a connection to them and the Gates. When I grew up, I tried to forget those memories, forget about voodoo, and all the bullshit that went with it. But somehow, I knew it would fall on me to complete this task someday. I know it sounds crazy, but I feel kinda relieved that I am getting it out of the way. It's like I am finally getting rid of an unbearable burden."

"Well, you know I love you, heart and soul. And it will kill me if anything is to happen to you. You know that. You are my best friend, the sister I never had. I hate that you have to do this alone," said Brandy.

"I will be fine. I promise you nothing is going to happen to me tomorrow. We will find out where Phillip and Mary are, go get them, and bring them home."

Now both women were close to tears. Brandy got out of bed and put on her night coat. "Ok, ok. But if you get yourself killed over this, I swear I will bury you in the ugliest, damn, cheap box I can find. You got that?"

"You would, too."

"Damn right, I will. Now I have to go to the bathroom so you can call down for our fucking coffee."

From inside the bathroom, Brandy heard Ethel start to sing. It was Etta James', *"At Last."* *God can that girl sing. The voice of an angel,* thought Brandy.

*

Outside, the sun was bright, but the morning air was still heavy with dampness. Just as Ethel had forecasted, Sam was standing across the street when the pair emerged from their hotel room. He was talking to a couple of tourists who had lost their way. Sam was pointing and talking. Then the woman would ask another question and Sam would point in the other direction. *Maybe he won't see us,* thought Ethel, waving to Brandy to hurry out the door. They walked briskly down the street, but they did not escape the watchful eye of the young boy.

"Ms. Brandy, Ms. Ethel," came the boy's voice from behind. Ethel could tell from the direction of his voice, he was making his way across the street quickly. Brandy, hearing the young man, and much to Ethel's annoyance, stopped and turned.

"Sam, I wondered if you would be here this morning."

"Yes, ma'am, I'm here. I know you need flowers and…."

"Don't tell me," said Ethel sarcastically. "You know the best shop in town."

"Well, yes, ma'am I sure do. But it's on Canal Street. We need to go the other direction."

"Fine," Ethel huffed. Brandy offered the boy an apple she had taken from the lobby. "How far is it? My feet are killing me."

"Oh, it's not far. It won't take but ten minutes to get there, I promise," said Sam crossing his heart. "It's Christmas Eve, you know, so everything will be closing early today. Good thing you are getting an early start."

"You are a sweet young man, but today, can we skip the history lesson on the way?" asked

Brandy. She took the boy's hand. "And if you want to, maybe we can stop for some ice cream before we get back. How does that sound?"

"That sounds amazing," said Sam.

Ethel shot Brandy a look of pure annoyance. "Really? Like we have nothing else to do today..."

"Get over yourself, Ethel. It's Christmas Eve," said Brandy jokingly.

Ethel smiled but was not amused. She was worried about making sure that they got just what was listed in the scroll. The thought of displeasing the spirits laid heavy on her mind.

"Ethel, Ethel," came a voice from behind them. It was her cousin, Rebecca, approaching at a fast pace. Ethel could plainly see that the woman was distraught. "It's Grandma. She's in the hospital. It doesn't look good. I am on my way up there now and thought you might want to join me."

Ethel stood in the middle of the sidewalk, unsure what to say.

"Go, go. Sam, and I will get the flowers," said Brandy. But when she turned to confirm this with the boy, he was gone. She looked up and down the street, but the boy had vanished.

"Oh, no need," said Rebecca. "I knew you would wait for the last day. Before I left to find you, I ordered them from a friend of mine. They will be delivered to your hotel this afternoon. Everything that was on the list. Trust me, I made sure she had everything you needed."

Ethel was hesitant, but with Brandy's

encouragement, she agreed to go with Rebecca. "Do you mind staying here and making sure the order comes in? And that it is correct?" she asked Brandy.

"Of course. Now go see your grandmother."

*

The flowers arrived right at noon. Brandy received the phone call that they were at the front desk. It seems that Rebecca had been kind enough to pay for the order upfront and Brandy thought it was a sweet gesture. After placing the bundle of flowers in their room, Brandy walked back out into the street. She was worried about Sam and his quick disappearance. Maybe she would find him again just to make sure that he was alright, but he was nowhere to be found. She ended up visiting some shops, searching for a gift she could give Ethel in the morning. She had already gotten her an additional phone line because she was sick and tired of her being on the Internet and not answering her phone. But still, it just didn't seem right her not getting something on Christmas day. Just as Sam had stated earlier, all the shops started to close at noon, so she ate lunch at a small restaurant known for their gumbo. She returned to her room around three, but there still was no Ethel. *Ethel's grandmother must be in bad shape for her to be gone this long,* she thought to herself.

An exhausted Ethel walked into the hotel room around ten that night.

"How is she? Is she going to be alright?" Brandy barely gave Ethel time to set down her purse.

"The old lady is going, it's just a matter of time. The doctor said he was surprised she is still here at all."

"Where is Rebecca?"

"Home. She is going back in the morning," said Ethel, plopping down on her bed.

"What about the Gates? Are we calling that quits?" asked Brandy.

"No, the Gates are still on. I will visit her when I am done, if she's still here," said Ethel.

Brandy gave Ethel a funny look., "You mean that you…"

"Hold it right there, old woman. She was the one who insisted I follow through with this. It took everything she had to tell me that I need to complete the Gates. Said she wanted me to tell her about it when I was done. So, don't be getting all high and mighty on me."

"But why would she care one way or the other? It's our friends, not hers."

"Hell if I know. She's half out of her mind, I guess," responded Ethel. "Either way, I'm going first thing in the morning."

*

There was a thick fog that moved in overnight that made it difficult for Ethel and Brandy to find their way down St. Louis Street. By the time they reached Basin Street, the fog was so thick, they struggled to find the front gate of Saint Louis Cemetery, No. 1. If it had not been for the unexpected sound of Sam's voice from within the cemetery, Ethel doubted they would have found the tall, white structure that was the tomb of Marie Laveau. "Ms. Ethel, Ms. Brandy, she's over here!" Sam's voice trailed through the mist.

Upon reaching their destination, Ethel was more than furious. She promised Brandy she could accompany her to the starting point, but no further. She never thought that Sam, too, would be waiting.

"Sorry, Sam, but you got to go!" exclaimed Ethel.

"Oh, I know. I'm sorry. I just wanted to help you get started. Everyone knows this is the first step," said the boy apologetically. "I'm not going to bother you, I promise. I will wait here with Ms. Brandy."

"No, I want you to walk Ms. Brandy back to the hotel," said Ethel. And to Brandy, "Dear, the rest I have to do on my own. Please take this little snot out of here. I don't want to start off on the wrong foot. Remember, I'll let loose spirits that can harm a lot of people if this is not done right."

"Yea and get drug to Hell if you piss them off," Brandy shot off.

"Come, Ms. Brandy, I will escort you home. Ms. Ethel is right' she has to do this by herself."

He tugged on Brandy's hand.

"Hold on, little man," said Brandy. Walking over to Ethel, she gave her an enormous hug and started to cry. "Ethel, please don't do this. I got a bad feeling. Let's just go home."

"Look, girl. I love ya so much, but you know this is something I gotta do. Phillip and Mary need me."

Finally, Brandy let her go. As she and Sam left, a panic came over Ethel. She wanted to run to her and flee to the safety of their hotel room, but she stood strong, gathering all her strength, and turned the other way. She didn't want Brandy to see her fear.

With all the courage she could muster, she walked up to the tomb of Marie. Next to the flowers, already there she laid some white lilies.

"May your bloodline do you proud," she spoke. "May you find it in your heart to give me guidance." And she began the ritual.

After Marie's tomb, Ethel pulled out the map from her grandmother. It was not easy to follow. The sequence of symbolic Gates had her running back and forth from Saint Louis Cemetery No. 1, Saint Louis Cemetery No. 2, Greenwood Cemetery, Cypress Grove Cemetery, St. Patrick Cemetery, then back to Saint Louis Cemetery No. 1. All of this she would have to do on foot.

Though she prayed the fog would lift, it did not. Ethel found the gate of Baron LaCroix, also known as the Baron of the Cross. As she neared the location on the map, she felt spirits moving along with her, following her, from her left and her right. Though she saw nothing in the thick fog, she could feel their presence. Once she arrive, Ethel took her time with the offering and words. More and more, she became aware that the spirits were waiting. Waiting for the slightest mistake that might set them free to wreak havoc on the city. Fighting back her fear, she left the gate of Baron LaCroix, guide of the dead and sexuality. As she left, she kept waiting for something extraordinary to happen, but nothing did. At least, nothing she could tell. *Thank goodness for Grandma and her map*, she thought.

From cemetery to cemetery, from grave, to tomb, to trees, she conquered the Gates one by one. For each gate mastered, the spirits came closer. It was not until the last gate, the gate of Baron Samedi, that she could finally see them through the fog. Spirits, numbering in the hundreds, followed her. Black men, women and children, all lost, as if she were leading them to some divine light that only they could see. Some wore the rags of slaves, while others sported the attire of rich merchants, prostitutes, ship captains. On and on, they comprised of all types of people from all walks of life.

The last gate was yet another tomb. Only this one so old and tattered that no epitaph remained. The red bricks had been removed in places as if someone had tried to search the tomb for treasure. This was the location that scared her the most, the gate of Baron Samedi, master of the land of the undead. If she could pass this gate, she would be able to ask her one question. Ethel prepared her offerings, a cigar and rum, and felt something touch her hand.

Ethel screamed, suppressing it in fear of angering the spirits. Especially Baron Samedi.

"Sorry, I didn't mean to scare you!" cried a faint, little voice.

Ethel knew at once who it was.

"Sam, I told you, you cannot be here. Where is Brandy?"

"Back at the hotel. Please let me watch. I will sit down right there and be as quiet as a mouse, I swear," he pleaded, pointing to a small stone bench across the path from the last gate.

Ethel didn't know what to do. If she did not complete the task, the spirits surrounding them would be let loose. If she finished and angered Baron Samedi, then she could be taken to the land of the dead, never to be seen or heard of again.

Damn this nosey little bastard, she thought. *I've not gone through all of this shit to stop now.*

All of a sudden, the spirits moved in closer. While Sam did not seem to notice the gruesome figures, Ethel, on the other hand, could feel her heart racing and her breath becoming more labored. She felt like she was going to pass out. Closer and closer they came from out of the fog, arms outreached, eyes blank, and faces drawn.

"Fine. Sit there and be quiet," she said to the boy. Working with urgency, she placed the cigar and rum on the grave, speaking the words from the script. A white, glowing orb, about the size of a small car, materialized in front of her. The gate opened.

"Dear Baron Samedi, I wish to ask a question of Doctor John. It is the right of my bloodline."

Slowly, the white orb dimmed. It formed into the shape of a man, though Ethel could not see his face.

"Proceed," spoke the figure.

Mustering all the courage she could find, Ethel announced, "Thank you, Doctor John, for coming to my aid. Yes, we need to find our friends Phillip and Mary. They were…"

"They were cursed by a satanic gypsy witch and have gone missing."

The voice was soft but direct. The face became clear. It was the kind face of a young, handsome man. "Did the witch sell his soul?"

"Yes," responded Ethel, shaking. The gate opening had not stopped the advance of spirits, and Doctor John's question was taking time.

"Did this witch complete the death, burial, and resurrection?"

"Yes, but please…."

"Did this witch have one of the three Grand Grimoires?" asked the spirit. He was obviously in in no hurry.

Just inches away, the spirit of an old man, whose head hung to one side, broken, reached out towards her. It startled Ethel.

"Yes, yes!" she exclaimed.

"And who is it the witch wants dead?"

"What?" said Ethel stepping away from the spirit. "Who does he want dead?" she pleaded.

Then the world seemed to stop. Her mind revisited the day Shawn stood on the table at the hotel. It was Shawn, but not Shawn. It was Banthom, possessing his body. She remembered his words to Franky: "Maybe I will save you for last so you can watch the rest die before you, just like that cunt mother of yours."

Just as the dead man grabbed her by the arm, Ethel closed her eyes and yelled, "Franky Lake! He wanted Franky Lake dead!"

In an instant, the man's hand was gone. When she opened her eyes, all of the spirits had disappeared, including Doctor John. From a distance, she still heard his voice.

"The question is answered."

Ethel dropped to the ground. *Phillip and Mary will be found wherever Franky is,* she thought.

"Now I will have a word with you," came a voice from behind her. It started out with the sound of a young boy, but turned into that of a grown man. There was no need for her to turn. She knew what she would see. Fear engulfed her whole being. Instead of a boy named Sam, there would be a large, black man in black tails, wearing a large top hat, his face painted with white, large teeth across his lips, a blackened nose, and white on his eyes. It was none other than Baron Samedi himself. An encounter with him was the one thing she had feared the most.

"I have done the Gates correctly. I have not strayed from my path," spoke Ethel, never once turning to look.

"You have done well. But your grandmother, bless her soul, is now dead. I have let her go, and you, my dear, are now the guardian of the Gates. You will never leave Louisiana again, or, the consequences will be rather harsh, my dear."

"But what about Rebecca? She is the heir, not me. I don't even know…"

"Stop. Do not anger me. The spirits chose the guardian of the Gates. This has always been your cross to bear."

"Please, I beg of you," wept Ethel.

"The deed is done; you are who you are. Leave home again and you, and all you love, will pay the price. Now go."

Ethel pulled herself up off the ground, looking for the man behind her, but he was gone. Weeping, she slowly made her way back towards Bourbon Street.

CHAPTER VII

WOMAN OF THE LAKE

Shawn was not quite awake when he and Franky, Vinnie, Malcom, and Luke all entered The Wooden Spoon. *The day after Christmas and I am stuck in the middle of Hooterville freezing my ass off, and so far, it's all been for nothing,* he thought. Franky called Captain Cowan the night before to let her know they would not be home for Christmas. Yet another person went missing Christmas Eve, a local boy who disappeared from his home in the middle of the night. Thankfully, they got a call from the parents that morning that the boy had been found. He apparently attempted to run away from home because he did not get what he wanted for Christmas. The boy did not make it past the neighbor's house next door. The neighbors, in Florida for the holidays, left their house unlocked and the boy took full advantage. *If only they would all be so easy,* Shawn thought.

The Wisemans had been more than gracious.

On Christmas Eve, Malcom broke out a bottle of his best scotch and Elma made a huge dinner, but all the time Shawn felt out of place. His parents had never celebrated the holidays, any holiday. Not Easter, New Year's, Memorial Day, the Fourth of July. The only person he had ever celebrated any holiday with was Samantha. She loved all holidays, but it had always been just the two of them.

"Malcom, I need to talk to you," said Marge, visibly distraught. "It's Dale. I haven't seen him for a few days and I'm worried. You know we were closed for Christmas, but I didn't see him the day before and he never showed this morning for his breakfast."

"You know Dale. He probably got drunk the last few days and is sleeping it off," said Malcom. He took a seat at the closest table by the door. "But I will have Luke go and check out his place this afternoon."

"It's not like him, Malcom. He has never, in all the years I have known him, gone this long without coming into town. No one has seen him for days."

"I'm sure he is just fine," consulted Malcom.

Marge seemed to take some comfort in Malcom's words. She sighed then grabbed her order pad. "Do you all want coffee?"

"YES, please!" exclaimed Shawn.

He needed something to warm him up. The morning strolls through the frozen fields had been hard on him. Even with the snowmobile suits that

Elma had offered on loan, the cold was getting to him. Yesterday, they had spent five hours combing the area near the boy's home for nothing.

"I think we all want coffee," said Franky. He smiled at Marge.

"The special today is shit on a shingle. Five fifty and that includes your coffee," said Marge.

Shawn watched Marge dart into the kitchen. "Is she related to this Dale guy? She seems awfully worried."

"She and Dale have one of those love-hate relationships," said Luke. "When this place was closed, Dale went over to her place and gave her five thousand dollars to make it through. He never even asked her to pay it back. Said it was a gift. The man has more money than he knows what to do with. He owns half the land between here and County Line Road."

"She still gives him hell every day, but deep down she cares a lot for him," added Malcom. "He's an odd one, drunk most of the time, but we are all family around here. He's been a part of our lives for a long time."

"If he has all this money and land, why does he live in an old trailer out in the middle of nowhere?" questioned Shawn.

"Well, his grandfather had a cabin out there. It was built a few years after that murder took place," said Luke.

"It was his grandfather who owned all that land and money. Dale's parents said it was to keep people away, but everyone knew they moved the old man out to the lake to get rid of him. To get him out of the way," said Malcom.

"They all said he was going crazy, forgetting stuff. Dale's mother and father had him found legally incompetent and took over the family fortune, moving him out of the way," added Luke.

"But that Dale loved the old man. He bought a trailer and moved in across the lake to look after him," continued Malcom. "About ten years ago, a tornado tore through those woods. It didn't cause much damage, but a large old oak tree landed on the cabin, went right through the roof, and killed the old man as he laid in bed. Dale was heartbroken."

"So why didn't Dale just move into the cabin?" asked Shawn.

"The cabin was a total loss and his parents never put any insurance on the place. So Dale took all the wood that was in the cabin and used it as firewood."

"All but the basement," said Luke. "He put an old barn door over the stairs and converted that into a storm and root cellar. Every year, Marge goes out of her way to make sure it's stocked with canned goods from her garden."

A few moments later, Marge returned carrying five cups of coffee.

"Do you know what you want, or do you need a few minutes?"

"Nothing for me," said Vinnie.

"I'll take the special," said Luke,

"Sounds good to me," said Franky.

"Me too," said Malcom.

"I'll just have two eggs, over medium, with white toast," said Shawn. *I don't know what shit on a shingle is, but it does not sound appealing to me*, he thought.

Once she finished writing down the order, Marge spoke to Malcom.

"You know the last time Dale was in here, he was raving about the Woman of the Lake again."

"I know, I know. He talked about her at the town meeting the other day," said Luke.

Marge walked towards the order window, but paused..

"Did he tell you she now looks evil and has red hair? He swears she is the one taking people."

Now it was Franky who spoke up. "Red hair?"

"Yea, pretty sure that's what he said.

"Hey Howard!" Marge yelled through the order window. "Didn't Dale say the Woman of the Lake has red hair?"

"The color of blood is what he said," called Howard.

"Shit," said Shawn.

Malcom glanced over at him. "That mean something to guys?"

"No," said Franky. "We just have a friend who is missing, and she has red hair."

Shawn was relieved that Franky had spoken up. He was at a loss for words.

"I see," said Malcom. "You don't think this has anything to do with..."

"I doubt that very much," continued Franky. "She went missing in Florida. She was from Ireland originally. And nothing against your town, but I highly doubt she has ever even heard of Phelton."

Malcom seemed to be satisfied with this explanation and quickly changed the subject.

"Ok, we are batting zero here. That storm they've been talking about all week is getting close, and it might even start tonight. I am afraid I will have to suspend the search. People will need to prepare for the storm today. I don't want any search parties until it's safe for people to be out looking again."

"We may just go ahead and head home if you are suspending the search. We will come back right after it clears. Is there anything you need for us to do before we go?" Vinnie asked.

"Well, if you don't mind, I would like for someone to ride out to Dale's with Luke. I know I sound paranoid, but I think it's best if we stay in teams."

"I'll go," said Franky.

"Tell you what," said Vinnie. "How about us three stop by before we leave town, that way Luke can help back here?"

"Sounds good to me," said Luke. "I have more important things to do than chase down that old nut job. I don't even know if there is gas for the school generator."

"That's fine with me. only you won't have a radio so if you could stop back and let us know before you go, that would be great," said Malcom.

"Yes, please," said Marge, bringing out the first of the orders.

"I guess we'll have to. If there is no cell phone service in town, I'm sure there isn't any way out there," said Vinnie.

Shawn was not crazy about the idea of going to a camper in the middle of the woods, especially one that is haunted by the Woman of the Lake, but he said nothing.

*

Elma was at the office when the gang of men walked in. They disclosed their plans to leave after they went to check on Dale. Elma was sorry to see them leave. It was nice having the house full again, but she was also relieved. She had not planned on guests and her pantry was running low. Meijer's was a long drive and she had hoped to make it through the coming storm before having to make the trip.

"Will you guys go and get the car packed?" Vinnie asked Franky and Shawn. "I need to talk to Malcom for a few minutes if you don't mind."

"The house is unlocked," offered Elma. "You can just leave your snow suits on the back porch and I'll take care of them when I get home tonight. By the sound of things, I won't have anything else to do. The weatherman is predicting twenty inches of snow and wind gusts up to fifty miles per hour."

"Damn," said Franky. "We may want to be quick about packing since it's a long drive home."

"Go ahead. You and Shawn take off. I won't be long," said Vinnie. "I just need a few minutes with Malcom."

With that, Franky and Shawn left for the house. Malcom led Vinnie to the back room and both men sat opposite of each other at the table. Elma made them a cup of coffee and then joined them at the end of the table.

"Elma, I think Vinnie here wanted to talk to me alone," insisted Malcom.

"Oh, no, old man. Not this time. I want to hear what he has to say, and I don't care if you are the sheriff or not. I am sure Vinnie doesn't mind, do you?"

Vinnie was taken back by this. "No, if Malcom doesn't mind, then..."

"Woman, you are going to be the death of me. You know that, don't you?" said Malcom.

"Now go ahead, Vinnie. Tell us what you got," said Elma.

"Well, I don't have anything, really. It's just, well, you know this isn't over. These people were taken by someone and you know as well as I do, they are probably never coming back. The snatches are clean; I mean really clean. I went to both locations and, just like you, I found nothing. That means these abductions were well planned out.

They are executed without a flaw. You are dealing with someone of higher intelligence, maybe a serial killer. I can't believe I am saying this after my dealings with them, but you may want to call in the feds."

"I thought about it, but you know… us small-town lawmen don't have the clout you city guys have. Missing is not the same as murdered. You know that."

"I do, but if you want, I could ask Captain Cowan to go to bat for you on this."

"What makes you so sure they are dead?" asked Elma.

"If it was just the White girl, I would say there is a case for a hostage situation. Maybe some kind of sex slavery. But with the old woman…, it just doesn't add up."

"Well, God rest her soul if that's the case. The woman was butt ugly; always was," griped Elma under her breath.

"Look," continued Vinnie. "I will be back, I promise you. But just think about what I said. Either way, I will be back. And if I must, I will dig until I find the evidence you need to call in the feds. In the meantime, you need to warn people, make sure they stay in their houses at night, and, for God's sake, tell them to start locking their doors."

"People around here have never…" started Elma.

"No, Vinnie's right. Right after this storm passes, I am putting a curfew in effect. Both women came up missing at night. Maybe it's part of his M.O." said Malcom. "And even if it isn't, it will put people on notice that there is a sicko out there."

Elma shook her head in agreement. She still was finding it hard to believe that something so awful could happen in Phelton. There had not been a curfew since Dolly Hurt was found murdered at the lake.

Just then, Malcom got up. He looked out the small window on the back wall. "I'll be damned! It's snowing already."

*

Franky was glad to be going home. Soon he, Josette, and Shawn would be able to set down and get caught up on all that happened since they left Florida. *Josette must big as a barrel by now,* he thought, packing his backpack. Shawn had finished packing his stuff and was ready to walk it down to the car.

"Can you grab Vinnie's suitcase out of the other bedroom?" asked Franky. "He said it was already mostly packed."

"Got it," said Shawn. "It seemed funny us sharing a room again after all this time."

"Yea, but next time I hope we at least have our own bed. Nothing personal, but you flip and flop all night."

Shawn smiled, picked up his duffle, and

walked out, leaving Franky alone in the upstairs bedroom.

Outside the bedroom window, Franky saw oversized snowflakes gliding gently to the ground. *Don't tell me this shit is starting already,* he thought. They had a long trip home. Hopefully, the weather would not turn before they got started.

Since he heard about the Woman of the Lake, Franky had been uneasy. *Red hair, the color of blood. Was it possible? Could all of this have something to do with Mary? No… that was ridiculous to even consider. That story started back in the '50s.*

Even though the odds were enormous, Franky could not rid himself of the idea. He and Shawn had talked at great lengths about all the possibilities. Both men knew that if they did find their friends, they may not be the same as they remembered them. They may be hurt and suffering, lost without memory, taken hostage, or even worse, dead. Shawn even shared his feeling that they might be better off dead. Even though it tore Franky up to think this way, he knew he may be right.

That fucker, Banthom, did something to them, but what? Franky remembered every detail of the day they found them hanging. They were stripped naked, bodies bloody from the deep cuts ripped across their chests. All though it all happened in a very short period, he could recall every detail, the pentagram on the floor, the animal bones, the broken pottery. He remembered feeling a pulse on Phillip, and Benjamin shaking his head no for Mary as he checked for one on her wrist. Thank goodness Shawn was smart enough to take the few quick shots of them gone, otherwise he would have always believed they died in the fire.

"Vinnie's back!" yelled Shawn from downstairs.

Franky quickly finished his packing, lifted his backpack, and left the room. Downstairs, he found Vinnie and Shawn standing by the front door.

"I'm warming up the car. Give it just a couple of minutes and we will head out. I called and left a message for Hazel that we are heading back until the storm clears. And look, you guys don't need to come back when the storm passes if you don't want to."

Franky walked past both men and headed outside. "I need to put this in the trunk."

"I left it open," said Shawn. Franky walked down the snow-covered sidewalk.

"Hell, it must be warm enough by now," said Vinnie. "It doesn't take long for that old beater to heat up. Did you guys hang the snowmobile suits back up?"

"All taken care of," said Shawn.

Shawn and Vinnie joined Franky at the car. The windshield was still covered in ice, except for a little wet spot right above the defroster. Franky, who had grabbed the ice scraper from the trunk, was already on his way to clear the rest. The snow was still falling in large flakes. And even though the sun had come up, it looked more like late evening or early morning. It was dark and gloomy.

Franky gave the windshield a quick scrape then hopped into the back seat of the car. "We better make this quick. I don't think the storm is going to wait until tonight."

"I watched the weather this morning with Elma. They said we would have early flurries, but the worst is still coming. High winds, subzero windchill, and a lot of snow," responded Vinnie.

All the three men knew for sure was that Dale lived about three miles out of town, his drive highlighted by two red reflectors and a mailbox mounted on a stone pedestal.

"Luke told me, and I quote," said Vinnie, making quotation marks with his fingers, "You can't miss it. The damn thing is in the shape of a manatee, like he lived in the heart of Florida or something. Crazy old asshole." Then Vinnie made the quotation marks again. "End quote."

It didn't take long before they arrived at their destination. The manatee mailbox was right where Luke had said, with the two red reflectors and the stone pedestal. Though the drive had not been bad, and the roads were still clear, the driveway was another issue. It had not been plowed. There had been no salt truck making the mile-long run up the two tracks, and with the morning snow, it was now covered. Franky knew the problem would not be getting stuck on the road, but being able to follow the hidden route. He knew if they got off the two tracks, then there was a strong possibility of getting stuck.

As they slowly made their way, Franky could see why someone might want to live this way. The woods were beautiful, the fresh falling snow covering the tree branches in a blanket of white. Somehow, the whole scene seemed dreamlike, like something out of a fairy tale of old.

"There's the camper," said Shawn. He pointed down the drive. "Look, there's the old man's truck."

"Well, at least we know he's here," said Vinnie.

"I'm not so sure," countered Shawn. "I've got a bad feeling about all this."

"Pull up next to his truck and we will get out and check on him," said Vinnie.

The camper was one of those old Silver Airstreams. It sat in the middle of a clearing, not thirty feet from the edge of the lake. It was bigger than Franky had envisioned. The front sported a large window covering its width, the door was near the front, and in the back, were two windows along the side, one above the other.

Vinnie stopped the car next to Dale's truck. The moment he put the car in park, Shawn and Vinnie jumped out of the car. "Hold on you two. Wait for me," said Vinnie hopping out.

"Remember, I am the one with the gun. God only knows who, or what, might be hiding in that trailer."

Franky heard but did not heed the warning. He ran up to the door of the camper and started pounding at the door. After only a few seconds of waiting, Franky flung open the door and went inside.

"Well, so much for listening to the cop," huffed Vinnie, finally reaching the front step where Shawn was standing.

After checking the entire trailer, including the bathroom, Franky was sure that Dale was not there. And by the looks of things, he had not been there for a few days. The moment he walked in, he noticed the unpleasant odor, but it took him a moment to find the source. A half-full glass of what was once milk sat on the kitchen table, along with a half-eaten bowl of cereal.

"He's not here," he yelled towards the open front door. Looks like he's been gone awhile."

That's when Franky noticed the crucifixes. At least one was hung over each of the windows and one over the front door. "Looks like he was even more afraid of the Woman of the Lake than we thought," he added. "Come in and look at this."

Vinnie was the first through the door. "What the fuck is that smell?"

Franky lifted up the glass of milk and rinsed it out in the sink. "Sour milk."

"What's with all the crosses?" asked Shawn, now making his way in.

"I don't know, but close that door. It's getting fucking cold in here," said Franky. "We need to talk about what we do next."

"I say we do what we said we were going to do, go back into town, tell Malcom he's gone, and be on our way," said Shawn sternly. "I'm telling you guys; I have the strangest feeling…"

That's when they heard the sound of a little girl's moan. It was coming from the outside, somewhere in the back of the trailer, just below the small kitchen window. All three men ran to the kitchen for a look. There, standing exposed in the freezing snow, was a little girl. Dressed in rags, she kept her head bent, cupping her hands over the top of her head.

"Please, can someone help me?" she pleaded.

Shawn at once jumped for the door.

"No, wait!" yelled Vinnie, but it was too late. He was on his way out the door. Turning to Franky, he pointed out the window.

"There's no footprints, see? She is standing in the middle of the fucking backyard and there are no damn footprints in the snow coming from either direction. Look."

Franky, staring out the window, picked up instantly on what Vinnie was saying. There was no wind, nothing to cover up tracks. She couldn't have gotten to where she was without leaving a trail. Franky, realizing the gravity of the situation, rushed towards the door.

"Shawn, no! It's a trap!" he screamed at the top of his lungs. As he was ready to make the jump out the door and over the steps, the front door came crashing shut, knocking Franky to the floor.

Outside, Vinnie watched as the child lifted her head, her face that of a putrid corpse. That's when he first saw the flash of white glide outside the front window. It was crossing from the front yard to the back. It was a woman, dressed in a white nightgown. She was barely visible through the falling snow.

"Shawn, no!" he yelled.

Franky pulled himself up off the floor and ran back to the window just in time to see Shawn standing in disbelief next to the girl. Franky watched in horror as Shawn realized what the little girl really was. Grimacing, he looked up at the two men in the window with a plea of help in his eyes.

"Look," said Vinnie. "Over by the lake, the woman. Do you see her?"

"Shit!" yelled Franky. He ran back to the front door. This time, it swung open with no resistance.

Franky turned the corner to the back of the trailer as the woman's form darted towards Shawn. Within a second, she was on him. She snatched him up as if he weighed nothing more than a paper bag and carried him off into the woods. Franky screamed, but to no avail. Shawn, the woman, and the little girl were all gone. Franky's first thought was to run after them, but then realized Vinnie and the gun were still in the trailer. He ran back around the trailer and ran headlong into Vinnie, who was running in the opposite direction with his gun drawn.

"What the fuck was that?" screamed Vinnie.

"I don't know, but we've got to find Shawn. We got to."

"Franky, I think we need to get back inside," said Vinnie.

Franky could see Vinnie's attention was now back on the lake. At its edge stood the little girl, and she was snickering.

*

Elma sat in front of her living room window watching the snow fall. It was past five and the men had not yet returned. As the wind started picking up, she cringed. Something was wrong. Vinnie and the boys would never have just left without giving their report on Dale.

That SOB of a lake, she thought. *Nothing good has ever come from that place.*

She remembered when the lake was the place to go. It was where she and Malcom had first made love. She lost her virginity that day. But after what happened to Dolly, the kids stopped going. Dale and his grandfather moved out of his parents' in the seventies and Dale parked the camper there. He has been there ever since. He never allowed hunting or fishing on his property, and posted "No trespassing" signs everywhere he could so to put an end to all the parties, skinny dipping, and young lovemaking that it had once been known for.

Tim, the newest member of the Sheriff's department, was working dispatch, so there was no need for her to stay at the office. No business was getting done today, anyway. Malcom and Luke were out there somewhere on a call, an accident way up on US 27. She worried about them being out in the storm, but after all these years, she had learned how to deal with the stress. It had always been her greatest fear that one of them someday would not come back.

When she had walked over to The Wooden Spoon for lunch that day, Marge informed her that they were closing early, and opening tomorrow was doubtful. By tomorrow, she knew the streets would be bare and the schools closed. And if the weatherman was right, the day after offered no better conditions.

Sipping her tea, she gazed out the window, waiting to see Malcom's truck pull up in front of the station. It was going to be a long day; of that she was sure. She didn't know how much longer she could play this game of wait-and-see. She had been nagging Malcom into retirement for the past five years to no avail.

"Next year, next year," he would always say. Elma made up her mind at that very moment that this would be her last winter in Michigan. If he didn't want to retire, then he could stay, and she would go visit her sister in South Carolina for the winters.

Elma heard a knock at the front door. She set her tea down on the coffee table and walked over to the door to answer, but when she got there, she saw Howard already kicking off his boats on the inside door mat.

"Sorry to bother you, Ms. Elma, but I got a bunch of food that will go to waste and thought you might want the rest of the chili and soup of the day. French Onion," said Howard. He held two large containers. I didn't want to leave it in the fridge. It won't be worth eating after a couple of days."

"Howard, that is ever so nice of you."

"Please, let me carry these to your kitchen. They're heavy. I thought with all the extra mouths you have to feed, it might come in handy," said Howard. He strolled across the living room towards the kitchen.

"Oh. Vinnie and boys have gone back to Jackson, or at least I hope so. But you know how Malcom and Luke can eat. Don't worry, it won't go to waste around here."

"I thought they were going to check on Dale. Marge is beside herself with worry."

"They were supposed to come back, but with the weather, they may have just headed home."

Howard walked to the counter next to the fridge and set them down.

"Could be," said Howard. They do have a long way to go. Doesn't that Dale guy have a phone?"

"Dale," Elma shook her head. "No, Dale don't believe in phones, or computers, or anything that might make life easier."

"My grandma was the same way. God, I miss her."

"I always liked your grandma. She was a good soul. A little out there by the end, but as sweet a lady as I have ever met."

"Yea, her dementia got pretty bad there at the end, I guess. Marge told me she was struggling to keep the restaurant going by the end."

"Well, Marge did everything after she got bad. She cooked, cleaned, waited tables. She loved your grandmother to death. If not, I don't think your grandmother could have kept it going."

"Really? I didn't know that. I guess I owe her a big, 'Thank you.'"

"Yea, I would say you do. By the way, I am glad you're here. You seem to fit in nicely. I do want to warn you, though. There are those in town who feel, well, you being a stranger and all, that you have something to do with the disappearances."

"I know, Malcom told me. It's kind of weird thinking people would think that of me."

"Well, it's a small town, and small towns sometimes have small-minded people."

"Well, I like it here," said Howard. He walked back towards the front door. "I think I am going to be around for a while." He smiled, then turned to leave. "If you do hear from Vinnie, you will call Marge, won't you? I'm worried about her."

"You got it, kid. I'm sure Dale is just held up in his camper. It's too darn cold for him to be anywhere else. And Howard…"

"Yes ma'am?"

"Thank you for thinking of us. Malcom loves your chili."

CHAPTER VIII

THE BODY

Sam was getting ready to leave when he got the call. The body of a man found on a golf course down in Concord was on his way to Sam's lab. From the description his staff had given, something had torn the man apart. Even though he knew the homicide took place outside of Hazel's jurisdiction, and today was to be her day off, she was the first one he called. She'd returned from Parksville where she had picked up Josette. They had plans to spend the day together.

Sam tore through the swinging doors to his lab and he hurried over to the body bag.

"We couldn't find a head," said Sam's lab assistant.

"Help me get him on the table," Sam ordered. His assistant and the two EMTs who brought him in hoisted the man up.

Unzipping the bag, Sam saw the sternum snapped in half like a wishbone. And most of the body's internal organs were missing. Sam politely asked his attendant and the EMTs to leave him alone with the body for a while so he could focus, but no sooner did they all leave, Hazel and Josette came rushing in.

"I got here as soon as I could," huffed Hazel, running up to the table.

"This is Josette, the one Franky talked about."

"Finally, I get to meet you," said Sam, walking over to shake her hand.

"Phillip always had such nice things to say about you," she responded. "I am so glad to finally meet you."

"So, what you got Sam?" asked Hazel. She seemed impatient.

"Brings back memories, don't it?" he asked. He pointed down at the body.

"Maybe you better not see this," said Hazel. She held up her hand, stopping Josette just short of the table.

Josette glared at Hazel.

"Please, I've seen my share of dead bodies. I think I can handle this."

Hazel nodded her head, lowering her arm. Josette waddled over to Sam, who was staring down at the cadaver.

Sam opened the bag a little further.

"Looks like Samantha Hastings, doesn't it?"

"Worse, I would say. At least that bastard, Fritz, didn't rip her chest apart," responded Hazel.

"True," said Sam. "But I am telling you

something ate this man. Look at the way the meat is ripped from the bone."

Sam walked over to the counter, took out a pair of gloves, and put them on. He walked back to the table, reached into the man's chest, and said, "If I didn't know any better, I would say they were after his heart."

"His heart?" questioned Hazel.

"Yes. I think who, or whatever, attacked this man was after his heart. It's the only remaining organ that isn't ripped to pieces."

"You mean they did all this and didn't touch his heart?" replied Hazel.

"No. What I am saying is, it's the only organ that is completely gone. I think that whatever it was clawed the man apart to get to his heart."

"Shit, Sam. What the hell?" gasped Hazel.

"Can I touch him?" asked Josette. Her question surprised Hazel and Sam. They stood aback.

"Sorry, but this man's body is evidence. As much as I would like to say yes, I must say no," said Sam.

"Well is there anything of his I can touch or hold?" asked Josette.

"You want to do a reading on him, don't you?" asked Hazel.

Josette walked around the table and stood by Sam. Looking down, she explained.

"Yes, something like that. Where is his head?"

"They didn't find it, just the body." said Sam. "And as far as you touching anything, I am sorry.

The answer is still no. I don't mean to be a pain in the ass, but…"

"No, no, I understand. I worked with the police a number of times," said Josette. "I don't know what killed him, but I have a feeling there will be more."

"Why do you say that?" questioned Hazel.

"Because, even standing near, I can feel the remanence of something evil. A dark cloud still hovers over this man."

"Fuck, I will be glad when Vinnie gets back," said Hazel.

"They are still coming then, I take it?" questioned Sam.

"As far as we know, we left a note at Franky's. It said that Josette was coming into town and to meet us at my house on their way back. But I think I will have to take her back to Parksville sooner than I'd planned. The roads suck and they are getting worse. I hope they make it ok."

"I am sure they will be fine," said Sam, still poking around the man's chest.

"Sam, you know I can't do anything with this case, but please let me know what you find. I have a bad feeling something terrible is about to happen." Hazel sighed and walked out of the lab.

*

Benjamin had always loved Romania and especially Budapest. He had traveled there a lot through the years, spending time wandering through the National Museum of Art, The Romanian Athenaeum, the National Museum of Romanian History, or visiting the Palace of Parliament. Once, he made the trip just to see Dracula's Castle. He ended up at both the Bran Castle and the real Poenari Citadel that was once occupied by Vlad the Impaler.

But now, all he wanted was for this Doctor Tobar to make his findings known. They had delivered the scroll by hand as soon as they arrived, and Benjamin felt he'd had the scroll for long enough. Even though Father Aron kept telling him that the man knew what he was doing, Benjamin was growing impatient. He had this feeling deep in his gut that he had to get back to the States. Something was going to happen very soon. He didn't quite know what, but he knew he needed to be by Josette's side.

"I think this is his office," said Father Aron. "Does this look right?"

"Yes, this is it." responded Benjamin. He didn't wait for the priest to open the door. He pushed his way in, only to find the short figure of the good doctor atop a bookshelf ladder.

"Mr. Burk and Father Aron, I am glad to see you. I think I have found everything I have on your scroll. Please have a seat and I will be right down."

Benjamin and Father Aron both took a seat front of Dr. Tobar's desk as the man made his way down the ladder. He carried a large stack of books in his left hand.

"Very interesting piece you brought me. Took me a long to decipher."

"Well we appreciate your time, Dr. Tobar," stated Benjamin.

"Well, let's hope you got what you paid for," joked Dr. Tobar. He retrieved the scroll from the top drawer of his desk.

"Let's see here. I made my notes on my pad. Where did I put it?"

"Is that it on the stack of books on the floor next to you?" asked Benjamin.

"Oh, yea here it is."

The man leaned over to retrieve a large black leather portfolio.

"I will try and translate from my notes here. What you have come across is truly remarkable. The top part, as you know, is written in Latin and talks about the Danior family history."

"Yes, we got that part," said Father Aron.

"Well the rest, it seems, is an ancient spell. It talks of two demons, one that possess only the living, one possessing only the dead. This spell is used to conjure these demons. It says both demons fear the light, one hiding in darkness and one hiding seen, but unseen. This part here really intrigued me."

This he said while pointing to a section of his notes.

"It says the demons mock the holy act of communion. It goes on about eating bread and drinking wine. Only, instead of the wine and bread representing the blood and flesh of Christ, the demons mock God by eating human flesh and drinking human blood, which represent the Antichrist. Fascinating stuff, really."

"So, according to the scroll, the Danior family had a means to raise these two demons from Hell?" questioned Father Aron.

"Yes, but please keep in mind that Danior is a common Romani name. This is just one family."

"Yes, yes. Father Aron told me a million times," said Benjamin. He was growing impatient.

"But what about this family?"

Tobar grinned. "They were a fascinating collection of individuals who practiced the dark arts."

"So, we are talking about a family that had a long history of witchcraft?" interjected Father Aron.

"Yes, but there is yet another caveat. Towards the end of the spell is a warning... about the inability to control the demons once summoned."

"Dr. Tobar, what if someone had, say, a book? A book that had the ability to give a witch the power to control demons. Would they then be able to control these particular demons?" asked Benjamin. He wasn't really sure he wanted to know.

"Ah, the Grand Grimoires. That is what you speak of. The magic book with all the spells throughout the known world, is that the book you speak of?" clarified Dr. Tobar. He smirked.

Father Aron and Benjamin both nodded in agreement.

"I'm sorry, but since I have never seen one myself, I am not sure I can answer your question. Hypothetically, I would say yes. The witch could give a command and the demon would need to do as told."

Benjamin took some time before posing his next question.

"And what if the witch died after giving the command? Would the demons still perform their task?"

Dr. Tobar stopped and thought a moment. "You know, I have no strong convictions about all this. I am not a believer, but if you are looking at it from a conceptual interpretation, I would yes, I believe so. A payment for a debt owed."

"Then the scroll must come back with me to Rome. Especially if it is used to raise demons," said Father Aron. He reached for the scroll.

"Wait just a minute, Father," protested Benjamin. He stood up in front of the desk, blocking the priest's arm. "The church is not paying for this, I am. And I need the scroll to take care of a difficult matter taking place in the States. I will return it when I am done."

"No, it goes with me," snapped Father Aron. "It is the property of the church."

Dr. Tobar stood with the scroll in his hand.

"Look, this is a significant historical document. I could not start to say what it is truly worth, but I don't see how this could help anyone."

"It can't," said Father Aron. He snatched the scroll from Tobar's hand.

"Our little adventure ends here, Benjamin. The scroll will go to Rome with me." The priest stormed out of the room carrying the parchment in his hand, leaving both Tobar and Benjamin sitting staring at each other in disbelief.

Benjamin got up to give chase, but Tobar grabbed him by his coat sleeve. "If you need to know what was in the scroll, why don't you take a copy of my notes? I will have my secretary make copies for you. They will serve you more than a scroll you, nor anyone else, can read. Father Aron left before I gave you my final word on the scroll, anyway. When you get time, read my notes."

Benjamin sat back down. What Dr. Tobar said made a lot of sense. He wasn't after the scroll for what it was worth, but for the information it contained. That information was now in the notes.

"Wait until you have time and read my notes till the end. I think you will find them rather revealing. I am sorry, but I have another appointment in a few minutes. I do wish you all the best in your quest."

With this, he picked up his phone. Within a few seconds, an older lady came into his office.

"Maleva, will you please make copies of these notes for Mr. Burk?"

Maleva smiled and took the papers. Through a thick accent she spoke.

"Right this way, Mr. Burk. It won't take but a moment."

Benjamin stood and shook Dr. Tobar's hand.

"I had a feeling he had an alternative motive

for helping. I can't thank you enough, Dr. Tobar. Really."

"Here is my card. Call me if you have any questions about the notes," said Dr. Tobar, handing him his business card.

*

The weather cleared somewhat as Josette and Hazel drove back to Parksville. The snow had slowed from a flurry to a fine dusting, and there was little to no wind. Josette had watched the weather that morning and knew it wouldn't last, but for now it was comforting.

If only the sun would shine, she thought. Josette was still contemplating what she had seen that afternoon in Sam's office. *The man was torn apart for his heart, but why? Was it going to be used in some sick ritual? Was it eaten?* Josette's mind raced with questions.

Just as the two passed Darin Road, halfway to Parksville, Hazel's radio called.

"Captain, Captain, I know you're off today, but I was hoping you were in your car. Captain, it's Jackson. Over."

Hazel snatched up the radio and pushed the receiver.

"This is Captain Cowan. What you got, Jackson?"

"A body," came the response. Josette could hear the tension in his voice. "The damn thing has been eaten. I'm in the woods just behind the Parksville University back parking lot."

"Do we have an ID on the vic?"

"No, but it's a young girl. Student at the university, probably."

"I will be there in ten," responded Hazel.

"Please, Hazel. Let me go with you. I gotta see," said Josette.

"Well," said Hazel. "I guess it would be ok. Besides, it's on the way. But please, you will need to stay as far back as you can. I am going to tell everyone you are here from London to observe our methods. Is that ok with you?"

"Sounds good to me. I am from London and I will be observing."

"Good. So much for a day off!"

Josette smiled at Hazel. "You are an amazing woman, Captain Cowan. The more I get to know you, the more I admire you."

"Admire me? Are you crazy? I'm pregnant and the baby's father is nowhere to be found."

"So am I. Currently, at least. No, I admire you for your strength. It is hard to find women who do not define themselves by traditional roles."

"There has never been anything traditional about me," Hazel said with a chuckle.

When the women pulled up to the lone police car at the back of Parksville University, Jackson was leaning on the hood of his car.

"Who is that hunk of a man?" asked Josette.

"That's Jackson. Nice guy. You'll like him."

"He is so big."

Hazel gave Josette a smile. "Yea, his wife told me that once as well."

Jackson looked confused when he saw Josette emerge from the car. Not only was she a stranger, but she and Hazel were laughing hysterically.

"Captain, I think this thing is starting all over again," he said as they approached.

"Jackson, this young lady is named Josette. She is from London and has come to observe our agency and how we conduct business. Be on your best behavior. Where is the body, and why are you the only one on scene?" asked Hazel.

"Glad to meet you," said Jackson. He nodded.

"Pleased to meet you as well, Mr. Jackson." replied Josette.

"Because everyone else is pulling assholes out of ditches or writing up accident reports. The girl's body is down there," said Jackson, pointing just beyond the tree line. "EMS is on their way. I think Sam's crew is, too."

Hazel started to walk through the snow that was now up past her shins. "How in the hell did someone find her in all this snow?" asked Hazel.

"I guess this is some kind of path the students use to get to the trailer park on the other side of the woods. A girl was walking the path and tripped over the body. She is in the admin building if you want to talk to her."

"No, I need to see this first," said Hazel. "Why

isn't the girl that found this out for winter break with everyone else? Did she say?"

"Well, according to her, she's been fighting with the financial aid department. And if she didn't get it settled before school starts back up, she would lose her classes next semester. She was on her way to the admin building to get it straightened out," said Jackson.

When Hazel, Josette, and Jackson all got to the body, it was laid half-covered in snow. Josette realized this body resembled the attack they found in Sam's office. The girl's chest had been ripped open and her organs devoured. Josette, mindful of Hazel's request, stayed back as the other two approached. It was by sheer accident that, as she stood there listening to Hazel and Jackson discuss the situation, she happened to look down to find one of the girl's joints stuck on the top of a small thorn bush. She reached over to pick it up and was about to alert the police officers when everything went dark. She could see the girl walking down the path. The girl screamed as some evil entity grabbed her from behind. Then, an image of Phillip: He crawled along the floor of some old house, his face full of pain and agony. He was covered in blood, weeping.

"Josette, Josette! Are you all right?" She heard Hazel's voice. Hazel, who was now kneeling, looked down at her. "You passed out and landed on your back in the snow."

Josette's mind started to come back into focus.

She grabbed Hazel by her collar and pulled her close so that Jackson could not hear.

"I know where he is, Hazel. I know where Phillip is."

Just as Josette finished, a large group of people, including EMTs, Sam's team, and four other police officers approached the scene.

"We will talk later. Now, do I need to have the EMTs take you to the hospital?" asked Hazel. Josette could see concern in her eyes.

"Hell no. I'm fine. Help me up and I will wait in the car until you're done," responded Josette. Jackson, who had been standing close by, reached out his hand and helped her to her feet.

"Thank you, sir."

"No problem," he said with a grin. "And don't go showing that big, old pregnant belly to my wife. She's already hounding for another baby."

"Will do," said Josette, returning the grin. Before the others reached them, Josette started walking back to the car. Smiling up at them as she passed, she thought, *They must all think I am crazy.* They must have all seen her hit the ground.

"Josette!" came a cry from Hazel. She ran after her. "Wait a minute. Here are the keys. I will make this quick and we will be on our way. Then, we can talk."

Josette took the keys and, without saying another word, went directly to the car. Easing into the passenger seat, she reached over, put the key in the ignition, and turned the car on. Hazel was true to her word, and within ten minutes, she was back in the car.

"Not much I can do at this point. They will scan the area, but to tell you the truth, I don't think they will find much. I will follow up with Sam when I get the chance. Now, what did you mean you know where Phillip is?"

Josette leaned back in her seat and put her hands near the heat vent in front of her.

"It's hard to explain. Yes, I can see and talk to dead people who have not passed. But I also get visions, especially when I touch something that has been handled by a victim. That is why I wanted to touch something of the man lying on Sam's table. It's not like I get a clear picture of everything. It's more like flashes, short snap shots of what has taken place. Does that make sense?"

"Yea, I guess so."

"Well, I found a joint in a bush by the body. I was going to tell you, but when I picked it up, I saw the girl. She was attacked by something. I don't know what, but it was horrible. The next thing I knew, I saw Phillip crawling along the floor of this house. Just before you spoke to me, I saw the outside of the house. It was an American style ranch house. Behind it was a lake, and on the far side, sticking out of the snow, was playground equipment. I don't know why, but I think the house is in Parksville."

When she was finished, she looked straight at Hazel for some kind of reaction. At first, she could not tell if she believed a word she had said.

"Playground equipment, and by a lake. The only playground like that I know of in Parksville is on Briskey Lake," said Hazel. "There are only a few houses there, and God help us, I hope it is not the one I am thinking of."

"Why is that?" questioned Josette.

"Because the last time I was in that house, I found an elderly couple with their heads torn off, their heads stuck between their legs. Their midsections had been eaten."

"Fritz?" asked Josette.

"Yes. After all that has happened, I know it was him."

"Well, then, let's hope it is a different house I am sick of seeing mutilated dead people."

"Oh, they are long gone."

"For you, maybe. With me, you never know. The body may be gone but it doesn't mean they are."

Neither one said a word the rest of the way. When they passed through Parksville, Josette half expected Hazel to turn left into Phillip's drive and tell her to get out, that it was no longer her concern. But she never even slowed down. They turned onto the road leading to Briskey Lake. Josette yelled. "That's it! That's the house!"

"Thank God it's the Yorkey's house." she heard Hazel whisper under her breath. "We found another victim of Fritz's here, but it was outside."

Hazel parked the car and pointed across the lake.

"The Gibsons lived over there. They were the

ones I told you about. I never want to go in that place again if I can help it."

"Well, hopefully you won't have to. This is the house. See the equipment in the background?" asked Josette. She threw herself out of the car.

"He's here, or was here. But I know what I saw."

Hazel, too, hurried out of the car.

"Ok, ok, I believe you." Pulling out her gun, she added, "But this is the part I tell you to hold back. Most of the people on this lake only live here in the summer, but I don't want to take any chances."

Hazel slowly approached the house, looking through the back sliding-glass window. The house was dark, there were no cars in the drive, and it looked like no one had even been down this road since it started snowing. Still, she knocked and waited for a response. When no one came to the door, she walked back to Josette.

"Now, what I am about to do could cost me a lot of headaches. So please, you will need to keep this one in your bonnet, ok?"

Josette nodded in agreement.

"Good," said Hazel. She made her way to the door once more, but instead of knocking, she pushed on it. When it would not give, she lifted on the left side glass door. With very little effort, the door came off its track.

"This is why I don't have one of these things at my house," she yelled.

Lifting it once more and pulling on the bottom, the entire door pulled out from the frame. Hazel sat the door down then reached around, undid the lock, and slid the door back on its tracks. With just a simple push, the sliding glass door was open.

"Bloody well done! Remind me not to piss you off, ok?" said Josette in amazement.

"Didn't your mom ever tell you not to judge a book by its cover?" asked Hazel, smiling.

Once inside the house, it was obvious that the owners were, in fact, gone, but there was a hint that what Josette had said was true. There were blood stains on the kitchen floor.

"Use your torch?" requested Josette.

"My what?" responded Hazel.

"A bloody flashlight! Do you have a flashlight?"

"Your accent comes out when you get your hair on end, doesn't it?"

"Sorry, I am not mad. Just nervous."

"Me too, sweetie. Me too." agreed Hazel.

They walked back to her car. A few minutes later, with the glow from Hazel's flashlight in front of them, they went from room to room searching for Phillip Parker. When they got to the back bedroom, they found their biggest clue. Like the kitchen, the master bedroom also had blood on the floor. There was even more on the Yorkeys' king-sized bed. The comforter was covered in it.

"See? I'm not crazy. He was here," said Josette.

"We don't know that for sure yet, but I think you might be right. I don't know. It just seems so strange. I mean, where in the hell would he be, and why is he covered in blood?"

"I'm telling you; he was in this house. I know it."

"Are you sure it was Phillip you saw in your vision?"

"Look, I'm telling you it was him."

"I believe you, but now what?" said Hazel, pacing back and forth in front of the bed. "I mean, I can't tell anyone about this. We are breaking the law as we speak."

Josette looked around the room, her eyes scanning for anything she could touch or feel. For the next ten minutes, she walked and touched, walked and touched, until at last, she threw up her hands in defeat.

"I can't get anything in here!" then, looking over at one of pillowcases with a small stain, she suggested, "Do you think Sam could run a test with that pillowcase and get a DNA sample?"

"Maybe," said Hazel. "If you could get him to do it. He is pretty much a by-the-book kind of guy."

"Well, we can still try, can't we?"

Josette removing the pillowcase. "Let's just hope it confirms what I believe to be true."

The women continued to search the house for a while, before Hazel had enough.

"We need to get back," she said.

"One question…" said Josette, looking around the living room. "How did he get in here? I didn't see any broken windows. Did you?"

"I wonder…" Hazel started. She walked over to the front door. She turned the knob and the door opened.

"I'll be damned! They left their fucking house unlocked."

"So, you did all that bloody macho shit with the back door for nothing?" Josette joked.

Hazel started laughing with her.

"Sometimes, I just like to show off, ok? But now, it is time for us to go."

"I would rather stay and see if he comes back," replied Josette.

"Well, I hate to lay this on you, but there is no way in hell I am leaving you here. We need you safe, I need you safe. So just get your pretty, little, limey ass out in the car. It's time for us to leave."

"But…" started Josette.

"But nothing. We are leaving. We can come back later, but for now, you're going back to Phillip and Franky's."

Josette reluctantly agreed and the two made their way back to the car.

"It's starting to come down hard again," Hazel said. She looked up at the sky. "I think this storm is starting round two."

*

No sooner did Josette and Hazel make the turn down to Briskey Lake, then Brandy Cartwright made the turn into Phillip's driveway. If she would have arrived only a few moments earlier, they would have seen Ethel's Cadillac in the driveway. The drive had been long and tiring. The weather got worse the farther north she traveled. She went from warm and humid, to rain, to downpour, to snow flurries, to downright blizzard. She made sure to get a running start before she pulled up the drive. She wanted to make sure the car was all the way off the road.

"If anything happened to Ethel's kitty, there will be hell to pay. That's for sure," she said aloud.

God, I don't miss this shit, thought Brandy finally, emerging from the car. Grabbing an overnight bag, her suitcase, and a bag of goodies she bought to share, she headed towards the front porch. Even after all these years, she still had a spare key to their house on her key chain. *Man, I wish Ethel was here,* thought Brandy. *She could help carry some of this crap.*

When Ethel returned from the Gates, she was in shock. Brandy had never seen her like this. Most of the time, she would just look out the window and cry. It was not until the next day that she confided in Brandy everything that had taken place. And that was only because Rebecca had stopped by the hotel to tell Ethel their grandmother had died. She died on Christmas day, just as Ethel was performing the Gates. Ethel was not at all shocked or surprised by the news. In fact, for the first time since returning from her task, she talked about everything that happened. Once she started, it was like a flood gate; she seemed to recall every last detail. When she was finished, there was a look of fear and anguish on her face.

Then came something she had not expected. Rebecca bowed before her.

"You are the new queen," said Rebecca as she rose. "I knew you were the one to take Grandmother's place. She did, too, and she told me many times. Her powers are in you now. You will need to learn how to use them. This is what they were trying to prepare you for so many years ago."

After Rebecca left, Ethel seemed to be in better spirits, though the tears still flowed off and on.

"Brandy, I finally found you again, and now I will lose you," she said. This was the first time she had talked directly to Brandy since they returned to the hotel.

"You are not going to lose me, you crazy, old woman. I'm going to sell those old, nasty trailers, and you and I are moving back to where it all started."

"I couldn't ask you to give up your home for me." Ethel pulled a hanky from her shirt sleeve. "God only knows what my life will be like now."

"Yea, yea, yea, like you didn't pack up everything you own to come and bug the hell out of me. You think I am letting you off that easy?" spoke Brandy.

Ethel smiled. "First, you need to warn everyone. They will find that Mary and Phillip are wherever Franky is. They are looking for him, and I think they mean him harm."

Brandy had left numerous messages on Franky's cell phone. She tried to call the house, but got no response. Finally, she made up her mind to just make the trip. It was Ethel who offered the use of her car, since that is what they'd arrived in.

"Take it. Go and tell them what we have learned.

If not, all I went through was for nothing," she said to Brandy.

Inside Phillip and Franky's house, Brandy laid down her overnight bag.

"Is anyone home?" she yelled. No response.

No wonder no one ever answers. They are never home! she thought. Brandy meandered into the kitchen. *I am getting that boy a damn answering machine before I go home. And God, I hope he has some beer.*

*

Benjamin sat gazing out the window of his private jet. His pilot, Rudy, had told him about the bad weather and the possibility that the small Jackson Airport might be closed, but Benjamin insisted they try. If they could not land there, then he had instructed Rudy to to get him as close as possible. One way or another, he was going to reach his destination.

As for Father Aron, he was long gone before Benjamin even left Dr. Tabor's office. *He must have taken a cab to the airport*, he thought. *What an asshole. All he ever wanted was the scroll and was tagging along, probably, for nothing more than to find a lead to locating the last book.*

As he sat on the tarmac, his thoughts went to Mary, her young and beautiful body pressed next to his in bed, the way she flipped her hair when she flirted, and the way she like to cuddled on the coach. She was, without doubt, the most beautiful lady he had ever been involved with. *If only I wouldn't have been such a fool*, he pondered. *I should have gone with Phillip the day they were taken. But who could have known that an ambush awaited them outside the hospital?*

Regardless of what happened, he would make sure she came back to him. This time, she would be his wife, and even the devil himself better not try and stand in his way.

Slowly, he pulled Dr. Tabor's notes out of his bag. After everything he had gone through to get these, he was sure as hell going to study them before he touched ground in the States. As he poured through the pages with intensity, he became more and more aware that what they faced may be far beyond their abilities. It was by sheer coincidence that he glanced out the window to see two men exiting a limo and approaching his plane. One of whom was Father Aron.

"You have got to be fucking kidding me!" he yelled, his voice carrying all the way to the cockpit.

"Everything alright there, Mr. Burk?" came Rudy's voice.

"Have you been cleared for takeoff yet?" commanded Benjamin.

"No, sir. They are holding us here," Rudy replied. "They haven't given a reason why."

"I think I know, Rudy. We have company."

CHAPTER IX

BLOOD, SWEAT, AND TEARS

Franky and Vinnie had been trapped in Dale's trailer for almost three days. Outside, the storm raged on, but it was not the storm that held them in check. Every time they made a move for the car, the little girl was there, waiting. There was no mistaking the fact that, if they tried to leave, the Woman of the Lake would have them. On the very first night, Vinnie spent most of his time consoling Franky who had, for all intents and purposes, lost his best friend. He pleaded with Vinnie to help search for him. But Vinnie, who had only known Shawn for a short while, was not as willing to forfeit his own life for a man who was almost certainly dead. Once, he had to physically restrain Franky who, out of the blue, made a mad dash for the door.

"You may hate me now, but when this is over, you will thank me. Trust me," he warned while pinning him to the floor.

Any hopes of leaving by car evaporated the next morning when they heard a loud crash outside. From the door window, they could see Vinnie's car, only it wasn't where he had parked it. Instead, it was flipped over in the brush like a discarded piece of litter. This devastated both men. Though Dale's truck was outside, it was of no use. They searched every inch of the camper trailer and could not locate his keys. Franky and Vinnie surmised that his keys were most likely on him when he was taken, if, in fact, he had been taken. Again, there was a very slim chance that the man was still alive. But neither held any hope that that was the case.

The search for the keys did result in some items that Vinnie put aside for self-defense. Yes, he had his gun, but somehow, it seemed that a gun would be little help against these unholy creatures. He found a claw hammer, a large pair of hedge shears, lighter fluid, an old nine iron, and one large butcher knife. All of these he placed by the front door just in case they might be needed. If the battle came inside the trailer, at least they would go down fighting.

Now, on day three, Vinnie was mentally exhausted. As he looked over at Franky sleeping on the padded bench under the front window, Vinnie started to cry. He didn't know how much more of this he could take. The sun had not shown since the morning they left for this little adventure. It was always dark and gloomy outside.

He knew it was only a matter of time before they would lose power, then the heat would be gone, too. The camper trailer was well stocked with nonperishables, so they didn't need the stove to make it through for some time. The furnace was another issue. Vinnie knew that if the woman got wise and cut the gas, they would also freeze to death.

SCRATCHHHHH, SCRATCHHH.

She was back, the little girl. She spent a lot of time dragging her fingernails against the outside of the trailer. Day or night, she would be out there, making that God-awful noise.

SCRATCHHH.

The first time they both heard the sound, it came in the middle of the night. It woke both men from their sleep. It scared them so badly, neither slept the rest of the night. When the girl wasn't dragging her nails, she would peek in through the bottom window, just above the bottom bunk in the back of the trailer. Without warning, there she would be, her cold, dead, black eyes gazing in on them, and always with that horrid grin.

Outside, the wind grew stronger. More than once he felt the trailer sway. And when it did, the only thing he could think of was the woman flipping the trailer the way she had his car. He knew it was the woman. After three days, Vinnie concluded that the girl herself was not the threat; it was the woman. The little girl had not shown any power remotely comparable to her. Vinnie remembered watching in horror as she snatched up Shawn with little, if any, effort. But the girl was different. Vinnie had not seen her do anything other than terrify the hell out of them. No, it was the woman who had supremacy. Vinnie was sure the girl was nothing more than a decaying dead body that the woman used as a puppet.

"Hey Vinnie," said Franky, waking from his slumber. Vinnie surmised that the scratching had once again awakened him. "Don't that little bitch ever take a break?"

"She was beating the side of the trailer a little while ago with a branch."

"Didn't hear that one."

"I don't think she is all that strong. It wasn't as loud as the scratching."

"Well, let's just hope she wears herself out some time soon. I could use a break from her shenanigans." With this, Franky got up and walked to the bathroom. Leaving the door open, he asked, "Has she shown her pretty little face in the window again?"

"She was there about an hour or two ago, but nothing since then."

"And the woman. Is she still out there?"

"Oh, I'm sure. But with the wind blowing the snow around, it's hard to see very far."

"I wonder why she doesn't come near the trailer," said Franky. He flushed the toilet.

"I think it's the crucifixes in the windows.

Notice how the girl only looks through the only window without one?" asked Vinnie. He stood and looked out the window of the door.

"Yea, that's what I thought as well."

"You know, it seems like, at some point, I would have seen her face by now."

Franky joined Vinnie at the window.

"You mean the woman? Yea, I know. Seems like every time I think I will get a good look at her face, she moves, and all that hair in her face makes it worse.

"There she is, again. Look right over there," said Vinnie, pointing out the window. "Only this time, she is lying on the ground, on her side, almost hidden in the snow."

Both men stood staring out into the darkness of the morning. The sun rose, but the sky was still dark, the sun hidden behind a thick layer of clouds. Then, it happened. The woman lifted her head. She was holding out her hand as if seeking aid.

"My God, it's Mary!" screamed Franky. "Oh, my God! It's Mary!"

"Help me, Franky!" came a soft voice, piercing the harsh winds. "Please! It's not what it seems. I need your help. Please, oh please, Franky!" came her plea.

The sound of her voice seemed to mesmerize Franky. He looked as if he was under a hypnotic trance. Without any notice, he made a quick move towards the door handle, but Vinnie quickly blocked his way.

"Look, I know you think it's this Mary girl, but it's not."

"Fuck you, Vinnie. That's Mary, and she needs me."

"But it's not her. Think about it, Franky. We have been hiding from this fucking thing for almost three days, so she might not be the Woman of the Lake, but that thing out there is still a monster."

"Franky, you let that bastard get me, and you let Phillip die," came the pleading voice once more. "You need to save me. Please, Franky."

This time, Franky surprised Vinnie with a hard shove that knocked him backwards onto the padded bench.

"Franky, no! She has put some kind of spell on you!" he cried. It was too late. Franky was out the door.

*

"Look, Elma, I can't get out to the trailer until all this is done," said Malcom.

"All I am saying is, those three were supposed to stop here on their way back. Now, I agreed to wait to see if they would call us once they got home, but it's been three days," huffed Elma.

"Now, we don't know if something happened to them. If something happened to Dale, which, by the way, Marge is driving me nuts about, or if they're all roasting marshmallows over an open flame singing 'Kumbaya.' We just don't know."

"I agree, we don't know. But I also know I and

every deputy and volunteer I got have been moving the old people to the high school in case the town loses power. Which, by the way, it is prone to do. Without that generator, these old people on oxygen and CPIPs..."

"It's called a CPAP, genius."

"You're pushing me, woman. I mean, really pushing. Pip, pap, I don't really give a shit. I know they need it. Now, let me repeat this one more time. As soon as everyone else is taken care of and safe, then, and only then, will I hop my tired, old ass on my Arctic Cat and go to Dale's."

"Malcom Wiseman, you know I don't like that kind of language in my house," snapped Elma. "And you make sure you do that."

"Fine!" Malcom snapped back.

"Fine!" said Elma. She stormed out of the room.

Malcom felt his son's hand on his shoulder.

"Dad, she is the only person I have ever met who can talk to you that way and still be standing."

"Trust me. I'm more afraid of that woman than any man in this town."

"Let me know when you go out there, and I will go with you. I got my Polaris all gassed up and ready to go," said Luke.

"I will. But I still got a shit load of stuff to get done before then. Can you run over to Howard's and see if he would be willing to provide some hot meals for the high school?"

"What if the power goes out? He can't cook in the dark."

"Don't worry about that. Old Lady Townsend had a nice, new generator put in before she died. The last few months, she couldn't make it upstairs to her apartment. So Marge talked her into installing one of those lift chairs for her staircase. The old lady agreed, but only if they put in a generator. She was afraid of getting stuck upstairs and freezing to death if she lost power."

"Smart lady," said Luke with a chuckle.

"Yea, like she could have ever got the damn thing started! They installed both about a month before she kicked the bucket. Just make sure he knows how to use the damn thing, will ya?"

"Will do, Dad. And I already did the call down list of everyone in town. So far so good. The Richards on Burch Lake Road are the only ones still needing transportation to the shelter, and Markowitz is heading out there right now."

"Well he better hurry. I know Mike can't keep up with his plowing now. Soon, he will be off the road as well."

"I'll make sure they get there. Is there anything else I can do?" asked Luke, walking towards the door.

"Stop being a bleeding-heart liberal, maybe," said Malcom. He grinned ear to ear.

"You know Regan was a dope-smoking homosexual, don't you?" griped Luke. He walked out the door before his father could respond.

*

Franky didn't remember much. He recalled running out the door of the trailer and straight into the dead girl sitting on the steps. He tripped and went headfirst down into the snow. He remembered looking up and seeing Mary across the driveway, only now, she was no longer lying on the ground. She was on her feet, like a predator waiting to pounce. Gone was the sweet face he had come to know. Her face turned blue, her ears enlarged, coming to tight points towards the back of her head. Her nose flatted until only huge flaring nostrils remained, and her two front teeth grew in length, sticking permanently outside her mouth. Her fangs were at least six inches long, coming to a point just below her chin. She started to move, and Vinnie flew between them. Franky heard a loud, painful squeal as Mary vanished somewhere into the darkness. Franky felt Vinnie grab him by his collar. Looking up, he saw Vinnie holding one of the grander crucifixes from the camper in his outstretched arm. Half helping him to his feet and half shoving him back into the camper, Vinnie got Franky up the steps and back inside.

While Mary was nowhere to be seen, her dead body puppet made its way off the ground and towards them. The girl leaped at Vinnie just as he ran up the steps.

"Look out!" yelled Franky from inside. "The girl is coming!"

Vinnie turned just in time. Her front teeth, while not as menacing as Mary's, were extended and seemed homed in on Vinnie's throat. Vinnie, with cat-like reflexes, took his right hand and held her at arm's length by her neck, her arms flailing at his to release her. Then, Vinnie lifted the cross with his free hand and slammed it hard against the girl's forehead. The girl shrieked in pain as her forehead started to smoke, the cross scorching into her grotesque skin. Franky, coming back to reality, grabbed the closest item he could find: the hedge shears. He leaped out the door. Vinnie must have sensed his intentions. He let go as soon as Franky flew out of the trailer and took a step back from the girl. With blades of the shears wide open, Franky plunged them deep into the back of her neck. The girl shrieked as Franky tried desperately to close the shears. It was not until Vinnie grabbed one handle and Franky the other that they forced them closed.

The two men could hear her spinal cord snap. The girl's severed head landed in the snow in one direction, her body falling limp in the other. Franky could see Vinnie looking once more into the darkness, making sure the coast was clear. Then, both men jumped back into the trailer.

Franky, still grappling with what had just happened, looked out the window. The body of the headless girl laid motionless. Franky, covering his mouth and nose, said, "My God, it stinks. We got to get it away from here. Do you think we killed it?"

"No, but this time I think we need to send a

message," said Vinnie. "You have a lighter by any chance?"

"As a matter of fact, I do."

"Grab the lighter fluid under the sink. The lady cannot use her if there is nothing left."

"Look! No blood! We cut off her fucking head and no blood." said Franky, still staring out the window.

"That's because whatever was in there, dried up long ago. Hurry up with that shit. She is stinking up the whole place."

Franky returned with the lighter fluid. They debated whether they could reach the body with the fluid while safe inside. In the end, they agreed not to take the chance of missing and would soak her outside. Looking all around with the crucifix stretched out before him, Vinnie gave the signal and the two jumped to the bottom of the steps. Outside the trailer, the body began to move. Franky, holding the head by its hair, gasped as the eyes opened and the mouth began to move. Vinnie, dragging the torso by the leg, had to deal with thrashing arms and kicking from the free leg. Once they reached the old-fashioned outdoor stone grill at the end of the trailer, Vinnie lifted the torso in the air and sent it flying on top of the grill's rack. Franky placed the head on the corpse's torso and took out his lighter.

"I didn't know you smoked," said Vinnie.

"I don't," he said, lighting the body on fire, "I've carried one of these since the day I had my little encounter with Fritz." The body went up with a loud whooshing sound. In the trees beyond the lake, both men could hear an ear-shattering scream that echoed throughout the woods.

"She's not happy we destroyed her pet; we need to get back in."

"Hold on," said Vinnie, "I want to make sure she is not coming back."

The body flopped but did not fall. After a few minutes it laid still. Franky watched the flesh of the face disintegrate.

"Fuck this. She's gone, and we need to get inside."

Then came the screeching once more. Only this time, it was close, just on the other side of the driveway. Without another word, the men ran back to the door. From the window in the back of the trailer, they watched the corpse burn.

"I don't know what your friend is, Franky, but we know she can make the dead do what she wants," said Vinnie. "To think that was once someone's little girl."

"Don't do that to yourself, Vinnie. Trust me. Whoever that little girl was, that thing out there was not her. It was just a body."

"Yea, I know," said Vinnie shaking his head. "Somewhere out there are parents that will never know just what happen to their little girl."

Franky started to respond but was cut short by the sound of ice cracking. They rushed to the front window. Placing their knees on the bench, they looked out over the lake. There she was. Mary cleared a spot of snow not far offshore and was stomping on the ice, making it crack beneath her feet.

"What the hell is she doing now?" asked Vinnie.

"I don't know! Sounds like she is trying to dig something free from the ice."

"Look, she's pulling something out of the water! Shit, it looks like another body."

"No, no, no, no, no" said Franky. He stood, pounding the top of his head with his fists. After a few moments, he stopped and walked towards the back of the camper.

"I can't take anymore, Vinnie." He laid down on the bottom bunk. "It's all just too fucking much."

Vinnie, who was still watching out the window, yelled back.

"She is dragging someone, and she is heading back to the woods on the other side of the lake."

"God help us. Vinnie, I don't think I can do this anymore," said Franky. He laid in a fetal position on the bed. "We are going to die here."

Vinnie walked over and sat on the floor next to Franky. "Look, I know things look bad. But don't you dare give up on me. I need you."

"But why Mary? Why here?"

"I don't know, man. I just don't know. But we will never find out if we give up. You have gone through more than any man needs to, and you've got to see there is a light at the end of the tunnel."

Franky rolled over without a response.

Vinnie reached up to the top bunk and pulled off a blanket. He placed it gently on Franky and walked back to the front window.

*

Howard was pleased with himself. He found the owner's manual for the generator and had it up and running in no time at all. When, and if, the power went off, he would still be snug as a bug in a rug. *Thank goodness Grandma was smart enough to buy this damn thing,* he thought. Now that he knew he could get it going, he shut it off. The lights flickered a few times that morning but stayed on. He knew it was just a matter of time.

Walking from the outdoor shed to the back steps of his apartment, Howard had the strangest feeling that his grandmother was watching him. He wanted so desperately to make her proud. He hoped she could see him looking down from heaven. *I am keeping your dream alive, Grandma,* he pondered as he made his way up the back steps.

His relationship with his father, Barbara Townsend's only son, took a turn for the worse when Howard was only twenty. His father walked into his dorm room one late afternoon and found Howard and Tad Turner, Howard's college roommate, both engaged in a sexual encounter with Cindy Preston. Howard and Tad were both drunk, and when Cindy had promised them both the dance of the double swords, neither one had any idea what she was talking about. By the time they realized her intentions, they sure as hell were not going to stop. They were in the heat of passion when James Townsend, Howard's father, walked in on them. James Townsend, being an overzealous God-fearing Northern Baptist, did not take it well. After he accused Howard of being a sexual deviant with homosexual tendencies, he told young Howard that his days at college were over and that he needed to find a job.

Though he tried for many years since then, he was never again in his father's good graces. When he found out that his grandmother had died and left the restaurant to him, he saw this as his chance to prove himself. If he could keep her business going and make it successful, then maybe, just maybe, his father would find it in his heart to accept him once more. He knew it would take time, but he had to try.

"Howard, Howard!" came a cry from the front door of the restaurant. Howard hurried back down the steps, through the back door, through the kitchen and dining area, to the front door. He caught Luke walking away from the building.

"Luke, come in. I was just out back making sure the generator started."

"Dad wanted me to see if you needed help with that, but you got it to work. Ok I take it?"

"Piece of cake, Luke. Did you guys ever locate

Dale? Marge has been worried as can be," said Howard, letting Luke in.

"We are heading out that way shortly. Dad also asked me to ask you about maybe fixing some meals for those people who will have to shelter at the high school."

"Sure. I got a meat order in just before the storm," said Howard, "I'll whip something up. When do you need it?"

"I imagine they will be getting hungry over there about supper time. Dad said to keep the receipts and the town will reimburse you," said Luke.

"Well, I'm not worried about that now. We can talk later."

"Thanks, Howard. That means a lot to all of us. By the way, I just ran into Marge over at the hardware store. Said she was coming over to help you. Hope you don't mind."

"Hell no. I can always use some help," said Howard with a grin.

Luke nodded and started out the door, but just before he left, he turned around again. "Howard, I just want to give you the heads up. That good-for-nothing Tom Phillip is putting in everyone's head that you might be the reason for people missing. Now everyone in town knows he's a troublemaker; he always has been. But there are some people having a hard time with this, especially Mike Shelly. So, keep one eye open, ok?"

"It's understandable, I guess. I am the new guy

in town, and few people know me. I will keep an eye out and call if I see anything. I promise."

"Good. Well you have a good evening. I'll make sure you get help getting that grub over to the school."

"Thanks, Luke." said Howard. Someone else yelled for him.

"Howard..."

It was Marge. She walked up the street, trying to hold one corner of her hood over her face to block the bitter wind. "Don't lock the door, yet. I'm coming in. Tried to call, but the damn phone lines are down."

*

Elma was busy trying to get the shelter ready. She directed volunteers at the War Hawks gymnasium. She remembered the winter of 1976, when a major ice storm devastated the small town. People were out of power for weeks. It was one of the worst experiences she ever had to endure. She remembered that three local residents, all seniors, died before the distressing event was over. Two of them froze to death in their own home. That was the year the town's emergency management board was created and the year she had been chosen to be its chair. She was young then, full of energy, energy she had lost through the years to old age. Still, she took her job very seriously. And even though her back hurt and her feet killed her, she pressed on.

She had been there for less than an hour, and already the cots were brought out. The extension cords placed anywhere there was an outlet. Blankets and pillows were brought out of storage but had yet to be laid out on the beds. This would have to be completed before she moved everyone from the auditorium. *Hopefully this storm will pass, and all of this is for nothing*, she thought. Elma reviewed her checklist. The meals would be served in the cafeteria. Hopefully, Luke had talked to Howard about the generator and cooking. Marge had just departed a few minutes ago, so she knew one way, or another, Howard would get the message and help with food preparation as well. Hopefully, the first of it would arrive before six. Elma had a good idea that, if it was later than that, the old people would start getting cranky.

Outside, the wind continued to blow. It was growing stronger as the day dragged on. The weatherman warned that things would get worse before they got better, and that the storm had basically stalled right over the Great Lakes. The sun had not shown in days. People were getting irritable, especially those waiting in the auditorium for word that their home for the next few days was prepared.

*

Mike Shelly was devastated with the disappearance of his new fiancé. As he walked Main Street with his doubled-barreled Remington Spartan 310 shot gun cocked and loaded, he had only one thing on his mind: *I will make that son of a bitch tell me where she is.*

For the past few days, his next-door neighbor Tom Phillips had been filling him with stories about Howard.

"A grown man, living on his own. what does that tell ya?" Tom Phillips asked. "Funny how all this happens right after he takes up residency in Phelton. Nothing ever happened before he got here."

At first, Mike, like most of the town, ignored Tom as he was known for stirring up trouble when there was none. But as time passed, Mike became more and more frustrated about Malcom's inability to locate Shannon. The stress of not knowing what happened to the woman he loved was becoming unbearable. He had been involved in every search and had taken it on himself to search when those involved were back home in their beds. Somewhere, there was an answer. And he was going to find it.

The only thing he had to pin his hopes on were Tom Phillip's words: "If he didn't do it, then I will kiss your bare ass on the county steps and give you ten minutes to draw a crowd."

If Tom could be so sure, then Mike was right to listen to what he had to say. As the days passed, exhaustion overrode all common sense he had. By the end, Mike was convinced Howard was the cause of all his problems, and he was going to take care of that right now.

As he approached the restaurant, his anger began to build. Mike was going to get the answers he needed one way or another, and if that son of a bitch hurt her, well, then, he would just have to blow his fucking brains out. *I will swear he came at me first,* he thought. *If not, then I will plead insanity.*

*

Malcom and Luke mounted their sleds to head out to Dale's when they heard the gunshots from across the street. In a flash, Luke had his Polaris gunned and was at the restaurant's front door with Malcom close behind.

Looking through the front window, Luke saw Mike Shelly with his gun pointed towards the kitchen. "Come out, you coward! I want to look you in the eyes," Luke heard Mike yell.

"Tell me where she is and I might just let you walk out of here with your face attached."

Luke put up his hand to stop his father from pulling up too close. "It's Mike. He is after Howard. That fucking Tom Phillips got to him."

"That son of a bitch. I told him to hold his tongue. Where is Howard?"

"Looks like he is in the kitchen. Marge is cowering behind the counter. I saw the top of her head."

"If he makes a move towards the kitchen, you will need to give a warning shot," said Malcom. He hopped off his Artic Cat. "I am going in; you stay here and cover me."

"I got you, Dad." Luke removed his pistol from its holder and aimed through the large front window. "If things go bad, I'll have to take him down."

Malcom gave him a look.

"You cool your jets, cowboy. I'll take care of this."

Malcom walked into the restaurant while Luke moved towards the front door.

"Mike, what the hell's going on in here? You're making one hell of a racket."

"This is none of your concern, Sheriff. This is between me and that mother fucker hiding in the kitchen," said Mike, giving no indications that he was willing to turn and lower his gun.

"Well, Mike, you see, I got a problem with you trying to shoot people in my town. Now put down that shotgun and let's talk," said Malcom. He hadn't yet pulled his pistol.

"I know you're hurt. Hell, who wouldn't be? But that don't give you no cause to go after an innocent man. You are making a very bad situation even worse."

"How much worse could it be, Sheriff? You can't find her, but I sure as hell can," responded Mike. His face was red and sweat dripped from his forehead.

Luke, now aiming from an open front door,

was sure that, at any moment, the man would turn and draw on his dad.

"Mike, you know me. You know I wouldn't steer you wrong. Please listen and drop the gun."

"Fuck you, Luke," said Mike. He never took his eyes off the small serving window.

"You are leaving, anyway. Everyone in town knows you took that job in Detroit. You don't give a shit about this town."

Malcom turned and looked at Luke for a brief moment. Luke had not said anything to him yet about his leaving Phelton. Looking back at Mike, Malcom said, "Mike, I'm tired of this. Tom Phillips filled your head with bullshit. If you're not careful, you're going to be in more trouble than you are right now. I said drop your weapon and come with me to the station."

"Look," said Howard from his hiding place in the kitchen. "I don't know what happened to your girlfriend. I never even met her. Please, let me go and I promise I won't file any charges."

"That's the best offer you're going to get, Mike. Please lower your weapon. Now." said Malcom.

"No, I want to see his face," Mike's voice trembled.

Before Malcom or Luke could say another word, Howard's face appeared through the service window. Luke could see his face was as white as a ghost.

"I swear, I never touched your fiancée or that other old woman. I swear on my grandmother's grave. I had nothing to do with it.

Mike stood there looking at Howard, his gun

pointed straight at his forehead. Luke was not sure what to do.

"Ok, Mike. He did as you asked. Do you still honestly think he had anything to do with any of this?" said Malcom in a calm voice. "Lower that gun and let us get back to looking for Samantha, ok?"

Mike lowered his weapon and fell to his knees on the floor. Laying down his gun, he cupped his hands behind his head and started to weep. Luke ran in, cuffs out and ready, but Malcom stopped him short of reaching Mike. "Come on, let's go over to the station," said Malcom. He helped Mike off the floor.

Marge now emerged over the countertop.

"Howard, you ok?" she yelled.

Howard walked out of the kitchen.

"Yea, I'm fine. Look, Sheriff, I meant what I said. I am not pressing any charges. He is a hurting man."

Malcom, walking Mike towards the restaurant's front door, said, "Thank you, Howard. Most people are not that thoughtful. I am going to take him over to the station and put him in the pen for a little while, let him get his mind straight. If you change your mind about pressing charges, then you just let me know. When this is all over, I will make sure he pays for that big hole in your wall."

Luke looked up, and, sure enough, there was a big gaping hole just above the service window. That's when the power went out. Luke watched every light in town go off all at once.

"Shit," he said. "We knew it was just a matter of time."

*

Vinnie sat in total darkness; he was surprised it had taken this long to lose power. He knew exactly where the battery powered lantern was. He needed a few minutes for his eyes to adjust before he would retrieve it out of the cupboard above the sink. Looking out the window, all he could see was the snow whipping by as the wind continued to strengthen. Franky, still asleep in the back-bottom bunk, did not stir. Hopefully, he would finally get some sleep. If not, Vinnie was afraid he would crack. There had been no sign of Mary. Not since she dragged the body from the frozen lake. *Maybe she is haunting someone else for a change*, he thought. Unfortunately, there was no way of knowing one way or the other. It was too dark to see very far, and the snow blocked the view beyond a couple of yards.

Then, Vinnie had a terrifying thought. *What if the light had been the only thing keeping the creature out?* In the darkness, he made a mad dash for the battery-powered lantern, bashing his knee on the dinner table.

"Oh, fuck me!" he said softly. He didn't want to wake Franky. Reaching into the cupboard, he grabbed the lantern. *God, I hope there are batteries in this damn thing*, he thought. But his mind was at ease once the trailer was illuminated by the soft glow of the light.

Returning to his spot on the bench below the front picture window, he noticed movement from outside. Vinnie's body tensed up. *For goodness' sake, can't this fucking thing ever take a break?* He put his face close to the window for a better view. Suddenly, a deer ran up to the trailer. It seemed to be in a panic, confused in the storm. Vinnie could only guess that she was disoriented and lost. Just then, a big buck, ten points from what Vinnie could see, walked out of the woods and stood at the forest edge. The doe, seeing the buck, took off on a run through the deep snow. It was past the buck and in the woods before the impressive male turned, looked around the yard, then followed the doe back into the woods.

A feeling of melancholy engulfed him. At any other point in his life, his heart would have been lifted with the appearance of the majestic buck. Now, all he felt was sadness. It reminded him how isolated they were, how cut off from the rest of the world they had become. All that he loved and cared for was just a few short hours away. It might as well have been a million miles.

*

Pastor Elijah Smith of First Baptist Church of Phelton was locking up the church when he saw Luke and Malcom whizz by on their snowmobiles.

He gave them a wave. *Fools. It's far too dangerous to be out right now, even with a snowmobile,* he thought. *If they aren't careful, they will get frostbite.*

Pastor Elijah mentally went through his to-do list. He'd already wrapped all the pipes in the basement, left the water in the bathroom on just beyond a drip, and secured all the doors and windows. If there was anything else to do to protect the church, he couldn't think of it. His house was only a stone's throw away from the church. He would run home, grab his cat, Buttons, and head to the shelter at the school. He'd promised Elma he would be there over an hour ago, but got behind when the lights went out and he had to finish his list with nothing more than a flashlight.

Walking the half block to his house Pastor Elijah got the strangest feeling of being watched. He did a three sixty turn and saw nothing. This did not relieve his perception that someone was watching him. He could feel eyes from somewhere in the darkness, fixed on his every move. He walked down the snow-covered street, stopping every few feet to survey his surroundings. It was not until he was near to his front steps that he saw her, a beautiful, young woman, naked as the day she was born, sitting on his front porch swing.

"I've been waiting for you, Pastor." She spoke just above a whisper. She parted her legs wide, exposing all of herself to the good pastor.

"Ma'am, I don't know who you are, but you'd

better get inside. You'll freeze to death out here. Why are you out here with nothing on?"

She got up and walked over to him. She put her hand on his crouch and started to rub.

"I just want to make you happy," she said.

"You can make me happy by removing you hand!" snapped Elijah.

"Ok," she said with a seductive smile. "Then maybe you want a turn."

She grabbed Elijah's hand, placed it between her legs, and started to grind.

Pastor Elijah tried to remove his hand, but she was too strong.

"Stop this right now. I am a man of God."

"God has nothing to do with this," she responded. She opened her mouth far beyond that which is humanly possible.

Pastor Elijah gasped in disbelief as her two front teeth turned into six-inch fangs. He tried to force his hand free, but she just kept rubbing harder.

"Please, just let me go," pleaded Elijah. "I can help you."

"Yes, you can." She spoke in a voice that was almost inhuman. With her free hand, she grabbed his face and pulled him close to her. The smell was beyond repulsive. Her eyes were now black, not just the pupil, but the iris and the sclera, too.

Pastor Elijah screamed, but his voice was lost in the howling wind. That's when she sunk her teeth deep inside his throat. He could feel the life being drained from his body, feel the blood running in streams down his neck and then his back. Though the will to fight was still there, there was nothing he could do. His head was getting light and all his senses started fading. As the cold, bitter wind blew, Elijah didn't feel a thing. He was dying and nothing was going to change that now.

CHAPTER X

TRUTH BE TOLD

Phillip Parker woke in a cold sweat, his body aching. He tried to pull himself up to a sitting position. The beast had left him hobbled once again; both his feet turned inward with no joint attached at the ankles. They were worthless, uncontrollable appendages doing nothing more than dangling at the end of his legs.

Phillip remembered the first time he awoke the morning after Banthom was killed at the empty restaurant. Cold, naked, and alone, he rose along the shores of the Hillsborough River, just outside of Zephyrhills, Florida. The beast had left him intact. Phillip had wandered aimlessly, looking for a road. Looking for some contact with the outside world, somewhere where he could find a phone and warn the others, to let them know about the monster bent on destroying them. Though he wandered tirelessly, he never found a way out of the woods. All he did was anger the beast. After that day in Florida, he would awaken to some form of crippling that would make any attempt of finding help impossible. Though the feet seemed to be the beast's favorite, there were times when his kneecaps were out of place, his hips pulled out of their sockets, and, of course, the fracturing of his femurs. They were all in his little bag of tricks. Through the most remote areas of Georgia, through the hills of Tennessee and Kentucky, the beast moved north. As the weather changed and the nights got colder, Phillip started waking up inside barns, people's houses, cabins, and sheds. Sometimes, the houses were deserted. Other times, he would wake to the sight of dead bodies mutilated by the beast, scattered around their living quarters.

The beast was clever; Phillip had to give that to him. There was no doubt the creature knew everything going on in Phillip's brain. He never left him anywhere that was not remote, far from any living person he could reach out to. And he never, ever, left a telephone line intact.

At first, Phillip was only aware when the sun was bright and he had awakened, but long before they reached the Ohio-Michigan state line, the beast tortured him with memories. Memories of towns and villages left in ruin, the hunting of human prey, the ripping apart of human flesh and bone. Phillip knew what the beast wanted him to know. He could see what the beast wanted him to see. Worst of all, he forced Phillip to feel his sick and deprived compulsions and animalist hunger for human hearts.

Unlike the spirit that arose next to him and occupied Mary's dead body, this demon was bound to Phillip. He needed Phillip alive. Alive, yes. The beast also took his pleasure in Phillip's torture, making him witness the sickness of its evil and the devastation of the human body. Then, there were the other things he showed him. Like the dark things brought with him from the very bowels of Hell, things so foul that it would make Phillip physically ill. Though the pain of being crippled was almost more than he could endure, it was his body enduring the suffering of transformation, the losing of one's body to a form never meant to walk this earth. That was the most painful.

Over the past few months, Phillip had made several attempts at suicide. It was not to be. It seemed even when Phillip was awake with the misconception he was in control, he was not. The first attempt was a butcher knife found on the floor of a cabin next to him one morning. Phillip wasn't sure, but he thought this was someplace in Ohio. As Phillip attempted to cut his own throat, a counter force pushed his hand back. The beast would not let him cause his own demise. Three more attempts yielded the same results.

The beast knew when the sun would shine. Phillip was always nicely tucked away before waking. Only the full sun would cause the beast to retreat. Any kind of cloud cover that blocked the sun was as welcoming to the beast as the dead of night. When darkness reigned, so did the he.

Looking around the room he now found himself in, Phillip saw, hanging on the wall, a family portrait of a young Asian couple with two small children. Phillip hoped they were ok; he didn't remember the beast taking any lives the night before. Then again, Phillip only knew what the beast wanted him to know. There was no large pool of blood anywhere he could see, so hopefully, this was a summer house, or the owners were out of town. He had no idea where he was. He was sure a few days ago that he was at the Yorkey's cottage, which meant the beast had reached his Michigan home.

Phillip knew the creature had yet to find Franky. He thought that was the one thing that it would elate in, showing Phillip his demise. Then, just as quickly as it came, the sun faded outside the windows and the clouds moved back in. Phillip shut his eyes and waited. The burning would soon start, the pain of his body being twisted and deformed was coming. *God, please, let me die*, was his final thought before the flesh started peeling from his face.

*

Benjamin's head pounded. It had been a long trip and nearing his destination in Parksville, a million thoughts rushed through his head. Meeting

with the Archbishop of Bucharest on Benjamin's
private jet had not been on his itinerary. It seems
the Church had its doubts about Father Aron's
intentions, the same as Benjamin. This had not
only been a quest for the man, but a test of his
loyalty. The Archbishop explained that Father
Aron's resistance to the evil, with his extensive
exposure to the Grimoires, was encouraging.
However, they wanted to make sure he had not
been compromised. During the expedition, they
kept a close eye on him. If he passed this test, there
would be a new job for him in Rome, one dealing
with the evil forces at work that the Church kept
locked behind closed doors.

It was not known to the church, at least not until
Father Aron traveled to Bucharest, that Banthom's
true name was Gunari Danior. The fact that the
pair started out looking for a script located at the
Banthom House only to make travel arrangements
to Bucharest, set up red flags. So, they, too, followed
the same paper trail that Mary, the year before, had
followed to uncover Banthom's true identity. At the
time Benjamin delivered the second book to Rome,
there was no inquisition into what had taken place.
The Church only cared about its return. That all
changed when they discovered Banthom was a
truly a Danior.

Over the centuries, Church leaders had
followed the Danior family closely. But Gunari
had slipped from view. They knew all about the
family's history. They knew about their historical

hatred of the Church. They knew Gunari was the son of the witch named Hester. Most importantly, they knew about the demons she conjured which resulted in the death of thousands. In detail, the Archbishop laid out what evil Benjamin was to face. The church kept quiet about folklore being embedded in truth. Many Romani people still believed the Church would give them no voice.

It seemed the tradition was to continue when Benjamin was asked to turn over his notes. The Archbishop insisted they be returned to Rome with the scroll. Then, just before departing the plane, the Archbishop informed Father Aron that he was to accompany Benjamin to the States. The look of astonishment on the priest's face was something Benjamin would never forget. Benjamin surmised that Father Aron's new position in the Church began that day.

Walking up the front steps, Benjamin was humbled by the house that Phillip and Franky called home. It had been a long time since he had stayed in such a modest abode. With Father Aron at his side, he knocked on the front door.

It was Brandy who met him at the front door.

"Benjamin! Thank God you're here," she said, throwing her arms around his neck.

*

Phillip was aware as the creature ran through the woods in search of prey. The cold, bitter wind and blinding snow kept most people inside, though he knew it would only be a matter of time before the beast would get the scent of human flesh. Phillip could not speak. He had no control over what the creature did, but he could hear, see, smell, taste, and feel everything the creature did. Helpless, he had no choice but watch once more as the horror unfolded.

The next victim was identified and stalked. An elderly man, late seventies or early eighties, walked from his house to his barn. He followed a path that Phillip was sure must have taken constant attention to keep clear. He was bent over, carrying what Phillip could only speculate was chicken feed. As the creature approached the old man, Phillip wanted desperately to scream out, "Run, you fool!"

But he knew this was impossible. Once again, he would be helpless to stop the onslaught.

As the old man entered the side door of the barn, the beast crept up behind him. Phillip was amazed at how silent the creature could move. Often, he would be with in mere feet of a victim before they even knew he was there. He was smart, too. He always took his time to scope out the area, making sure the victim was alone. He knew how to kill quickly and flee, only to kill again. Not once had he been seen. Of that Phillip was certain.

The beast waited outside the door. Phillip could smell the old man and hear his breath from inside the barn. *Please, you old son of bitch. Stay inside,* Phillip thought. But it was not to be. The old man gave a cursing lesson to his livestock and Phillip could hear him approaching the side door. He could feel the beast anticipation, its joy in finding a victim. Long, sharp claws protruded from the beast's fur, raising his left hand in anticipation.

The attack was over in a matter of seconds. The beast was on the old man before he could raise a hand in his own defense. It ripped at the meat of his chest, grabbing the right side of the rib cage with its fangs and the left with his claws. He snapped the ribs apart at the sternum. The old man, still screaming in fear and pain, laid on the ground, his chest cavity fully exposed. That's when the beast assaulted the man's lungs, digging and biting his way through to the heart. Reaching it with his front teeth, he pulled it from the man's chest, raised his head, and swallowed it whole.

Phillip was repulsed by the taste of blood and flesh. *God, please don't let me remember this one*, thought Phillip. *I can bear no more.*

He and the beast heard an elderly woman yelling from the house. She stood on the back porch. "Willy, don't forget the eggs!"

The beast crouched down on the path in the blinding snow. It hid low to the ground.

"Willy! Damn it, can you hear me?" she yelled again. Then, she started down the path herself.

*

"Vampire? You mean to tell me we are looking for a fucking vampire?" asked Hazel in disbelief.

Benjamin had tried to be as delicate with the whole situation as he could. This was his first meeting with Hazel and Sam. Even though Josette and Brandy seemed mortified with his conclusions, and had assured him that Hazel and Sam knew about the situation and could be trusted, Benjamin remained a little skeptical about their participation in this get-together at Phillip's and Franky's. He looked over at Father Aron for confirmation, but the priest stood next to him quietly. The man seemed in a daze as if he, too, was still gripping the reality of their situation.

It had not been his idea to wait until this meeting to make the findings known. That had been at the Josette's insistence.

"They are a part of the team, Benjamin. We all need to hear your findings together," she had told him more than once.

Now, Benjamin had an awful feeling about it.

"Look, we knew that Banthom's real name was Gunari Danior. Think about it. It all makes sense. A gypsy from Romania, the legends of vampires, and…" Benjamin gave an extensive pause.

"Oh, for goodness' sake! Spit it out, Ben," said Josette.

"A hound of Hell, a lycanthrope," finished Benjamin.

"Holy shit!" shouted Hazel. "You mean he is a fucking werewolf?"

Benjamin was becoming frustrated.

"Look, I was there the day we killed Banthom.

Everything was just like in Doctor Tabor's notes... the pentagram on the floor, the animal bones, and the broken pottery, all part of that bastard's ritual.

"What was the pottery for?" asked a confused Hazel.

"It's Babylonian. The name of the victim to be cursed was written over and over again in clay pots with the victim's own blood. As the witch invoked the curse, they would fill the bowls with blood from the victim and drink it, only to shatter the bowls on the floor when the curse was complete.

"If the fucking place hadn't burned to the ground, I bet we would have found the animal bones to be that of a bat and a wolf. I have little doubt now that those bones were used to perform the carvings on Mary and Phillip's chests, bleeding them for ink for the pots and blood for the drink."

"Believe it or not, it all makes sense," said Sam. Up to this point, the man had kept to himself. "I mean, if you were living at that time and in that place, it would have been the evil spirits that you were most fearful of. Think about it. A demon that possesses only the dead."

"Mary was dead when I found her; I'm sure of it," said Benjamin, having a seat next to Hazel on the couch.

"Drinking human blood in defiance of holy communion... that sounds like a vampire to me," continued Sam.

"Then that means Phillip..." said Josette.

Benjamin could tell she was on the edge of a breakdown; tears welled up in her eyes.

"Is a werewolf, a shape shifter," said Benjamin. He looked at Josette sympathetically.

Josette took a deep breath.

"Franky said he was still alive, the one that possesses only the living."

"Wait, that's the one that eats the flesh, correct?" asked Hazel.

"Yes. He mocks the act of holy communion by eating human flesh," said Benjamin.

"Did it say anything about eating hearts?" questioned Sam.

Benjamin was surprised by this question.

"Yes, as a matter of fact. It says in the notes that the flesh the creature desires is the human heart."

"That might explain the two I have setting in my lab," said Sam, rubbing his chin.

Hazel shook her head and stood up. Walking around the back of the couch, she said, "Hold on. I mean, I know I am newer to all this than the rest of you, but you're talking old superstitions here."

Sam turned his head, so he was talking directly to Hazel.

"Think about it. If the family had the secret to summon these two demons, who's to say they haven't done it before? If, indeed, they did accomplish this back then, like the Archbishop described to Benjamin, and it resulted in the death of thousands, then that would be a hard tale to die, if you know what I mean. For God's sake, there are still places in Romania where they eat the hearts of loved ones to keep them from coming back as vampires. That kind of belief system is usually rooted in some form of reality, don't you think?"

"I know, it's true. I saw the destruction this Hester left behind her. I think one of the creatures ended up killing her," said Josette. "It was horrible."

"His mother didn't have a Grimoire so she couldn't control it," said Benjamin.

"But Banthom did," said Brandy. "That is what I have been trying to tell Josette. The two people we know, and love, have been ordered to kill Franky Lake. Why they didn't do it in Florida when he was there, I am not sure. But it cost Ethel a lot to get this information and I think we need to heed her warning. If Franky is down in Phelton, then maybe that is where we all need to be."

Hazel stopped pacing and sat back down next to Sam.

"Ok. We have missing persons down in Phelton, which, if you were traveling from Florida, would make sense. It is out of the way, but still south. The two dead bodies we found with their hearts eaten out were in Pulaski, then at the college, moving closer and closer to Parksville. Ok, you're all starting to win me over on all this."

Josette, no longer able to hold back her tears, muttered, "Yes, and you said yourself you have not heard from Franky, Vinnie, or Shawn since before Christmas. Maybe they are dealing with Mary now. Maybe they need our help."

"What about Phillip? if he is, indeed, a werewolf, then he is here, not Phelton," said Benjamin.

"I don't think so," said Hazel. "There haven't been any more bodies found. For all we know, he has picked up Franky's scent and is on his way to Phelton. I am going to have Jackson run a search and see if anyone has been found half-eaten or missing between here and Phelton."

"No, I am not going to wait. I am going to head down there now," said Josette. "We may not know where Phillip is, but we know where Franky is. And if he's their target, if he's the one Banthom sent them to destroy, then I am going to be by his side."

"Oh no you're not, young lady," said Brandy. "I know you love Franky. We all do. But you have more than yourself to think about."

Brandy reached over and placed her hand on Josette's belly.

Benjamin was relieved that, at last, the group was coming to a consensus. Doctor Tabor and the Archbishop were correct.

"I think we need to do a little planning before we just head out."

Sam got up and walked over to Josette. Putting his hands on her shoulder, he said, "Look, my dear. I know you have special abilities, but have you looked outside? This is Michigan. That means, while they have been able to keep Michigan Ave. out front here plowed, those back roads on the way to Phelton are not. I doubt that even Michigan Ave. will be clear by nightfall. See how it's coming down?"

"See? That's what I'm talking about," said Benjamin. "We need to plan how to get down there, figure out what we need to kill the bloody creature, and keep Phillip intact."

"What about Mary?" asked Brandy.

"That spirit only possesses the dead, which means Mary was dead before she ever left that restaurant. There is no bringing her back," said Benjamin. His voice wavered. Now it was Benjamin on the brink of tears. After all this time, reality finally came crashing home. When he found her, she was dead. Nothing that happened since then had changed that. His hopes of reunification were shattered. There would be no Mary and Ben, no children running around Burk Manor, no wife to share his life with.

Josette pulled herself up and went to his side.

"Oh, Ben. I am so sorry."

Ben welcomed her in his arms. Together they cried while the others simply sat quietly, still processing the situation. After ten minutes, it was Sam who broke the silence.

"We will need a good four-wheel drive truck, a jeep maybe," said Sam. He was creating a mental checklist.

Releasing Josette and wiping his eyes, Benjamin nodded in agreement.

"That will get us down to Phelton, maybe, but how do we kill these bastards? That's what I want to know."

"Not Phillip. If he is possessed, then you will

need to exorcise the bastard," said Josette. She looked directly at Father Aron.

Father Aron, who had yet to speak a word since their arrival, nodded.

"I have a copy of the Roman Ritual with me."

"Well, we know that both hide from daylight. The scroll talked about one hiding in shadows and one in plain sight. I assume Mary would be the one hiding in the shadows, and Phillip..."

"The demon is hiding in plain sight, alright. Only he's using Phillip to do it," alleged Brandy.

"Ok. So, if they hide from it, it must kill them... or at least cause them pain," added Sam.

"Well sunlight hasn't exactly been readily available this past week," remarked Hazel.

"Granted, it's not much. But what else do we have to go on?" asked Benjamin.

"What about all the old wives' tales about vampires and werewolves? Does anyone think any of the old lore would apply? I mean, we know what they are, so maybe some of the old stories are true," offered Sam.

"Well, they are demons, so they will have a strong urge to avoid any religious artifacts. I think we would be safe to say that crosses warding off vampires may be true," offered Father Aron.

"What about the silver bullet? That was used to kill a werewolf," said Hazel. "It's believed silver represents the 13 pieces offered to Judas to betray Jesus."

"Good," said Sam. "Now we are getting

somewhere. In the old days, they would have cut off the vampire's head and put a stake through the heart."

Hazel gave a quick rebuttal.

"I would not take a chance with the whole 'stake through the heart' thing. Cutting of the head, maybe. But I say we stick with sunlight since we know that affects them."

"You can't see anything?" whispered Benjamin to Josette. The others continued the debate.

Josette closed her eyes. After a few minutes she looked up at him.

"No. The evil possessing them is also hiding them in a veil of darkness. I fear I will not be much help. If only Kip was still here."

"What about the one about a werewolf only being able to be killed by someone who loves them?" asked Brandy, not sure if the others would even hear her.

"So, loved ones can kill werewolves," asked Hazel.

"No, the man or woman with the curse. Without them, there is no werewolf," replied Brandy.

This last statement caught Josette's ear.

"Brandy! Do you hear what you're saying?" she exclaimed. "This is Phillip we are talking about!"

PART TWO

CHAPTER XI

Calm Before the Storm

Ethel walked around the dark kitchen of Rebecca's modest home. The small amount of light from the streetlamps gave her just enough glow to move around. She had checked out of the hotel the day before. Until she could find a more permeant location, she decided to visit with Rebecca. Looking up at the clock on her cousin's wall, she noticed the time: two in the morning. Making herself some tea, she sat down at the kitchen table and waited for the water to boil. It was not her intention to be up in the middle of the night, but the nightmares were endless. Over and over, she walked the path to Samedi. Over and over the spirits followed, only this night, she saw Brandy among them, her tortured body hobbling among the crowd.

The kettle began to sing, and the lights came on around her. She jumped. Rebecca stood in the doorway, dressed in only her nightgown. She rubbed her eyes.

"Why are you up at this time of night? Nightmares again?" Rebecca asked. She walked into the kitchen and took a seat at the table.

"Oh, I am so sorry, my dear. I did not mean to wake you. Go back to bed," responded Ethel. She rose to make her tea.

"I will, I will. But first, tell me what's on your mind that you feel a cup of tea is needed in the middle of the night. And how you thought you were going to pour hot water in the dark."

"It's just those dreams again; I've told you about them."

"Yes, you have. Make your tea and sit down. I know there is something else going on, so you may as well tell me. That way we can all get some sleep."

Ethel did as she was instructed. She put a tea bag in a mug, poured the boiling water, then returned to sit next to Rebecca.

"I saw Brandy tonight in my dreams. She was among the dead."

"Well, that's understandable. You're worried about her," said Rebecca. She took Ethel's hand. "Trust me, your new powers do not include seeing the future."

"Powers," said Ethel, shaking her head. "I still can't get used to you saying that. Besides, what good does it do to be a witch queen if I can't even help those I care about?"

"Who says you can't?" asked Rebecca, grinning. "You forget. You have the power, but I was the good student. You are not helpless."

"Say what? Are you telling me I can do something to help?"

"Yes, I think we can." Rebecca patted Ethel's hand.

"But we are not doing anything tonight. In the morning, we will talk." Rebecca got up from the table and headed back to her room.

"But…" started Ethel.

"In the morning, Ethel," Rebecca called. The door shut behind her.

*

Brandy was the first to get out of bed. In Phillip's and Franky's kitchen she started making a pot of coffee. Looking out the window at the endless storm, she noticed the snow had stopped, but the freezing wind continued to blow under a sunny sky. Just as she was pulling a coffee cup from the cupboard, Benjamin made his way into the kitchen and sat down at the modest, round, kitchen table.

"Good morning, sunshine," said Benjamin. He smiled.

Brandy reached for another mug and walked over to the coffee pot to pour them both a cup. "Black, right?" she asked.

"You got it."

Brandy made her way to the table, one mug in each hand. She placed them down on the table and sat down across from Benjamin.

"I didn't want to say anything last night and

look like a fool in front of that Captain Cowan and that Sam guy, but I want you to explain this all to me. So we are looking for two demons, correct?"

Ben took a sip of his coffee then offered a response.

"Yes, I would say they are demons. Make no mistake, they are pure evil."

"Ok, so these demons are where the story of vampires and werewolves started, right?"

"I guess. The Church thinks that's how the legends started, the ones you find in books and movies."

"Ok, so if they are demons, and this Banthom conjured them and sent them to hunt down Franky, then why use Phillip and Mary?"

"Do you remember that day at the hotel when Shawn got up on the table?"

"Hell yes. I will never forget that." Brandy shuddered.

"Phillip Parker. You cocksucker. You will pay for killing the Judas. I have special plans for you," said Benjamin.

"Those were his exact words. He had his sights on Phillip because he holds him responsible for the death of his partner, Fritz."

"Ok, I understand that," said Brandy. Her coffee cup remained untouched.

"But why Mary?"

"I think Mary was nothing more than collateral damage. He needed two vessels, one for each demon."

"Last question and I will quit bugging. Do you think we have a chance to save Phillip?" asked Brandy. She was working hard to control her grief.

"I don't know, Brandy. I just don't know."

Josette walked in, rambling, just as Benjamin was finishing his sentence.

"Don't know about what?" she asked.

"Oh, I was just wanting to know when we might be leaving, dear," said Brandy. She looked at Benjamin with a look that said, "You better keep your mouth closed."

"Would you like a cup of coffee?" she asked, not waiting for an answer.

Brandy jumped to her feet and headed for the cupboard.

Josette grabbed the back of the nearest chair and eased herself down.

"Oh, Brandy. It is nice to have you around again! You always did brighten up my day. But you never did finish telling us about Ethel. Is she doing ok? Will we see her soon?"

Brandy thought about what she should say. There was enough going on, and she didn't want to add to the stress.

"I presume so. She is having a little problem with leaving New Orleans right now. With her grandmother dying and all, she will need to get her affairs in order."

"Understood," said Josette. "I miss her almost as much as I missed you."

"Flattery will get you everywhere with me.

You know that, don't you?" Brandy chuckled and handed Josette her coffee.

"I will be renting the jeep today. As long as the snow holds off and they get a chance to clear some of these roads, I will pick it up this afternoon. That is, if you are kind enough to drive me, Brandy."

"Sure, no problem. Just as long as we take our time. I don't want anything to happen to Ethel's kitty; she would never forgive me if I brought it back with damage," responded Brandy.

"Aren't you afraid of driving in this shit?" asked Josette.

Brandy balked. "Dear, I've been driving in this shit since I was knee high to a grasshopper."

"We still need to meet with the others to get things planned," said Josette directly to Benjamin. "These are good people and we need their help."

"I know, I know. It's just hard having someone else involved in all this. But if you trust them, then I trust them," said Benjamin. He placed his hand on hers.

"I do, Ben. I really do." replied Josette. "It's Father Aron I am still up in the air about."

*

Vinnie opened his eyes to daylight streaming through the front window of Howard's apartment above the restaurant. For a moment, all the horror from the past few days was gone. Life seemed almost normal. There were no eerie corpses staring at him through the window, no scratching sounds, no late-night banging from the outside. Just quiet. The sun helped bring back some normalcy as well.

For the first time in almost a week, the sun shone brilliantly across the Michigan countryside. It was almost as if the nightmare was over, like the devil himself had pulled up stakes and returned to the very bowels of Hell. Unfortunately, this feeling of life-as-usual quickly dissipated. Franky, dressed in the pajamas Howard let him borrow the night before, came strolling in from the bedroom where he had spent the night.

"We have to make some plans on how to kill that fucking thing."

"Relax, Franky. Let me have a cup of coffee or something."

Last night they were at the end of their ropes. When the power went out, the two felt the cold creeping into the trailer. When the lights of snowmobiles danced across the ceiling and through the windows, it was Franky who ran to the front door. Fortunately, Mary must have been out spreading her terror elsewhere, because when they made their mad dash to the sleds, there was no trace of her anywhere. Before Luke or Malcom could dismount, the two men were running at them, begging them to hurry and get them the hell out of there.

Without a word, the two men made room for them on the back of their snowmobiles. Freezing cold, neither one dressed for this ride, they made the trek back into town, where the two were left at Howard's doorstep. Retelling the story of their encounters at the lake seemed only to legitimize the fact that it was all real. Neither Vinnie nor Franky were sure the men, Luke, Malcom, or Howard believed a single word of what they said. Regardless, he and Franky felt better saying it.

"Howard said he has coffee and breakfast ready down in the diner, but I just wanted a chance to talk to you alone first."

"Franky, it can wait. Give me a few minutes before we jump back into the frying pan, will you?"

"But I just want…"

"Franky, I don't give a shit what you want right now." He got off the couch and made his way towards the bathroom.

"I said give to it a fucking break. We have time to talk about all this. Look outside, she is not out there right now."

"I know the sun is out, but who knows how long…"

Vinnie shut the door in Franky's face, ignoring the rest. He proceeded to take a pee. When he was done, he took his time and washed his hands. Looking in the mirror, he sighed heavily.

I look sixty years old, came the little voice inside his head. His face was thin and pale. He missed home and, most of all, he missed his dog, Harry.

When Vinnie came out of the bathroom, Franky was not there. Vinnie surmised that Franky must have headed downstairs. He felt bad about the way he had talked to him. The man had lost so much, and he knew Franky was just trying to find a way to end all of this. But after the few days they had just endured, breathing space for Vinnie was a necessity. Taking his time to get dressed, Vinnie finally made his way down the back steps, through the back door to the kitchen, and into the dining room. He found Franky and Howard deep in conversation.

"So how does one go about killing a vampire?" asked Howard. He then noticed Vinnie approach. "There is fresh coffee in the pot and eggs and sausage in the kitchen."

Vinnie smiled and headed for the coffee. Breakfast would have to wait until he was more awake.

"I don't know. I know how it is done in the books, but this is no fucking fairytale. I know what we saw," responded Franky eagerly. "I mean, the only thing I know for sure is that, in all the stories I remember, they can't tolerate the sunlight. I think we need to trap her in the sun."

"I agree," said Vinnie, sitting down at the table with a full coffee cup in hand. "We need to get her into the light."

Howard rubbed his chin.

"Luke was in this morning before either one of you got up. He came to grab the breakfast I made for the shelter. They found that preacher guy that lives next to the church dead on his front steps this morning, all the blood drained from his body." He took a deep breath and continued. "I think I am starting to buy into your story."

"She's not even bothering to hide them anymore," said Franky, just above a whisper. "I think she will come back in town tonight. She knows we are gone and this is the first place she'll look."

Vinnie, ignoring Franky's comment, turned to Howard.

"And did Luke seem to believe?"

Howard grinned. "Yes, I think so. But Malcom is not convinced. He swears there is a serial killer on the loose."

"That's what they thought about Fritz," said Franky. He looked at Howard. "It's hard when superstition becomes reality, but trust me, that bitch is real, and she will be coming back."

"Got any tape?" asked Vinnie.

"Yea, I think so. It was behind the counter last I knew. Why?" responded Howard.

"Good, we can hang these in the windows," said Vinnie, pulling out a pocket full of crucifixes. "I grabbed these from Dale's trailer as we ran out. We know they keep the bitch outside."

"I thought vampires weren't allowed to enter a house unless invited by the owner?" asked Howard. He got up to retrieve the tape.

"Look. I wouldn't put my trust in what might work. These have been battle-tested," agreed Franky. "I say, we stick with these."

*

Sam received the call around nine that everyone was meeting at Hazel's around noon. That rich Irishman, it seems, would be picking everyone up in the brand-new Jeep Explorer he rented. When he told Linda he was going to be gone for a couple of days, she was less than thrilled. Sam had not been home much during what the Weather Channel called "the worst storm to hit central-lower Michigan in decades."

For Sam, it was not easy skating against the truth. He told her he was involved in an investigation down in Phelton that may or may not be related to the recent killings in Jackson. Not the complete truth, but not a lie, either. Even though the snow had stopped for most of the day, the wind was still bitter, and the skies had started to turn grey.

Sam was not sure about the Irishman. He seemed nice enough, that's for sure. But Sam still did not have a grasp of how he and the priest fell in with Franky and Phillip. As for Josette, he liked her. She was somewhat brash at times, but always seemed to approach things with a sense of innocence. If they all made it through this latest adventure, he hoped she might join him at church with the family.

Now looking down at the body of the college student, he wondered if he was making the right decision going down to Phelton with the others. He had so much more to lose than he did back in '89. Linda and the girls meant the world to him.

What would they do if, for some ungodly reason, he did not return?

Yes, he had money saved, and yes, he had life insurance. But he knew Linda would be devastated. The girls would have no father to scare away unwanted boyfriends, watch as they graduated, or to walk them down the aisle. *Then again*, he thought, *what happens if we fail? What will the creatures do once their mission is complete? Would anyone, anywhere be safe?*

Sam had little time to contemplate this when his pager went off. His ride had arrived. He quickly grabbed his jacket and the satchel he had packed with supplies and headed for the door. Before he even got to the hall, with the elevators, he saw Hazel and Benjamin walking toward him.

"Sorry, I was afraid you wouldn't get the page," said Hazel. "Make sure you cover up good. It's colder than a witch's tit outside."

*

Elma walked into the office to find Malcom in the back breakroom staring at the remains of Pastor Elijah Smith. Lost in thought, he did not even notice her walk in.

"I remember the last time we had some one lying in this room waiting for the meat wagon to take them away," she said.

Startled, Malcom turned to face her.

"Yea, I was just thinking about that." Turning

back to the body, he added, "But this one... I don't know. It's just not right. Look at the way his neck is ripped open. Did you know all of his blood is drained?"

"Yes," replied Elma. She put down her purse and walked over to him.

"Luke filled me in this morning at the shelter. Malcom, I think you need to listen to Franky and Vinnie. If they say something supernatural is taking place, then I am inclined to believe them."

Malcom stood there rubbing his unshaven chin. Slowly, he walked around the body. It was placed nicely on what was normally used as their break table.

"The plow should be through here soon, then we will call for the pickup. Personally, I will be glad when they get here. Damn, body gives me the creeps."

"What about him?" asked Elma, pointing to the sleeping Mike Shelly laid out on the bunk in the cell.

"I am going to give him a little more time. Maybe by tonight, it will be safe to let him go home."

For the first time, Elma took a good look at the body even though she told herself she wouldn't. Elma had never done well with facing death. She hated funerals, though she often went for the sake of friends and family. Never once had she ever agreed to go to the grave-side services. The thought of sticking loved ones in the ground was too much; she always had an excuse.

"He looks empty," she said to Malcom. "And his color... it's just not natural."

"Well, that's what happens when you have no blood in your body," said Malcom. He walked over to meet her. Putting his arms around her, he said, "Mother, I think it's time I get out of this business and leave it to the next generation."

"Old man, I think you're right," agreed Elma. "When this is all over, you and I are pulling up stakes."

"Yea, but for now we need to deal with this," Malcom said, letting go of Elma.

"If this fucking thing is supernatural..."

"Malcom, language."

"Sorry. I just mean, if it is a vampire like Franky says, and which I still cannot bring myself to believe, then I fear I won't be able to protect the ones I love and the town I have spent most of my life dedicated to."

Not since the day his mother and father died in a car accident back in '77 had Elma seen Malcom cry. She could see he was on the verge of tears this morning. His eyes were moist and turning red. She was lost. She didn't really know how to converse with this side of Malcom. She had always relied on him to be her rock; she had never had to be his. Before she could formulate a response, Malcom put on his hat and headed for the front door.

Elma started to follow him, then stopped. *He needs time to work this out*, she thought. Instead, she snatched her purse off the table and walked over to The Wooden Spoon. The sun shone as she made her way to the restaurant. It was nice to finally see the sun, even though the weather forecast called for an additional six inches of snow later that day. It was nice to get a break. She would help Howard and Marge with the lunch for the shelter. Elma knew he was making BLTs and homemade chicken soup, and that was a lot of work for just the two of them. Just before reaching the front door, she ran into Marge, who was also on her way there.

"Morning, Marge!" said Elma. "I hear you are helping with lunch as well?"

"Yea, there is not much else to do around here with all the lights off. Unless you are lucky enough to have someone to do something in the dark with, if you know what I mean."

"Good morning," said Howard when they entered. "You here to help with lunch?"

"Yea, thought I would give you a hand," Elma replied.

"Me too," said Marge, tossing down her purse.

"Oh, thank you, Marge. Thank you, Elma," said Howard. "Franky and Vinnie said they would help as well when they get back."

"They're back? Why didn't you tell me? What about Dale? Is he ok?" questioned Marge.

Howard hung his head.

"Sorry, Marge. They didn't find him."

"Then why are they back? They were supposed to report on Dale then head home."

"Well, it seems they ran into a little trouble

at the trailer," said Howard. "Something attacked them out there."

Marge, putting down her things, took a seat at the counter.

"Attacked? By what?"

Howard hesitated, then looked over at Elma.

"They don't know for sure" Elma interjected. "I think it's best you ask them when they come back."

Luke walked through the front door of the restaurant.

"Howard, Dad wants to know if you can make a few extra sandwiches for the police station. A lot of deputies have been pulling doubles and most have not eaten."

Howard shrugged his shoulders.

"I already planned on making extras. You just never know when something like this happens." Then, looking over at Elma, he asked, "Did they like the scramble I sent over to the shelter this morning?"

"Yes, and thank you," responded Elma.

Howard grinned and walked into the kitchen to work on the sandwiches.

"Mom, why are you here and not the station?" asked Luke.

"The station is covered. Markowitz is manning the phones. Ain't nothing we can do, anyway. And besides, Howard's been working hard, so I thought I would lend a hand."

"Oh," said Luke. Turning to Marge, who was still sitting at the counter, he suggested, "I hear you and Tom had an argument outside the restaurant."

"What?" said Marge. "Who told you that?"

"Tom. Well, he didn't tell me directly. He went down to the shelter this morning to get his breakfast and I heard him telling his buddies how he warned you to stay away from Howard. He said some pretty nasty things about how you were banging the guy, and was probably in on the kidnappings. Thought you might want to know," said Luke, putting his hand on her shoulder.

Marge's face turned beet red with anger.

"He came here to tell me that Howard was dangerous. I told him to go fuck himself. That was about all there was to that conversation."

"That's about what I thought happened. He is such a dick." said Luke with half a grin.

"And a perv," added Elma. She was furious and couldn't even confront Luke on his language.

"Never trusted that butt head. Not since Malcom caught him looking into the girl's locker room."

Marge almost responded when Howard walked out of the kitchen with a plate full of BLTs wrapped in aluminum foil.

"Hope this is enough for the crew," he said, walking over to Luke.

Seeing the looks on Elma's, Marge's, and Luke's faces, asked, "I'm sorry. Am I interrupting something?"

"No, no," said Luke. "Just catching up with Marge."

Grinning ear to ear, Luke took the sandwiches and headed for the door.

"You got a great girl working for you, Howard. Thanks again for the plate." And with that, he was gone.

Marge quickly changed the subject. "Look, it's getting cloudy and it's starting to snow again," she said, pointing out the front window.

"The sun is gone!" cried Howard. With a look of dread on his face, he added, "Holy shit. Where are Vinnie and Franky?"

"They're over at my place going through our shed, looking for things that will help them when she comes back," said Elma.

"When who comes back?" asked Marge, confused. "And why are all these crosses hanging in the front window?"

*

After everyone left her alone at the house, Josette sat in the large armchair in the living room. This was her favorite location in the house. It was not that the chair was all that comfortable or had better placement, but it sat high for an armchair. And it was easier to get in and out of. The couch was nice, but without someone there to help, getting off it was a chore.

Josette rubbed her belly and thought about her situation. Here she was, in a distant land, extremely pregnant, and not one person knew about the danger she was facing just carrying the lives inside her to full term. At first, it hurt when the group decided she would not be joining them, but she came to grips with the fact that she would be more of a burden than help. Brandy, on the other hand, had not been so easygoing. When Benjamin told her he thought it best she set this one out, Brandy promptly reminded him who had saved his rich ass last time. Still, even she seemed to give in when they broached the possibility of hunting the creatures outside in the woods. Though Brandy still had not committed one way or the other, Josette was sure she would be left in Parksville to keep her company.

"Do you think they will have a chance against the monsters they will face?"

Josette, lost in her own thoughts, almost jumped out of chair when she heard the voice behind her. She quickly turned around and there, standing in the kitchen, was little Bobby.

"Oh, honey. We need to make some rules about you showing up unannounced like that," she said to the half-sized specter. "You would think, after all these years, I would get used to it. But damn, you about scared me out of my wits."

"I'm sorry," replied Bobby. He regretted startling her.

"Oh, no, no. Don't feel bad, sweetie. You just gave me a start, is all."

"You can't see your friends, can you? I know you have been looking for them."

"No, I can't. The team seems to have an idea of where they might be, and they are leaving sometime this afternoon."

Josette pulled herself out of the chair and walked to the kitchen.

"Why are you in here, Bobby?"

"I get a good feeling in this room. I think this is where that Phillip guy spent most of his time."

"Was there something you needed, or are you just here for a visit?"

"I am here because I want to talk to you. I have some questions I need answers to, and I am hoping you can help."

"I will try, honey. What is the question?"

"When this is all over, will I go to that other place? The place Richie is?"

"Richie was your brother, the one who killed all those people? Is that correct?"

"Yes, but it wasn't his fault," said Bobby. "I know he did some bad things, but it was only because those people did what they did."

"You miss him, huh?" said Josette. She could see the pain on the boy's face.

"You're afraid he went to that place that evil people go to, don't you?

"I don't know. I just want to see him again and make sure he is happy."

"Oh, I wish I could give you an answer, Bobby. But I just can't. That's beyond my abilities."

"Ok, I was just wondering…" said Bobby, lowing his eyes.

"Is that why you haven't moved on, Bobby? Because you're afraid of where your brother went?"

"No. I told you, it's because of Hazel," said

Bobby. "I am afraid for her. She was the only person I can remember who was ever nice to me. For a little while, she was, like, I don't know… like my mother, I guess. I know she will be a good mom, but these things that are out there, I'm afraid they will kill her and the baby."

"Look, I know she means a lot to you. But she is a policewoman. Her job is dangerous."

Bobby looked up at her and then out the kitchen window. The storm raged outside.

"This is different, and you know it. If these things kill her, she will never rest. Not until the monsters have been sent back to Hell."

"What do you mean they will not rest?" asked Josette. She was taken aback by the boy's insights.

"People who die at the hands of something that evil cannot pass. All spirits know that," said Bobby, as if it were common knowledge.

"Do you remember the girl in your dreams? The one who showed you what they can do?"

"Yes, but how did you know?"

"Because I talk to her all the time. She follows you, but she will not let you see her again."

Josette remembered that day she first met Ethel and the words of wisdom she gave her: "You can see and hear those spirits, my dear, who want you to see them. And then, there are always more that will never be seen."

"Why is she following me? Kip sent her to me, so why is she still here? I got the message."

"She was trapped here for a very long time,

waiting for someone to send the Hellhound back to, you know, that place. When they finally did, she could have passed on, but chose not to. She told me she will not rest until some scroll with a curse is destroyed. She wants to make sure they never rise again."

"So, she saw their demise. Did she say how the monsters were killed, Bobby? It's very important we know how to send them back to where they came from."

"No, I don't think so. I could ask her when I see her again."

"Oh yes. Yes, Bobby. Ask her for me, ok, sweetie? It is so important that you do."

"Will it help Hazel?" asked Bobby, softly.

"Yes, it will. Please, go now and try and find her again. Ask her Bobby. It is very, very important."

"Ok," said Bobby. Without another word, he was gone, and Josette was once again all alone.

*

Franky and Vinnie, with the permission of Malcom, combed the shed behind the Wiseman house, looking for items that may help defend them from a vampire. Franky felt bad about not telling Malcom exactly what they were looking for. He knew that Malcom did not believe their interpretation of events. He only hoped that Malcom would come around before it was too late.

In the middle of the shed, they had started a pile of items they thought might come in handy. There was an old pitchfork, well beyond its years, an old shovel, a nail gun, some rope, and a brand-new axe. How they would use these items was still unclear, but they looked like they could do damage. The last thing they looked for, but could not find, was any wood that might be shaped into a stake. Franky doubted that the old tales were true. But if need be, he would jam one through that bitch's cold, black heart.

"What about this?" asked Vinnie. He held up a hacksaw with blade.

"That will only work if we convince her to hold still while we saw her head off," said Franky. He tried not to sound sarcastic. He knew Vinnie was starting to be stretched thin. He could see it in Vinnie's eyes. His manner had changed since the house trailer. He was far more irritable and oftentimes distant.

Franky had known Vinnie for years and had never seen him this way. Then again, Franky never knew him when he was on a case. *Maybe this is the way he is when he is working*, he thought.

"True, true. Guess I'm reaching at this point. Still, I like the idea of taking her head off. I guess that's what you're for, little buddy," said Vinnie. He reached down and grabbed the axe.

"I think we are done here. There is not a lot," called Franky. They picked up the meager pile of weapons.

"Well, I still have my gun. Not that I think it will make much a difference," added Vinnie. "I still like your idea of fire. It worked on the dead girl. She was still alive, but went up like a house of twigs."

Franky nodded.

"It worked on Fritz and Banthom, but they were witches, not vampires."

"Shit," said Vinnie, looking out the window. "The sun has gone behind the clouds again. We need to get back to the restaurant."

*

Hazel rode upfront with Benjamin while Father Aron and Sam rode in the back seat of the Wagoneer. For the first hour or so, not a word was spoken. Parksville's roads were covered with deep snow. The going was rough and tensions high. More than once, the Jeep seemed to lose all traction and slid dangerously close to the side of the road. It was not until they reached the highway, which had at least been plowed and a thick layer of salt laid down, that they began to relax.

"How far do I have on the highway?" asked Benjamin.

"You have a ways to go. Unfortunately, the last thirty miles are backroads," responded Hazel.

"Yea, those roads make Parksville look like downtown Detroit," added Sam.

"That's all farmland."

Benjamin shifted in his seat.

"God, I hope Franky and Shawn are ok. I can't tell you how much I missed them," he muttered, trying to get comfortable. Even though the Jeep was a good size, he could feel Father Aron's knees pressed against the back of the chair.

"I will be glad to see them as well," said Sam. "As well as Vinnie."

"I will just be glad to get there," said Father Aron.

Hazel turned around to face the priest.

"So, what is your part in all this? I mean, I know what you told us at the house. But why would the Church trust you with this quest, and why did they put you in charge of the Grimoires?"

Father Aron hesitated for a moment.

"Experience, I guess. You see, I was very young when I performed my first exorcism."

"Exorcism!" exclaimed Hazel. "You mean, you have actually performed an exorcism?"

"More than one, my dear lady," replied Father Aron. "Most of my assignments in Cape Town turned out to be nothing more than hysteria, mental illness, or some other reasonable explanation. Sometimes, though not often, they were not. When I went to Rome, they knew about all my encounters. I guess they figured I was strong enough to bless the books. I have been performing that task since the first one arrived."

"You mean, since I delivered Banthom's copy to the Church?" asked Benjamin. "That was right after I returned from the States and purchased the Banthom House."

"Wait, I thought you said that you delivered

Banthom's book just this summer?" questioned Hazel. "At least, that's what you said yesterday."

"No, that was not Banthom's original copy. That was Fritz's copy that Phillip had hidden. Banthom got his hands on it down in Florida. It's a long story, but I delivered two of the books to Rome. The other one, I have no idea where it is at," explained Benjamin.

"One book for the dark lord, one for the Judas, and one for the false prophet," said Father Aron. He stared out the back window.

"Well, none of the books would be in Rome if it wasn't for all of us working together. Phillip, Mary, Josette, Shawn, Franky, Ethel, Brandy, and even Hoffman, I guess," continued Benjamin.

"Hoffman was the man killed by Banthom, correct?" asked Sam.

"Yes. I cannot say that I was broken-hearted when he passed. The man had caused me nothing but pain for many years, but no one deserves what happened to him. The other man killed from our group was Joe. He had been aiding Banthom all along, right under our noses."

Benjamin thought back to his first meeting with Phillip, Franky, and Shawn then grinned. He could still picture the look of horror on Hoffman's face when Benjamin embarrassed him in front of everyone. He remembered Franky's and Shawn's attempts to stifle their laughter.

"Franky, Shawn, Josette, Ethel, Phillip, Mary, and Brandy, they are all now my family. They were the first people I let get close to me after my parents died. You see, when you're wealthy, people come out of the woodwork. But this group of people l knew liked me for me. That was something new that I had never encountered before."

Tears welled up in Benjamin's eyes.

Hazel looked over at Benjamin as he was wiped a tear from his eye.

"You know, I really didn't trust you too much until just now."

Wiping his eyes with the back of his hand, Benjamin said, "Funny. I didn't trust you too much at first, either."

CHAPTER XII

MEAT PUPPETS

Mike Shelly woke up in the cell. Over on the table was the body they had brought in that morning. Supposedly, they were coming to get it, but with the storm, who knew when they would arrive. Malcom had said something about letting him out later in the day, and Mike hoped he was good to his word.

It was not the confinement of the cell as much as it was the isolation that went with it. Other than the deputies that came in that morning for breakfast, Mike had not seen a soul. He was sure that, at some point while he was sleeping, he had been awakened by the sound of Malcom and Elma's voices. But taking no notice at the time, fell right back to sleep.

Looking out of the window on the other side of the room, Mike could see that it was getting dark. Outside, snow was falling. The storm had not yet given up.

What a fool I was, he thought. *If Malcom wouldn't have showed up when he did, I would have killed him for sure.* Mike hung his head. In the past few days, his entire life had been turned upside down. The only thing that made a difference in his life was gone. All his life's plans included the missing Shannon. He loved her long before she was aware, watching her hang out with her sister after school, and lying about going to see his sister play softball when it was Shannon he wanted to see. It seemed that all his hopes had been focused on her and now his life was empty. He hated the fact he did not know the truth. Not knowing if she was alive or dead, and, worst of all, knowing there was not a damn thing he could do about it. It was as if he was caught in a trap that had no door, no way out.

That's when he heard the sound of someone opening the door to the back room. Though the lights were on, they were playing tricks on his eyes. The first thing he thought he saw was a delicate, blue hand pushing the door ajar. When at last the door opened completely, he saw her.

It was Shannon. Her hair was matted, her clothes tattered, and her complexion, like her hand, was a bizarre shade of blue. Mike didn't know what to do. It was her, yet, it wasn't.

Without a sound, Shannon reached up and grabbed the keys from their hook by the door. Then, as silent as the grave, she approached. Mike didn't know whether to laugh, cry, or scream. Adoration and terror both engulfed him all at once. She unlocked the door to his cell and it swung open with a loud bang. Mike sat quietly on the bed, afraid to move. That's when the other woman walked in. She was the most beautiful woman he had ever seen. Unlike Shannon, her color was vibrant, full of life.

"Come," said the woman. Shannon reached out for his hand. "I am giving her back to you. Come."

Still in shock, Mike reacted to the woman's soft, assuring voice, and stood. He took Shannon's ice-cold hand in his and offered her a nervous smile. Shannon lead him towards the door, past the redhead with the amazing blue eyes. Looking over his shoulder, he could see the woman bend over the dead body lying on the table. Upon placing her hand on the man's forehead, the man on the table opened his eyes.

*

"Dear, you have not touched your dinner," Brandy scolded Josette. She got up to clear the table. "You have to eat something."

"Oh, Brandy. I wish I could. My stomach is in knots."

"Look, I know you are worried. So am I. But for now, we are on the sidelines."

Josette got up to help Brandy with the dishes, but Brandy would have none of it.

"You just go in the living room and have a rest."

"If it's ok with you, I would rather just sit here and talk," said Josette.

"Fine with me if you want to sit there and watch me do up these dishes. You want something to drink?"

"No, I'm good, Brandy. I know this is an off-the-wall question, but why didn't you ever remarry? I have sat and listened to you and Ethel talk for hours about the old days, but I never heard you say why you never fell in love again."

"Who said I never fell in love? I was head over heels for Ethel's brother for years, but I could never have married again."

"Why would you say that?"

"Because, I married the man I wanted to spend my life with, and the one I hope to spend my afterlife with. How awkward would it be, if I am so blessed, to show up in glory, only to have two men waiting there for me? No, I know the one I want to walk hand-in-hand with for eternity. And if he has to wait for me to get there, then he will just have to wait."

"I guess I never thought of it that way."

"Well, I am a little strange in my thinking. I know," said Brandy. "But that's the way I feel."

"You loved him a lot, didn't you?"

Brandy closed her eyes for a moment.

"I can still remember the day he asked me to marry him." Opening her eyes, she looked over at Josette.

"He had just picked me up for our date. He was going to propose over dinner, but then admitted he couldn't wait, and asked me the minute I sat in the front seat next to him. He always did wear his heart on his sleeve. I never felt so complete in my life as when I said, 'Yes!' to that man."

"I feel that way with Phillip," said Josette. "Brandy, this not knowing is killing me. I have tried to think of life without him, and I can't. I just can't."

Josette buried her head in her hands and sobbed.

"Oh, dear," said Brandy, pulling up a chair. She put her arms around her.

"I wish I could give you some comfort. Remember, if for whatever reason Phillip does not make it through all this, he will be pacing the floor in glory waiting for you to join him. That, I promise. You have to be strong. Strong for those two innocent lives you and Phillip are bringing into this world."

Josette looked up.

"I know, I know. But it's just so hard. With everything going on with Phillip and Mary, and the doctor's warnings, it's just so much."

"Warnings? What warnings?"

*

"Luke Wiseman and his daddy are a couple of incompetent cunts," said Tom, sitting at his sister's kitchen table.

"Sandy, I can't believe our lives might depend on those two finally getting something right."

"Please. I've heard this shit all week. Give it a break," said Sandy.

Tom walked over to his sister's house because he knew she might have beer, and if he was lucky, some weed to go with it.

"Fuck that! Someone needs to do something."

"You're just pissed off because Marge won't have anything to do with you anymore. And you know she is sweet on Luke. That's what this is all about, so just admit it." Sandy snapped.

"First, it was poor Howard, because he is good-looking and working with her. Now, it's Luke. For fuck's sake, get over it. Marge does not want you."

With this, Sandy got up and walked in the other room, only to return a moment later with a blanket wrapped around her.

"Damn I will be glad to get heat again."

"Why? You'll still be a cold-hearted bitch whether the heat is on or not," said Tom.

His day was not going as he had planned, and everything Sandy said was hitting home.

"Fuck you, Tom. You know what? You can get the hell out of here. I don't need this shit from you today. Grab a beer and go home. I know that's the only reason you come over."

Tom jumped to his feet and slapped Sandy across the mouth with the back of his hand.

"Look, I've had enough of your shit!" Tom shouted.

Sandy fell hard to the floor.

"Open that mouth again and see what happens."

Sandy, who was holding her hand over her bleeding lip, yelled at him.

"Get out! Get out! You son of a bitch, you hit me for the last time. Don't think for a minute you can run to mom and have her change my mind again. I never want to see you again, you bastard."

Tom became enraged and started kicking her, over and over, to the face, the stomach, and any open area she was unable to cover in time with her hands. Finally, after she laid writhing in pain on the kitchen floor, Tom stopped.

"You're not telling mom anything," he barked, as he reached down and undid her belt.

"Nothing's changed. No one is going to believe you. They never do."

Sandy cried out in pain as Tom rolled her over and pulled down her pants, revealing her bare buttocks. Then leisurely, he undid his pants.

"Bitch, you've had this coming to you for a long time."

At that very moment, he glanced out the kitchen window above the sink and there, watching his every move, was Dale Harris. His eyes were sunken deep into his skull and his color was a strange bluish-green. Tom screamed, but Dale did not flinch. From the front of the house came the sound of an opening door. He heard someone else at the back. Tom quickly did up his pants.

Dale, still standing at the window, let out an unnerving cry. Around the corner of the living room came Helen McCallister. She looked long dead. Tom started backing away as she approached, her hand outstretched, as if pleading for help. As his backside made contact with the sink, he heard behind him Dale moaning. The handle of the back door turned.

Sandy, who had managed to pull herself up with the aid of the kitchen table, seemed oblivious to the old woman making her way into the kitchen.

"You bastard!" she yelled, grabbing a steak knife that rested on the kitchen table. As the back door opened, Tom saw Mike Shelly, still bleeding from an open wound on his neck, making his way into the house.

Tom watched Sandy muster her strength to make a move in his direction. Still holding the knife, she lunged at him. Tom knew she meant to kill him, but she never got the chance. Seeing Mike Shelly, she stopped. That's when Helen grabbed her around the waist from behind.

Mike, now turning his attention from Tom, also moved on her. That's when Tom started to regain his composure. While the two vile creatures pawed at Sandy, he ran past all of them, through the living room, and out the front door, leaving his sister to fend for herself. He heard her desperate pleas for help, but was untouched by them. His only thought was that of self-preservation.

*

Elma and Marge trudged the quarter of a mile from the high school to the restaurant. Dinner had been served and they were returning the steam pans to Howard. Marge did not have a car and Elma wasn't going to try and get anywhere in hers. It was buried up to the bumper in the driveway and would remain there until the plow came through, or Malcom and Luke shoveled her out. She never did like driving in the snow. *That darn car can stay there till spring for all I care,* she thought to herself.

That's when the strangest thing caught her eye. It was Tom Phillips running in the direction of the police station, with no coat and no shoes.

"What the hell is he doing?" asked Marge. She'd seen the same thing.

"I don't know," said Elma. Even from a distance, Elma could tell the man was in a panic.

"Let's get these to Howard then go over to the station to see what the heck is going on."

"Look!" yelled Marge. "Is that Dale following him?"

"Hurry, Marge. Let's get to the restaurant."

"No, I want to see Dale. The son of bitch has been missing all this time, scaring the daylights out of people…"

"Stop. Look," said Elma, grabbing Marge by the sleeve. From behind the church came Elijah Smith.

"It's just the pastor," said a very confused Marge.

Elma pulled on Marge's sleeve so that she was forced to turn and look at her.

"That man was dead as a doornail and lying on the table in the breakroom of the station this morning. Now, listen to me. You run to the restaurant and get Vinnie and Franky. I will be right behind you, but God knows you can make it a lot faster than me. Now go!"

"I don't understand, Elma," petitioned Marge.

"Darn it, girl. Listen to me! Go, go now!" shouted Elma.

That's when the priest, who had been so focused on Tom, heard Elma yell. He spotted the women and walked towards them.

*

Malcom and Luke stood staring down at the body of Deputy Markowitz laid out on the floor of the station. Next to him, on the floor, was the smashed remains of their radio system.

"It looks like someone tore out his fucking Adam's apple for piss' sake. Look at all the blood."

"I don't get it. If this woman is a vampire, why rip the guy's throat out so the blood ran out all over the floor? I mean, the pastor didn't look anything like this," asked Luke.

"Maybe he was not the one they were after. You said that Mike and the pastor were both gone. Maybe Markowitz was just in her way. Anyway, they knew enough to take out our last means of communication with the outside world."

That's when Tom Phillips came running

through the double glass doors. His body was shivering from exposure, but Tom didn't even seem to notice.

"Sheriff, thank God you're here. These crazy bastards are chasing me. They came at us at Sandy's place. I tried to fight them off, but I couldn't. I just couldn't."

"Now just slow down, Tom. Catch your breath. You are not making any sense."

"When did he ever?" added Luke, just above a whisper.

"These things… they came after us. One of them was that Helen woman who went missing. I'm telling you; they are out there."

Sobbing, Tom plopped down in one of the two chairs in the breezeway, put his head down, and covered his face with his hands.

"Let's go have a look," Malcom said to Luke. "Tom, come with us and show us what you are talking about."

"Hell no. I am not going back out there with those things. They're dead. I mean, fucking dead. No, you two go. I am staying right here."

"Ok, stay here and keep Markowitz company, then. But just so you know, they got in here too," said Luke, pointing over at Markowitz's ravished body.

For the first time, Tom saw Markowitz and noticed he had been sitting with his feet in blood.

"Fine, fine. But can I at least get some shoes and a coat?"

Malcom looked over at Luke and smiled.

"There is an extra coat hanging in my office," he said to Tom.

"And I have a pair of galoshes in the closet of the break room," added Luke.

*

Looking from the front windows of the restaurant, Franky saw Marge running towards the front door. Behind her, Elma was doing her best to keep up. Seeing the two women in distress, he ran to the front door and opened it. He was hit by a frozen blast of air that half chilled him to the bone.

"What's wrong?" he yelled to Marge through the howling wind. In that moment, he saw Mary. She approached the two women from behind.

"Run! For God's sake, run!"

But it was too late. Elma was stopped dead in her tracks as Mary's claw-like hand impaled the old woman from behind. It was obvious that Mary was no longer concerned with feeding. She only meant to kill.

Franky looked on in total disbelief as blood gushed from Elma's mouth. The look of shock on her face filled Franky with dread, but that was soon overshadowed by his fear. Franky saw Marge pause to look behind her, but Franky knew any delay would mean her death. Frantically, he made a mad dash for Marge. That's when he heard the first gunshot.

"Get her inside!" yelled Malcom. He was twenty yards up the street, standing with Luke at his side. They shot round after round at the herd of lifeless bodies approaching from all directions.

Reaching Marge, he grabbed her by the arm, and pulled her towards the front door. On the ice-covered front stoop, he slipped. Going headfirst into restaurant, he and Marge landed hard on dining room floor. Vinnie and Howard, both of whom had been in the kitchen, ran into the dining room. Franky jumped to his feet.

"Elma! They got Elma!" he yelled.

Vinnie slammed the front door shut as Howard helped Marge to her feet.

"Malcom is out there, but there are so many, he needs our help."

"She made more of those fucking meat puppets," said Vinnie, looking out the window.

Franky watched as gun fire from Luke and Malcom knocked them down. It was only momentarily before they got back on their feet, advancing towards the restaurant. Suddenly, the door burst open and in flew Tom Phillips. He slammed the door behind him.

"Those fuckers just won't die!" shrieked Tom. "I saw Malcom plug that old bitch at least half a dozen times!"

Franky, pushing Tom aside, reached for the front door.

"What the fuck, dude! Don't open that door!" yelled Tom in protest.

Franky gave no notice. He opened the door and yelled for Malcom and Luke.

"In here! They can't come in here! It's protected."

Luke, who was closer to the door, managed to hear Franky's plea over the harsh wind and gunshots.

"Dad! Come on!" Franky heard him yell.

Malcom let off a final barrage of gunfire, then followed Luke to front door. Once inside, he turned to Franky.

"I am starting to believe your theory," he said. He looked up at the crosses taped to the front window.

"What about the school? Half the town is there," said a frantic Luke.

"Mom is at the school; we need to get to her."

Franky hung his head. It was obvious that neither Luke nor Malcom saw Elma's demise.

"Luke, Malcom, sit down." said a shaken Franky. "There is something I need to tell you."

*

CHAPTER XIII

Battle of The Wooden Spoon

Outside on the rickety old porch of their grandmother's house were tributes of burning candles, photos, flowers, and small statues of the Virgin Mary. Ethel was amazed at the outpouring of sentiments left by the locals.

"Grandma was a very beloved woman," said Rebecca, reaching the front door. In her arms were boxes they would use to collect her things.

"Through the years, I've had an endless number of people come up to me and talk about how she had helped them get through the tough times in life. She was an extraordinary woman."

"Wow. I always just thought of her as that mean, grumpy, old woman," said Ethel, following her into the shack.

"That is because she was your grandmother. You did not know her like the people she spent her life helping."

Is that what they will expect of me? thought Ethel.

She plopped her purse on the small table. *She had not asked for any of this, and there was no way in hell she was isolating herself out here in the middle of the bayou.*

Rebecca seemed to anticipate her troubled thoughts.

"Don't worry. You can live wherever you wish. Grandma chose to live out here because she loved the bayou and hated the city. It does not matter where you go. Those in need will find you."

"Look, I don't think I am ready for all this. You're the one…"

"Stop, Ethel. You where the one chosen. You are the one with the power of a queen. That this has been laid upon you is not a curse, but a blessing. The spirits chose you as the guardian of the Gates. Like it or not, you have no choice."

Ethel looked around at the old woman's meager existence.

"Ok, well right now there are people I would like to help. You said that in all this mess, there might be a way to protect them. So I accept my fate, but if I have to be this person, then I want to start by stopping my friends from being slaughtered."

Rebecca gave Ethel a reassuring grin.

"Grandma always found a way, and usually, it was found in the pages of all these books and endless papers."

"Then let's stop talking and start packing so that I can find what I need, "said Ethel. She grabbed an old, dust-covered journal that was placed on the shelf above the table.

"And what if the answer is not here?"

"You have other resources at your disposal," said Rebecca. "Let's just hope it doesn't come to that."

Ethel was a little unnerved by this comment. *What other resources?* she thought. *What in the hell did that mean?*

*

As the night dragged on, Vinnie kept a vigil at the window, watching as the creatures continuously walked back and forth in front of the restaurant. Each time they passed, they avoided the crosses hanging in the window. Sometimes, they would stop to bare their perilous fangs; sometimes they would give out an unbearable screech. Most of the time, they simply passed as quietly as a cat waiting for the pounce.

They had barred the back door with a two-by-four, bracing it between the door and the steam table. It took a few good hits with a hammer to get it in place, but no one was entering after that. Then they hung a cross on the inside of the door for good measure. Franky said the only thing to do now was wait. Any attempt at trying to escape the fortress would be a death sentence. Though it was the middle of the night, no one dared close their eyes.

Malcom and Luke had been mostly silent after learning about Elma's fate. Both men were beyond consoling, so the rest of the group left them alone.

Everyone, that is, except Marge. She had been instrumental in calming them and it was she who stopped them numerous times from running out the front door.

"Do you see Mary?" came Franky's voice behind him. Vinnie turned to find him sitting in the booth behind him with Howard.

"They are all connected to her. I think she is out there trying to find a way around our defenses."

"Defenses? What? Some crosses hanging in the window?" asked Howard, butting into the conversation.

"Yes, that is what I mean. If it weren't for those crosses, we would all be dead by now," answered Vinnie. He twisted in his seat so he could look at Howard.

"Thank God you were thinking clearly when we fled Dale's, Vinnie. You saved all our asses," added Franky.

"What about the school?" came a voice from the counter. It was Malcom. "They are unprotected. I've got to get to them."

"No, I don't think they are worried about them. Notice how they are all staying close," said Vinnie. "That bitch is out there; I see her every now and then. For some reason, her focus is on us."

"Has anyone noticed how alive she looks?" asked Marge. She sat between Luke and Malcom at the counter.

"I mean, the rest… they look dead. But she looks… alive."

"She is not letting them feed," said Luke.

They all turned and looked at him. These were the first words he'd uttered since learning about Elma.

"They want to; you can tell. Though she doesn't let them. If they did, they would look more like her."

"But why?" asked Marge.

"Who knows? Maybe she is just a heartless cunt," said Luke.

"I think as long as they are hungry, they are easy to control," said Franky.

"Where's that fucking Tom?" asked Malcom.

"Hiding in the kitchen," responded Marge.

Luke got up and walked to the front window.

"That bitch killed my mom. I am going to rip her fucking heart out."

"Right," said Tom, now walking out of the kitchen with a hand full of chips.

"It's only a matter of time and we are all going to die."

"Shut up, Tom," said Marge.

Getting off her stool, she walked over and put her arm around Luke.

Tom shrugged his shoulders.

"I'm just being realistic. You've seen what she can do."

Malcom stood and walked over to Tom. Without say a word, he slammed Tom's face onto the counter.

"Say another word and I will personally toss your ass out that door and watch them feed on your rotten corpse."

Vinnie and Franky pulled Malcom off Tom.

"Malcom, no. This won't solve anything," said Franky.

"Fuck you, Malcom!" screamed Tom.

Vinnie and Franky held Malcom back. "It's your fault your wife is dead."

Unseen by everyone except for Marge, Luke had made his way across the restaurant from the front window. With one swift jab to his face, Tom went flying backwards, landing hard on the floor. Blood gushed from his nose.

"I've been waiting to do that for ten years."

Vinnie and Franky let Malcom loose and ran over to Luke, but Luke already had his hands in the air.

"We're good! I'm not going to hit him again," he said with a smile.

"At least, not right now."

"Oh my God! Look out!" screamed Marge.

A large stone hurled through the front window. This was followed by another, and another.

Vinnie had to jump of out the way, as glass rained on top of him. Cold air rushed into the restaurant. That's when Vinnie realized that the crosses were scattered across the floor.

"The crosses! Grab the crosses!" he yelled.

It was too late. The first one through the window was Dale. Baring his fangs, he lunged for Marge.

Vinnie started looking for crosses on the floor, but seeing none, he grabbed the axe from Malcom's shed that was resting on the seat next to him. He rushed toward Marge. Dale's head exploded as Malcom's shotgun blasted in the background. Dale hit the floor just as Mike and Shannon climbed in the window. Behind them was the rest of the herd.

Vinnie took a step back as they approached.

So, this is how it ends? he thought. He lifted his axe. *If I am going to die, I'm taking some of you fuckers with me!*

Suddenly the room was filled with light. Vinnie watched in total disbelief as a Jeep crashed through the front of the restaurant, plowing over the gruesome figures. Within seconds, Hazel jumped out of the passenger side, firing round after round. To Vinnie's amazement, a priest appeared out the backseat. In one hand he brandished a crucifix, and with the other, a bottle of holy water that he sprinkled on the surprised creatures. Upon contact with the holy water, the creatures screamed in pain.

Dale, slowly raised to his feet, half his face gone. He hissed at Malcom. A splash of holy water landed on the part of his face that was still intact. It slashed his face as if the priest had carved him with a knife. From the front window came a loud screech, and for less than a second, Mary appeared just beyond the back of the Jeep. Vinnie's only thought was how pissed off she looked.

Her bottom jaw seemed unhinged as she opened her mouth to expose her large fangs. Within seconds, all her goons started their retreat. Vinnie managed to finish the job on Dale. With one swift swing of the axe, he decapitated him, leaving his still-twitching body standing for a moment as his head hit the floor.

Vinnie saw Tom make a rush for the back door. Without any consideration for the others, he kicked out the two-by-four blocking the back door. Swinging the door open, Tom gasped in disbelief. His dead sister, Sandy, grabbed him and slowly pulled him out the back door. Vinnie saw Tom fighting with all his might, but it was to no avail. He was gone.

Those creatures trapped in the room now started to crawl their way past the Jeep. The priest continued to douse them with holy water.

"It is he who commands you!" Vinnie heard the priest yell.

Their screams of pain were overbearing, and at one point, Vinnie had to cover his ears. He kept an eye out for Mary's return. Riddled with gun shots, the remaining herd scrambled outside. Within mere seconds, they were all gone in the night.

*

It was Hazel who first saw the onslaught taking place at the diner. Pulling into town, the creatures that gathered outside the diner left no question to their intent. Mouth gaping open, their hideous teeth bared, she realized that the vampire story was all true. It hit her like a ton of bricks.

"Hurry, Benjamin!" she cried.

"I see them!" responded Benjamin, hitting the gas.

"I have a feeling that Shawn, Franky, and that detective of yours might just need our assistance."

From the back seat, Hazel heard Sam and Father Aron gasp. They leaned forward to observe the sight from the front window. As they approached, Hazel watched as rocks flew through the restaurant window and the herd descend on the gaping hole left behind. Closer and closer, they sped along Main Street. In the last few yards, she realized that Benjamin had no intention of stopping. They braced for impact.

Bodies landed on the hood and under the car, but most, still climbing over the windowsill, got thrown inward. The Jeep came to a stop inside the restaurant and Hazel jumped into action. The first person she saw was Franky, fending off a would-be attack from an elderly woman. Hazel pumped a couple of shots into the woman's chest, but it didn't seem to faze her. That's when Father Aron stepped out of the back seat and hit the old woman with a shot of holy water. The woman winced in pain and fled towards the front door.

Benjamin fired from the other side of the car, but Hazel was sure he was doing no more damage than she was. *It's the priest and the holy water,* she thought to herself. *That is the key.*

"Father! Over here!" she yelled. A man was approaching Malcom. She watched in total shock as the water split the man's face wide open. Then Vinnie cut the man's head off.

When the group of living dead realized what they were dealing with, they quickly retreated, leaving Hazel and Benjamin to shoot aimlessly into the darkness. Sam, who had no weapons to fight with, finally emerged from the back seat.

"Holy shit!" was the only thing he managed to say.

"Well, it's about fucking time," came Vinnie's familiar voice.

"If I knew it was you in here, I would have kept going," joked Hazel.

"My restaurant! Look at my restaurant!" said the man Hazel would later learn was Howard.

Hazel took a moment and looked around at the devastation. The whole front of the building was now scattered on the floor, alongside broken tables, chairs, and any number of shakers and tablecloths.

Also, on the floor, was the remains of the man Vinnie had decapitated. He was still moving. His torso seemed to be searching for the head that was a few feet away. Franky, who must have seen it at the same time, kicked the head out of the torso's reach.

"We will need to burn Dale," said Franky.

"Damn it, Dale," said Marge, emerging from behind the counter. "You always were a pain in my ass."

She burst into tears and buried her face in Luke's chest."

Oh, God. What is going on?"

That's when Hazel first saw Malcom, sitting alone at the end of the counter, his shotgun by his side. She made her way over to him.

"Malcom, we have to get to a safer location. How many men do you still have in the field that we can call?"

Malcom sat unresponsive.

"We lost mom, Hazel," said Luke, still holding on to Marge.

"Malcom," Hazel said again. "I know it's hard, but we have got to get a plan in order. Elma was a great lady. I met her many times. But right now, you are the law in this town and we need you."

Malcom turned his tear-stained eyes to meet Hazel's. "What's the use?"

Hazel now raised her voice firmly.

"Now you listen here, Malcom. I've known you for many years. You dedicated your life to this town. Just when the town is in need, just as things get as fucking hard as its ever going to get, you want to run and hide. You need to get your shit together. There will be a time to grieve for Elma, but it's not now. We are in the fight of our lives, and we need our strongest assets. Get up, brush yourself off, and let's get to a secure location."

Malcom stood and grabbed his rifle.

"We can move everyone over to my office," said Malcom. He looked at his feet. Without a word, he started towards the front door.

Luke, letting go of Marge, walked over to Hazel as the others made a move towards the door.

"I hate you right now," he whispered.

"I know you do, Luke," said Hazel. "I know you do."

As the rest of the group left for the Sheriff's office, Vinnie and Franky stood back. Each grabbed one of Dale's legs and pulled the still-twitching body out of the door.

"Grab his head, will ya?" requested Vinnie.

"Watch the teeth, though," added Franky, "Grab him by the hair."

Hazel felt her stomach turn as she reached down to grab Dale's head. *In what world is this even fucking possible?* she thought to herself. Even with her newfound awakening to the supernatural, this was beyond anything even she could imagine in her worst nightmares.

As she grabbed his head, Dale's jaws snapped open in a feeble attempt to inflict damage. Hazel cringed. Holding the head out at arm's length, she followed the two men to the middle of the street.

*

Rosie Galbreath and Mick Reed sat quietly in their ice fishing shack. Rosie had insisted that they try fishing on this lake, even though they knew it was not allowed. He rightfully reckoned that no one would see them drive up and slide the shack to the middle of the lake. And even if they did, with the current weather, no one would come to chase them off.

The shack was designed with two runners along the bottom, so that even when the ice was too thin to drive on, they could simply pull it to their desired location. Even though the blizzard had covered everything in snow and ice, Rosie knew that, just because it was cold, didn't mean that the ice was thick enough for his full-ton Chevy.

Lit only with the battery-powered lantern placed strategically in the middle of the shack, hanging just above the open hole they had just dug, the homemade shack seemed even smaller on the inside. They had enough room for their folding chairs, beer, bait, and poles.

Outside, the wind had died down and the snow had finally stopped.

"I think we will need to call it a night pretty soon," Rosie said to Mick, who was reaching for another beer. "We have to get out of here before light."

"That's ok with me," responded Mick. "I'm freezing my ass off anyway."

"Shit, I already have enough bass to fill my freezer till spring."

"Hell yea! Great catch tonight," said Mick. He held up his sealable storage bags filled with fish.

A strange growling noise came from somewhere out in the darkness. It was deep, like the grunt of a bear.

"Did you hear that?" questioned Mick.

"No, I'm fucking deaf. Of course, I heard it. That sure as hell wasn't the wind. Something is out there."

"Well, open the door and take a look!" Mick said to Rosie.

"Bullshit. Whatever it is, it's not friendly."

"There is no bear around here, is there?" questioned Mick. He already knew the answer.

Suddenly, the sound came once more. This time, it came from the opposite side of the shack.

"The fucking thing is circling us," said Rosie, adjusting his Lion's cap.

"Maybe it's just moving past us," offered Mick. Rosie could hear the dread in his voice. "This is bullshit."

"Shhhh," said Rosie. "Quiet."

Rosie stood and looked out of the small pane of glass. For a few moments, he heard and saw nothing. Then came the sound of something coming at them, its feet pounding the ice as it ran. In the last few seconds, Rosie saw it coming out of the distance, a large, dark blur of fur. It was coming closer.

"Run!" Rosie screeched, making a mad dash for the front door, and almost knocking Mick off his feet. Both men cleared the front door when the shack slid across the lake. Rosie only saw a dark figure, as black as the night, rushing the shack towards the shore.

He knew if the creature would have come on the side opposite the runners, the shack would have blown apart right there. It seemed not to even notice the two men now laying on their backs on the snow-covered lake. It had taken both of them to pull the shack to the middle of the lake, and within seconds, the shack was across the lake, tipped at the edge. It disintegrated as it slammed onto the uneven shore.

Rosie laid still. If the thing had not seen him, then he may have a chance. Once the creature rummaged through the demolished shack, it turned. For just a moment, the moon came out full and bright, and Rosie saw the creature standing ten feet tall. It was human in stature but covered in hair. Its face was like that of an enormous dog, large fangs shining in the moonlight.

But it was those eyes. Rosie could see its red eyes glaring back at them over the lake. Mick saw it as well, for he stood and started to run in the opposite direction. Rosie yell at him to stay still, but it was no use. The beast was on him before he got halfway to the other side of the lake. With one foul swoop of a claw, Mick crashing down onto the frozen lake. Rosie watched in horror as his lifelong friend was ripped apart, Mick's screams echoing in his ears.

Rosie was torn. Should he run away while the creature ripped his friend apart? Or stay as still as possible?

The choice, unfortunately, was made for him. The creature raised his head and gobbled down some unknow part of Mick. And turned again.

His red eyes focused directly on Rosie. Rosie stood and turned to see which way to flee. Rosie picked the wrong direction. In his desperation, he turned and stepped straight into their fishing hole, his leg disappearing into the lake underneath the ice. Before Rosie could respond to the excruciating pain from his leg, the monster was on him, clutching his head in its mighty jaws. Rosie could feel the blistering pain as the beast pulled him all the way back onto the ice. He saw red eyes glaring down at him as the beast tore him apart.

CHAPTER XIV

A New Day Dawning

The night drew slowly to an end. No one in the Sheriff's office, other than Sam, who laid in the cell bed snoring loudly, got any sleep. Even though the priest had put a generous amount of holy water on every door and window, every noise from the outside was considered by the team to be a threat. Franky knew everyone's nerves where shot. He remembered his mother's words that she so often spoke: "God never gives us more than we can handle."

What a bunch of crap that was, he thought. *I am at my limit, and it won't take much more to send me over the edge.* Next to him sat Hazel. He was so impressed by the way she took control at the restaurant. The more he grew to know her, the more attracted he found himself. *That's the kinda girl my mom would pick for me*, he thought.

Malcom, for all his grief, seemed to put his focus into a new place. Since returning to his office, Malcom took a leading role.

"We have this one door to protect," he said. "Entering the office, the only window is the small one in the break room."

He then took inventory of every firearm and handed them out like a good neighbor handing out Halloween candy. Everyone, including Howard, Marge, and Sam got a weapon. Though Howard did reject the offer at first, Malcom gave him no option. The small revolver he handed him was the same one that Elma had used for target practice at the local firing range. Benjamin and Hazel kept their personal handguns, but now they also carried shotguns.

The night was spent talking about how to put an end to Mary's terrorization. Ideas of how to evacuate the town came up. Luke always went back to the school and the people there who had no idea what was going on. It was Hazel who kept assuring him that the creatures probably had no interest in them at this point.

She said that they were the ones that she was after because they were the ones who killed her pets. But as Franky listened, he could tell that everyone who came in the Jeep seemed to know a little more than they were saying. Franky would ask Sam what was going on once they were by themselves.

Father Aron insisted that only he could put an end to the demon.

"I am the only one here with the power of the Church," he repeated.

To Franky, it seemed that Father Aron was a little overconfident in his abilities. Franky knew firsthand the power of prayer; it was prayer and flame that killed the witches responsible for all of this. Still, Franky doubted that the priest had ever dealt with such an adversary.

It was close to morning when Malcom pointed out of the small breakroom window.

"Stars are shining in the night sky," he said to the group. "Stars mean no clouds. Whatever we do, it must be done as soon as the sun rises. We cannot endure another night like this."

Franky remembered watching Dale's body burn in the middle of the street. He was doubtful that Mary would be as easy to kill.

"Sunlight is our key," he offered.

"Exactly," agreed Malcom. "Daylight and surprise... They are our only hope of killing that evil bitch. I agree with Vinnie. If she goes down, they all go down."

"There is only one demon," spoke Father Aron from the break room table. "She is doing nothing more than manipulating the dead. I will send the demon back to Hell, and the rest will fall."

"But where is she?" asked Hazel. "Do we have any idea where she might be?"

Marge, who was resting her head on Luke's shoulder, said in a timid voice, "Dale knew. He said he saw the Woman of the Lake almost every night, but no one believed him."

Franky jumped to his feet.

"That's it, Marge! You are a genius. Why would she spend so much time at the lake? The only one she could kill there was Dale, but his trailer was well-protected. I think her hiding place is somewhere around that fucking lake."

Malcom smiled.

"The old basement! That's got to be it."

"You mean that old cellar? The one he uses for my canned goods?" asked Marge.

"Fuck! I forgot all about that. He built that thing because he was so afraid of another twister, especially after what happened to his grandfather. It would be the perfect spot for them to hide."

"Then at first light, we hunt her down. If she is hiding down there in the dark, then we will find her and drag her evil ass into the light."

"That's easier said than done," offered Vinnie. He leaned against Malcom's office door. "I'm telling you; she is strong. She turned over my car like it was nothing."

"What if we find a way to bring the light to her?" asked Hazel.

*

Rebecca woke with the morning sun. It was a beautiful morning and outside her window, a small bird sung his morning song. It was hard to believe at this moment that anything sinister or evil could possibly happen on such a wonderful day. Getting out of bed, she made her way to the kitchen, only to find Ethel already at work. Ethel poured through the documents left at their grandmother's.

"You are up early this morning," Ethel said as Rebecca walked in.

"I see you're already at it this morning. Find anything yet?"

Rebecca walked to the coffee pot.

"Not really," confessed Ethel. "But there is one thing that just keeps bugging me."

"What's that?" asked Rebecca, taking her seat across from Ethel with her full cup of coffee.

"The response I got from Doctor John. I can't put my finger on it. I know I was in a panic, but there is something I am missing."

"Well, I am sure you will figure it out. Did you find anything of interest in Grandma's stuff?"

"A lot of things dealing with healing, something on love potions, and, I even found a recipe for gumbo."

"Grandma's crawfish gumbo recipe? I want that. Best gumbo I ever ate."

"Yea, I remember her gumbo. It was damn good. But I am only a short way through; maybe something will show up that will help me help the others."

"Or maybe you will find her Étouffée recipe as well? That shit makes her gumbo taste like dog food."

Both women laughed for a minute, then Ethel said, "Now *that* was the best."

When the laughter died down, Rebecca brought up a fact that she had been waiting on. She was not sure how Ethel would take it.

"If you cannot find the answers you seek in Grandma's stuff, you know you can always ask Baron Samedi himself."

"What!" exclaimed Ethel. "I never want to be in his presence again."

"Settle down. I am just saying that, as the guardian of the Gates, you have the right to call upon him at any time. He cannot deny you an audience."

"Look, I have never been so frightened in my life as I was with him standing next to me."

"I know, and sometimes the spirits speak in riddles, but you are the queen. You can get the truth out of them."

"Look, Rebecca, I appreciate your help with all of this. I truly do. But I don't know that I can go through all of that again."

"Silly, you don't have to do the Gates again. You are queen and can summon Baron Samedi anywhere, anytime."

"Still, I choose not to," said Ethel, defiantly.

"That is up to you. But remember, even Grandma's knowledge only went so far. Anyway, I will look with you this morning. We will carry all this stuff to the store, at least as much as we can review in one day. That way, we can take our time and I don't have to worry about what is going on there when I am gone."

"You are a blessing, Rebecca," said Ethel. She stood to give her a hug.

*

As Benjamin backed the Jeep out of The Wooden Spoon, the boards and remnants of the front window fell to the dining room floor. It was amazing to Franky the damage inflicted on the restaurant, and how little damage was actually done to the Jeep. It still ran even though the front end was in disarray. Only one headlight worked, the left right fender was gone, the windshield was cracked, and one of the side mirrors lay on the floor of the restaurant.

Franky stood outside of the building next to Hazel. She watched the entire thing with great intensity.

"Is it still drivable?" he heard her yell to Benjamin. His window was down. The sun was shining so bright that both Franky and Hazel had to shield their eyes from the glare bouncing off the snow.

"Yea, I think so. Not sure what I am going to tell Avis, though," joked Benjamin.

Sam, who had just arrived on the scene, looked up at Hazel and Franky.

"Looks like you will be buying a Jeep."

"Sam, glad you're here," said Hazel. "I need you to do me a favor. Do you think you could drive this thing back to Jackson? We need help here."

She is calling in the Marines, thought Franky.

"I don't know," responded Sam. "It's not exactly safe, is it?"

"I know it sounds crazy, Sam," said Hazel. "But in a few minutes, people are going to be coming out of their houses and the school. People are going to want answers as to what happened here and will want to know where their family members are. Malcom is a good man, but I don't think he has the capacity to deal with this situation. Besides, the town has no means of communication. If you can just make it up the highway to a phone, call the state police, and call Officer Jackson. Tell him we need help down here, and we need it *now.*"

"But the major..." started Sam.

"Screw the major," said Hazel. "Benjamin, do you mind if Sam takes the Jeep back to Jackson to get some help?"

Benjamin, who had parked the Jeep across the street, walked up to the group.

"I don't care, just don't scratch it," he smirked. "It's a rental."

Franky could see Hazel's bewilderment.

"He's joking, Hazel. You need to know Ben's sick sense of humor."

Sam started to chuckle. When Hazel got the joke, she joined him.

"Franky!" came Malcom's voice from down the street. He stood in front of the Sheriff's office, loading a small sleigh he had hooked to the back of his snowmobile.

"Can you come down here for a minute? I want to run down some of the items we will need to load up."

"Be right there, Malcom," Franky yelled back. He turned to Sam.

"Sam, if you go back, will you just stop by and check on Josette and Brandy for me? I am sure they are dying for some news."

"Sure thing. I will leave right after your little posse pulls out," said Sam.

"Be careful. Remember, the important thing is just to get to a phone. Hopefully this fucking thing will be over before they get here, but this town will need help," said Hazel.

She hugged Sam.

"Watch your ass, Hazel," said Sam. "You too, Franky. I want to see both of you safe and sound real soon."

"Franky!" came Malcom's voice once more.

"Good luck, Sam," said Franky, shaking the man's hand.

*

The twins had chosen this particular morning to start their wrestling match, at least that is how Josette felt. Both babies had been flipping all morning. Brandy, who had taken every opportunity she could find to put her hand on Josette's belly, made the prediction that she would give birth to two football players, both kickers.

Even though the sun was out, Josette's spirits

where not light. She discovered that the phones were now down.

"Well, at least we still have power," offered Brandy. "I was more afraid of losing that than the phone. You don't freeze to death from not making a phone call."

It was around ten in the morning when Tod Davis, a local farmer driving a pickup with a plow on the front, showed up at their door. Brandy had known Tod for years. He plowed her drive when she lived in Parksville.

"Mrs. Cartwright, as I live and breathe! What are you doing back in town?" asked Tod when Brandy answered the door.

"Just came for a visit. You here to plow?"

"Yea, the professor is one of my customers. I was wondering if you could move your cars out of the drive, or I could do it if you like."

Brandy smiled broadly at the man.

"You know the answer to that one, Tod. You don't even need to ask. Here are the keys to the Cadillac and I will get the keys to the other one."

What a nice man, thought Josette. She rummaged through her purse for keys to the rental. She wondered if this was what living in a small, American town was like… people helping people. She walked over to the front door and handed Tod her keys, but as he took them from her, a feeling rushed through her, as well as a vision of the house that she and Hazel had visited in their attempt to locate Phillip.

"Have you been plowing down by Briskey Lake?" she asked.

"Now how did you know that, young lady? As a matter of fact, I just finished down there. They pay me to plow that whole road and their drives. All the families chip in. I don't know why, since there aren't many of them there this time of year, and hardly anyone goes to that old cemetery. But how did you know?"

Josette was at a loss for words. Thankfully, Brandy stepped in.

"Tod, how are Lori and the kids?"

"Oh, doing about as good as can be expected, I guess," Tod said.

Josette, seeing her way out, walked back through the living room into the kitchen. After a few moments, Brandy joined her.

"That Tod is a nice guy," Brandy said walking into the room. "He is always right on top of it when bad weather hits. Glad Phillip uses him."

"Brandy, I had the strangest vision!" said Josette. "Remember when I told you about Hazel and I going to the house on the lake?"

"Yes, dear. I remember."

"I suddenly got the strangest feeling that we overlooked something, a clue."

"You're not saying you want to go back to that place, are you?"

"Oh, Brandy. Of course not. It was just a strange feeling, is all. You know me enough to know that I get these things from time to time. Might mean nothing at all."

Brandy stared as Josette. She could sense the

woman was holding something back. Josette knew that look. She saw it often when shit hit the fan.

"Sorry the holidays have been such a mess," said Josette. "I was so hoping for all of us to be together."

This was an obvious attempt to change the subject, and Josette knew that Brandy would see right past it. But for some reason, Brandy let it drop.

"Well, there will be more holidays, my dear," smiled Brandy. "Just think of those boys waking up on Christmas morning, waiting to see what Santa brought them."

Josette seemed to glow with this thought and a large smile appeared on her face.

"You know, I never really gave much thought to having kids. Now, I am so happy when I think of what my life will be. I so want you and Ethel a part of their lives."

With this, Brandy got off the couch and walked into the kitchen. Josette could see this was Brandy's feeble attempt to avoid Josette's statement.

"Ok, what's wrong?" Josette asked over her shoulder. "I just said I wanted you to be a part of my children's lives and you walked away."

"Dear, come in here and set at the table. I have something I need to tell you about Ethel."

*

The sun was still shining bright when the group arrived at Dale's trailer. The convoy of snowmobiles lead by Luke pulled up to the trail just before noon. The snow was deep, and the wind had made drifts so high across the drive that the troop had to converge along drainage ditches and the woods to avoid them. Behind Luke came Franky and Vinnie on Elma's snowmobile, then came Hazel and Benjamin on an old 1974 Massy Ferguson that Malcom had restored. Malcom brought up the rear, with the priest on back, pulling the sled that Malcom had used mainly to give rides to the kids of Phelton.

Now it carried guns, rope, Vinnie's axe, wooden stakes whittled by Malcom, a gas-powered ice auger, snow shovels, Luke's cross bow, and other items handpicked by the team. Though none of them knew exactly how to kill a real vampire, they had no choice but to rely heavily on the old traditions.

The priest, however, made it clear to Luke, and anyone else who would listen, that the only tools he needed were his Bible, the Roman Ritual *Rituale Romanum,* and holy water. The only item that the priest and everyone else agreed on were crucifixes to hang around each one of their necks.

"We leave the snowmobiles here and walk the lake. The old cabin is just past the tree line on the other side. I am pretty sure I can find it without too much of an issue," Luke said, pulling off his helmet.

"I don't understand why we can't just ride the snowmobiles across the lake. That's quite the little ways," countered Vinnie.

"Just a precaution," replied Luke. "We don't know where they are for sure, but I, for one, would rather approach without them knowing."

"I agree," said Hazel. "Remember, if it starts clouding up, we all hurry back here and get the hell out of here. Best we live to fight another day if it comes down to it."

"I'm taking that bitch down today," said Luke. "She took my mother. Now I will send that whore back to Hell."

Malcom, who had already started unload in the sled, added, "And all her pets."

"There is only one demon. If I drive her out, all will fall," said the priest.

"I hope you're right on that one, Father," said Vinnie, grabbing his axe. "There are too many for us to fight all at once."

"As long as the weather holds up," responded Hazel, "I would feel a lot better if we got started."

The group headed off in pairs, each carrying a share of supplies. Malcom had filled a backpack full of stakes; Luke had the shovels; Franky had Luke's crossbow and the guns; Benjamin had the gas cans; Vinnie his axe, more guns, and his pistol; and Hazel had the rope and the crosses.

Malcom marched next to Luke. Not a word was said between the two as they trudged along. Luke wondered about their future after this ordeal was over. After all, his mother had been the glue that held their family together. What would it be like without her?

Tears welled up in his eyes though he tried to push them back. His mother was gone. She was really gone, and now life would go on without her, even if he wasn't sure what that life would be like. The poorer, for sure.

"Look!" exclaimed Franky. He walked next to the priest. Luke turned to see Franky pointing down at the frozen lake. "There is someone down there! A body!"

Luke ran over to where Franky stood, dropped to his knees, and wiped away the snow. There, laying with arms crossed and eyes open was the body of a young man.

"Oh my God!" exclaimed Franky. He fell to his knees. His voice cracked. "It's Shawn."

*

Ethel screamed; that's what woke her. Rebecca, who was working in the shop below, ran upstairs to the office to find Ethel sitting up straight in her chair. Ethel had fallen asleep while pouring through her grandmother's trove of Voodoo documents and books.

"I know now what was bugging me!" she said to a concerned Rebecca. "I dreamed I was back at that moment talking to Doctor John. When I was talking to him, it all became clear."

"Slow down," said Rebecca, huffing from her run up the steps. "You scared the shit out of me."

"When Doctor John said I have the answer, it

wasn't the answer I gave him, but the answer he gave me. Only, he formed it in the form a question."

"I told you they speak in riddles sometimes."

"He asked, 'And who is it the witch wants dead?' I though he was talking about my reply, but he wasn't. He had already answered the question. Oh my God. I have to do something."

"What are you talking about?" asked Rebecca. She was losing her patience.

"He didn't send the demons to kill Franky. He wanted all of us dead, especially Josette. She is in as much danger as Franky. Brandy, Shawn, Benjamin, and Brand..."

Ethel buried her face in her hands.

"You need to call this Josette to warn her and the rest of them," replied Rebecca. "Are you even sure you have it right?"

Ethel stood up, the papers on her lap falling to the floor. "I don't know, but I think so."

"There is only one way you will know for sure," said Rebecca, taking Ethel by the arm. "It's time to use the gifts given you. Call him. You know who I mean. Make him answer true."

CHAPTER XV

WAR OF THE DEAD

The vision of Shawn would not leave Franky's mind. His body was blue from the frozen lake and he stared up at him. It was burned into the fabric of his brain, a forever imprint that he knew would never be forgotten. Thinking of it sent chills through his body. He and Vinnie had seen her busting the ice and pulling out a body while they hid in the trailer, but it never even crossed his mind that there might be more bodies. Vinnie knew, Franky had watched him walking with his head down across the lake. At the time, he thought nothing of it. Vinnie knew there might be more and was looking for them.

"This way," said Luke, from the front of the group. They traversed the lake. The snow was deeper here, and the going was slow.

"The old cabin was right over here."

Franky felt his heart sink. So many times, he had come face-to-face with unadulterated evil, yet he never once felt any braver. He knew he would have to see this through, but it did not mean that the fear wouldn't keep building within him. So far, in the face of danger, he had stepped up to the plate, mostly out of self-preservation. What about this time? How many tests would he have to endure before it all came to an end?

"Look," said Vinnie. He passed Luke in the procession. "There's a hole over here, see? No snow. This must be the spot that Marge was talking about, the way down into the basement."

"I'll be damned! They must have ripped the door right off," said Malcom.

"Stop!" Franky shouted. Vinnie approached the identified location. "We need the shovels."

"You still think your plan will work, you fool?" spouted the priest. "I need to deal with this my way."

"Father, I don't mind you wanting to do things your way, but you need to let us do things our way, as well," said Hazel.

"I agree with Hazel," said Malcom. "You just say your prayers while we burn the floor off this damn cabin, and let the light shine on those fuckers."

"Are we even sure they are there?" questioned Vinnie.

"They're there. I feel it," said Franky.

"I smell it," said Malcom. He looked down the hole. "It smells like death down there."

Luke took the flashlight off his belt, pointed

it down the hole, and turned it on. There was nothing there except snow accumulated on old, dirt floor. "I don't see anything," he said. "But Dad is right. It stinks."

"That is the smell of the damned," said the priest, taking his turn to investigate. Without another word, he opened his book and walked dangerously close to the hole. Taking out a bottle of holy water, he sprinkled in down the opening while chanting.

Franky grabbed a shovel and started clearing the snow of the top off the floor. The snow was deep and heavy. *If we can just clear off enough to burn the middle, light will cover the whole basement. If there are some left, we can fight them in the confines of hidden corners*, he thought.

The others helped him to clear a spot. The priest shouted. A hand, hidden from below, had reached out from the hole and grabbed him by his right ankle. The hand, in reaction to the sunlight, burst into flames, but did not stop its assault. The priest was pulled from his feet, landing squarely on his bottom, his leg immersed in the hole, gone from view. Franky and Vinnie rushed over to prevent his demise, but it was to no avail. Whatever had a hold of him was strong, and he disappeared in seconds. The next few minutes were filled with the priest's screams. He was being tortured. Everyone who stood near the hole could hear him being ripped apart.

"We need to keep going!" yelled Franky. "Don't let this keep us from what we came here to do."

Everyone seemed to come back to their senses and started to shovel faster. Only half of the floor was cleared before Vinnie poured the gas on top. When he was done, Franky took out his trusted lighter and set it ablaze.

Then, something totally unexpected happened. Out of the hole came a cloud of darkness. It skirted the ground, then began to rise.

"What the hell is that?" shrieked Hazel over the roaring blaze. The cloud of darkness continued to pour from the opening.

"It's the smoke?" offered Malcom.

"No, Dad. The smoke is going up. This spreads before ascending; this is something else."

The dark cloud expanded inches away from them when Franky came to a devastating revelation.

"She's putting out protection! We need to get the fuck out of here!" he yelled. But it was too late. The first of Mary's demon defense climbed out of the opening. It was Shannon White.

*

About the time that Franky and the gang were listening to the priest's screams, Josette was taking time out for an afternoon nap. She knew the warning signs of preeclampsia. She was tired, she had belly pain on the right side, her head was pounding, she had not urinated for two days, and although she had not vomited, she was constantly nauseous. With her feet propped up at the foot of the bed with two pillows, she closed her eyes ready for a needed rest.

That's when the uncanny feeling of being watched crept over her. Opening her eyes, she beheld, standing at her bedside, Bobby. Next to him was the little girl from her dream. She stood with her head bent, avoiding Josette's gaze.

"I found the girl," said Bobby to Josette. "Just like you asked me to."

Josette raised herself up to a sitting position and looked over at the girl.

"Thank you for coming."

The little girl seemed not to hear, or simply ignored Josette's comment.

"She doesn't want to talk to you," said Bobby. "She wants to know where the scroll is."

Josette leaned in closer to the girl. "Sorry, but the scroll is in Rome. The Catholic Church has it now, dear."

Rage engulfed the girl, her eyes glaring at Josette.

"She is mad. She wanted the scroll destroyed. As long as it exists, she cannot rest."

Bobby spoke for her.

"I'm sorry, my dear. We had nothing to do with it. The church took it." Josette spoke directly to the girl.

"But please help us. We need to know how to send the demon inside Phillip back to Hell."

The little girl stood silently; Josette was sure she would not answer. Then, the girl turned to Bobby and whispered something in his ear.

"She says the only way to send the demon back is to kill the vessel. Wait..." said Bobby. The girl once more whispered in his ear. "The vessel must be killed by someone who loves them."

"No, that can't be! We have a priest. We can expel him and send him back!" snapped Josette. "Tell her we have a priest."

Before Bobby could say another word, the girl vanished.

"You scared her away," said Bobby, surprised at Josette's outburst. "I don't think she will be coming back."

"Oh, Bobby. What am I going to do?" asked Josette. She buried her head in her hands and started to cry.

"Please don't cry. I know there has to be another way," said Bobby sympathetically.

"Please leave, Bobby. Thank you for all your help. But right now, I need to be alone."

When Josette again raised her head, she was alone. Her mind raced. *There has got to be another way.* The nap now forgotten, she raised herself out of bed. *I know the priest can cure him. The girl just didn't know all the answers.*

The vision of the house by the lake she had at Tod's touch came back to her. *Why that house? Why now? Was it because she had been there, or was there something else, something she had missed?*

*

The dark cloud that had ascended from the opening of the cellar continued to grow. It raised no more than a few yards off the ground, and another few yards in each direction. Above the darkness, the sun still shone brightly, but it was no longer keeping Helen, Shannon, Mike, Sandy, and Pastor Elijah Smith in their hole. They now stood a few feet away from the group, staring at them with their cold, dead eyes. They were covered in the darkness.

Franky stepped back. The darkness once again expanded, and Mike moved closer to him until he was inches away. The sunlight would burst Mike into flames.

"What the fuck do we do now?" asked Hazel.

Though their outlines were faint in the darkness, Franky watched each one of the dead matched up with a counterpart. In front of Franky was Mike; Luke had Sandy; Hazel had the pastor; Benjamin had Helen. For Malcom, Shannon now became his pledge. Again, the darkness grew. And again, the group backed away.

"Where's mine?" asked Vinnie.

"I don't think she has come out yet," cautioned Hazel.

Franky knew at once who she was talking about. Mary had yet to show herself.

"She must still be in the cellar," said Franky. His voice wavered.

"I'm tired of all this shit!" griped Malcom. Holding up a wooden stake he'd grabbed from his backpack, he ran directly into the darkness. The group lost sight of him. A paralyzing scream, so pierced the darkness. Franky fell to the ground, cupping his ears. The group looked at one another as the darkness expanded further. This time, it didn't stop.

Franky was torn. Should he rush in and save Malcom, or run for his life? This was soon answered. Malcom appeared out of the darkness on a dead run.

"The fucking things work!" he yelled, passing Franky on his way towards the lake. Franky and the rest of the group took his lead and ran. When they reached the lake, the darkness halted.

She must have a limit on how far she can go, thought Franky. *Surely there were limits to her powers.*

Franky called for a regroup.

"Everyone over here!" he hollered, while waving his hand above his head.

"The stakes work on the puppets. I doubt they will on the puppet master, but we will deal with her when she shows her face." Once the rest approached, he instructed them.

"Everyone grabs a stake."

Everyone did as they were told and grabbed a stake from Malcom's backpack. Still standing together, they took inventory of their other weapons.

"The crosses! I lost the bag of crosses!" yelled Hazel.

"Nothing we can do about that now!" said

Franky. "We should have put them on before we got here."

It was true. They'd agreed to put them on once they reached Dale's trailer, but, in their excitement, the crosses were forgotten.

"Franky…" urged Benjamin. He used his stake to point towards the other end of the lake. "I think we have an issue."

Franky looked across the lake. The darkness approached them. Turning around, he realized it was now coming from every direction. She encircled them.

"What the hell are we going to do now?" croaked Hazel. The group formed a circle, each member keeping watch. The darkness creeped in, methodically encroaching upon the lake.

"Franky, I have an idea," suggested Benjamin.

*

Sam pulled into the Pop Shop in Parksville and was making his way inside when he saw Brandy and Josette drive by in a Cadillac. They were heading out of town. *What the hell?* he thought. *Why would they be out in this mess?* Sam had done as he was told, even though it took him stopping at six different locations on his way back to Jackson to find a phone that worked. He finally got the chance to talk to Officer Jackson, and as far as he knew, the troops were on their way. Sam hoped they would get there on time. His last duty was to check on Josette and Brandy, but obviously they were doing rather well after the storm.

Where in the hell could they be going? he speculated. *Jackson is the other way, and God knows there was nothing out the way they were heading.* Sam shrugged and walked into the Pop Shop. He needed coffee.

*

The group remained in the circle, only this time Franky stood in the middle with Vinnie. Everyone stayed on guard as the darkness crept in. In a few minutes, they would be blanketed in the unnatural blackness. Vinnie knew they were taking a chance on Benjamin's plan, but they were out of options. Benjamin confessed that the demon was on her way to Franky when they unknowingly came to her. He was her only true target, her reason for being there. Above, the sun shone through a brief respite of darkness.

How could this all be happing on such a nice day? thought Vinnie. That's when Vinnie heard the ice break. He knew what was going on: That bitch had made friends on her long way up here, friends that she probably still had laying suspended beneath the ice. God only knew how many of them there truly were. The ice cracked repeatedly, and Vinnie was sure that, each time, Mary was retrieving another warrior of the dead. *Stay focused*, he thought. *You have to get this right, or we all die.*

The darkness mere inches away, the group started calling out names.

"Here comes Shannon!" yelled Luke.

"I've got Helen over here!" replied Malcom.

"I see that Mike guy over here!" added Vinnie, pointing to a spot in front of Hazel.

"Get your stakes ready!" yelled Malcom.

A lone figure walked up. It was Shawn, still blue from the cold waters. He stopped in front of Benjamin, fell to his knees, and hung his head low.

"Please, Franky. Please, Benjamin. I am your friend. I love you guys," pleaded Shawn. "I want you to be with me forever."

"Don't listen, Franky," snapped Benjamin, holding his stake at the ready.

Behind Shawn, other faces approached. These faces were unfamiliar. Vinnie guessed there were ten to fifteen new people they had not counted on, all hidden beneath the lake.

"She must have been collecting them for a while," said Malcom.

"It doesn't matter; stick to the plan," ordered Benjamin.

The last of the sunlight hid behind the veil of darkness. The group struck out at the walking dead as they came forward. Vinnie and Franky remained protected in the middle but jabbed out at the hoard as it approached. One dead body after the other hit the ice. They fought on, plunging the dwindling number of stakes deep into each dead chest.

A screech rang out from nearby. Vinnie felt it in his bones. It was her. As he turned, he saw her in the darkness just in front of Malcom, her enlarged ears pointed and pressed back against her skull. Her hands were claw-like, and her teeth exposed over an unhinged, gaping mouth. Vinnie moved behind Franky. He reached his stake out to protect Malcom, but Malcom had already plunged his stake deep into the creature's heart. For his efforts, Malcom met his fate. Mary withdrew the stake and stuck it through Malcom's head before fleeing back into the darkness.

"Stay with the plan!" yelled Benjamin. He fought off Shawn, who was now on his feet, charging at him.

Then came the loud screech once again. This time, it seemed to come from the opposite side of the lake. And it was speeding in their direction.

"Here she comes!" yelled Vinnie.

Franky stood between Vinnie and the approaching Mary.

"Wait for it!" Benjamin shouted. "Wait for it!"

"Now!" yelled Luke. Mary came into clear view.

Franky dropped to the ground just as Vinnie swung his axe. It barely missed Franky's head, but found its target with Mary. Her head slid across the ice and her body fell to the ground, still ripping at Franky. Almost immediately, the darkness began to rescind.

The body that was clawing at the helpless Franky attempted to scurry across the frozen lake.

"Her head! She wants her head!" yelled Vinnie.

When Luke realized what was happening, he ran over to the head. Before taking two steps, Mike was on him, sinking his teeth into Luke's neck. Vinnie took off after the torso and Benjamin and Franky ran to Luke's aid. As he ran, he observed the darkness fading further. If he reached the head before her torso, it would soon end. But the body scurried quickly.

It was Hazel who launched herself and grabbed it by the foot. The foot kicked, sending Hazel backward on the ice. She had not given him much time, but it had been enough for Vinnie to reach the head first. Like a field goal kicker at its best, he sent the head sailing across the lake. The sun's beams broke through the darkness. All around them, bodies combusted. Fires erupted where each body lay.

Vinnie heard Mary release one more blood-curdling scream. What he saw next was apocalyptic. A demon was being sucked back to Hell, taking with it large portions of what was once a human body. The only thing that remained was smoldering bones and burnt flesh.

After a few moments of astonishment, Vinnie heard, "Luke didn't make it."

Hazel stood over the man's body. A large portion of the man's throat was shredded.

"Fuck! Why is it always the good ones?" wept Franky. Hazel approached him and wrapped her arms around his shoulders.

Benjamin, however, did not walk over to Luke. Instead, he found Mary's remains. There, he dropped to his knees and started to cry.

Vinnie, too, teared up. The battle had gone as planned. Even though Vinnie was terrified that he would hurt Franky and leave the bitch intact, it worked. They knew she would come for him. The whole thing came down to timing. Benjamin was a smart guy, but if Vinnie didn't step up to the plate, they all would have been vampire food. The stress, lifting, was replaced by sorrow. A family he had come to care for was dead. Three people came into his life, however briefly. Now, they were now all gone. It wasn't fair.

*

Brandy and Josette trudged through the thigh-high snow to the front door of the Yorkey's Cottage. The sun was shining bright, but a small group of clouds were moving in from the west. Secretly, Brandy wished the cottage was locked, even though Josette has sworn she and Hazel had left it just as they found it. She didn't know why she had let Josette talk her into this bullshit. Though if it gave her some comfort, then maybe the trip was worth it.

Tod did not lie. The road had been plowed as well as the driveways, but no one was around to shovel the walk to the front door.

"Stop," said Brandy. She pointed to the edge of the lake. "Look at that."

On top of the deep snow was the remains of what Brandy could only figure was a broken-up pile of lumber. It appeared to be a fishing shack at one time, and its destruction concerned Brandy.

"Please, Brandy. We need to hurry. I don't want to get caught breaking into a stranger's home."

Brandy paused. "Ok, but I still don't like this."

With Brandy in the lead, they pushed their way forward until they reached the door. Checking the knob, they found the house still unlocked.

"Now, you just wait out here until I check this place out," said Brandy. She stuck her arm out like a crossing guard. "I will let you know when it's safe to come in."

"Oh, Brandy. I've been here before."

"Still, just humor me this once," said Brandy. She opened the door took a step inside. Groaning came from the back bedroom. Brandy turned to see if Josette had heard the agonized painful moans as well, but Josette had already pushed past her.

The women flew to the master bedroom. Neither was quite prepared for what they saw next.

Laying on the Yorkey's king-sized bed was Phillip. He laid naked on top of the covers, drenched in blood and sweat. From their first glance, both women could see he was unnaturally twisted. It was as if someone had tried to snap him in half. His legs and feet were laid nearly halfway to the man's back, making an almost perfect "L."

Josette ran to him and fell to her knees by his bedside, weeping.

Brandy had never been so frightened in all her life. It was not that she feared Phillip. Whatever had ever done this to him was evil to the core.

That's when they heard the sound of footsteps. Someone else was approaching from down the hall. Brandy ran to the door to see who it was. A sigh of relief left her lips when she saw Sam.

"I thought you two were up to something! I saw you come this way from town. What the hell are you doing back here? I thought Hazel told you to stay away," said Sam. Brandy stood in the doorway.

"We found him. We found Phillip," said Brandy on the brink of tears.

*

Just before the survivors from the lake reached town, Hazel pulled over her snowmobile. The others followed suit and, coming to a stop, stood and removed their helmets. In the middle of the road, they planned their way forward. Hazel wanted to make sure their story was straight: They went out to the lake to investigate the disappearance of this Dale guy and found the burnt bodies on the lake. It was that simple. And she wanted to make sure everyone was on the same page. The group took less than ten minutes to repeat their side of the story to Hazel, each following the script. Hazel felt confident that she could pull them all through this without getting too far into the truth.

"Ok, I think we have it down pretty well. Remember, don't talk to anyone unless asked. And then, answer the question as briefly as you possibly can, then clam up. Agreed?"

"Agreed," they all said in unison.

"You said that the demons were after me. That they wanted me dead," said Franky to Benjamin.

"That's what Ethel told Brandy, yes," replied Benjamin.

"Sorry, but I got to…"

He took the opportunity to relieve himself on the side of the road.

"So why isn't Phillip here?" asked Franky.

"I thought you said that this Mary woman was on her way to Parksville when Franky came to her?" asked Hazel. "Maybe he is just waiting for him in…"

"Parksville," said Vinnie, completing her sentence "Maybe he isn't on his way here. Maybe he is lying in wait up there," added Vinnie.

Hazel watched Franky pace back and forth in front of her. Finally, he stopped and turned to her.

"Mary was sent to kill me, but if Phillip is what you said he is, then maybe he had another target. Think about it. The two people he hated as much as me were Phillip and Josette. She was the one who could see his thoughts. She was the one he threw the champagne bottle at. She was the one he told to get the fuck out of his head."

"And Phillip?" questioned Hazel.

"Phillip? Well he was just as involved in killing Fritz as I was," replied Franky.

"It makes sense," said Benjamin, zipping his fly.

"What better way to get revenge than to make you kill the woman you love? That would be the cruelest thing he could think of."

Hazel came to the revelation that she would need to take this on herself.

"Look. Change of plans. I know this is a strange request, but I want all of you to go straight to Howard, pull your snowmobiles behind the restaurant, see if you can borrow his car, and get the hell out of town unseen. I know this sounds crazy, but if I know Jackson, he is already on his way, if not there already. If you want to help Josette and Brandy, you need to avoid detection."

"So, you're saying we should avoid a murder investigation?" questioned Vinnie.

"If you want to save the women, then yes," responded Hazel.

*

Ethel looked out the window at the rain. Back at Rebecca's store, she had made up her mind. If she was going to help the others, she needed help, his help. From the one entity that she feared the most, Baron Samedi. She had lied to Rebecca about why she wanted to return home. She knew Rebecca would forgive her once it was all over. After all, she was the one pushing for this to happen.

Ethel didn't know exactly how one called on Samedi, so she simply closed her eyes and spoke.

"Come to me; I need your aid."

She did not know if this was going to work, but it was worth a try.

Opening her eyes, she continued staring out into the pouring rain. She thought of Brandy. She thought of what life might be like without her. After losing so much, her husband and her child, the thoughts of losing her dearest friend was too much. Her eyes welled with tears and a sadness weighed on her chest. All the new people who had come into her life, Josette, Shawn, Phillip, and Benjamin, they had all taken a part in filling the void left in her life. Now she could only hope to see them all once again. Ethel was about to try again, to use some other plea to contact the only one with answers, when she saw a figure making its way down the street. It was a small boy.

CHAPTER XVI

LOVE AND DEATH

Sam had seen a lot of things in his life, but nothing could have ever prepared him for Phillip's broken body. *How can he bear the pain?* he thought. Brandy had gone into the bathroom and returned with a wet washcloth.

"He is burning up," she said. She patted his head with the washcloth.

"We have to call an ambulance."

Sam shook his head. "I don't think that would be a good idea. Don't forget, he is not always Phillip. Not anymore."

Josette had not moved from the side of his bed. She held his hand in hers. Josette sobbed. Phillip had tried to speak more than once, but nothing seemed to come out. He gasped in pain.

"What do we do?" asked Brandy.

"Sam, you're a doctor. What do we do?"

"I don't know. I mean, if he were at the hospital, we could..."

"We wait for the priest," demanded Josette. "That is his only hope. We need to get this demon out of him."

She took Phillip's hand and placed it on her belly.

"These are your two sons, Phillip. They need you to hold on."

"But we can't even get ahold of them. They are down in Phelton, for God's sake," said Brandy.

"I love Phillip as much as anyone, but I don't think we can wait here for them to come find us."

"It will be dark soon," added Sam. "If what we've learned is true, then as soon as the sun goes down, all bets are off. I say we leave him here, go back to his house, and try to contact the others. For all we know, they may be on their way now with Father Aron as we speak."

"I am not leaving him!" protested Josette. "I finally found him; I am not leaving."

"Josette, I think you need to listen to Sam. I think he is right. This is dangerous, and we are not equipped to deal with it right now. If his best hope is the priest, then let's find him and come back."

Sam could tell Brandy's pleas were landing on deaf ears. There would be no way of getting her out of this house unless they drug her by her feet. That's when he heard a sound coming from Phillip. He was trying to speak again.

"RRRRRRR…"

"What are you trying to say, Phillip?" begged Josette.

"RRRRRRRR…"

"Oh, Phillip," said Josette, placing her cheek on his hand.

"RRRRRRun," Phillip got out at last. "Run!" he repeated. just above a whisper. As he said this, a dark shadow came over the room. The small group of clouds they saw approaching from the west arrived.

"Kill me or run!" shouted Phillip, so loud it took them all by surprise. Suddenly, his back snapped back into place. Sam watched in horror as the man's eyes turned blood red.

"Let's get the fuck out of here," said Sam, grabbing Josette forcibly by the arm and pulling her to her feet.

Brandy instinctively grabbed Josette by the other arm, helped Sam drag her out of the room.

"There is no choice, my dear. We are leaving."

Sam looked back once he reached the bedroom doorway. Phillip's face had split open from forehead to chin.

"Holy Shit!" Sam exclaimed as he ran. Whatever was trying to come out was something he didn't want to see.

Down the hall and through the front door they fled, following the same path through the snow they had made going in. The women instinctively ran to the Cadillac, while Sam ran for the Jeep. Both vehicles were parked side by side and he wished they had followed him.

But wait! Maybe they were better off in the car. It

was new and wasn't as tore up as the Jeep. God knows the Jeep has seen better days, he thought. Abandoning the Jeep, he ran to the car and managed to hop in the back seat when Brandy hit the gas.

"Hold on!" she yelled.

The car leaped backwards a couple of yards, then Brandy hit the brakes. The car slid the rest of the way out of the drive and across the road, where it crashed into the snowbank left by Tod's snowplow.

Damn, thought Sam. *She is going to get us stuck sure as shit.*

Brandy threw the car into drive and hit the gas once more. Off they flew. Clearing the hill up to Michigan Avenue, Sam saw it. The creature busted out the bedroom window as they escaped. Landing on all fours, it looked up at them.

"Gun it, Brandy! Get us the fuck out of here!" screamed Sam.

That's when Brandy took a hard right on Michigan Avenue and gunned it. Sam could not see the creature at this point but was sure he had seen the direction they were heading and was in pursuit.

Any doubts about Brandy's driving were now gone. She handled the Cadillac like it was the last lap of the Daytona 500. She flew down Michigan Avenue at a speed Sam wouldn't have attempted on a clear summer's day.

In a matter of minutes, we'll reach Parksville, thought Sam. Without warning a blow came from Josette's side of the car. None of them saw the creature as it ran out from behind the

Brickman's old farmhouse. The blow sent the car spinning down the median like a child's top on a hardwood floor. It did not stop until it came to a hard landing in the drainage ditch that followed Michigan Avenue out of town. The back end of the car pointed towards the sky while the entire front end was buried in the snow. Sam was quick to check on the women. He could tell they were both shaken, but both seemed to be unharmed.

"I am so sorry, "cried Brandy. "I never saw him coming."

"No, it wasn't your fault," said Sam reassuringly. "Are you both ok?"

"Fine," said Josette.

"Me too," confirmed Brandy.

That's when they heard the heart-stopping sound of heavy footsteps crunching the deep snow near the road. Out of the back window, Sam could see nothing but open sky, but heard the creature's heavy breath bearing down on them. The first glimpse he got was of the wolf-like ears protruding over the ditch's edge. Next came the overly elongated drooling snout. Snarling, it exposed enormous rows of long, canine-like teeth. The women, both horrified by the sight, screamed. Sam closed his eyes and braced for the creature's inevitable charge; however, it did not come. Instead, Sam looked up to see the beast tipping its head to the sky, as if it were looking for something in the clouds. The creature ran away.

Everyone stayed where they were, listening, waiting. After a few minutes, the reason for his departure became abundantly clear. The sun shone brightly down on them, the small group of clouds had moved on, and somewhere close by, they all knew Phillip was laying somewhere in the dark. He was in pain once more.

*

Ethel found herself stripped naked as Baron Samedi painted her body with symbols. There were multiple snakes, skulls, rivers, mountains, stars, and quantities of shapes and circling lines, all painted in white, black, and red. From the moment he had walked into the small, modest house, the Baron had taken a dominating tone. She knew she had no choice but to do as he commanded. She had asked for his help. If that meant standing naked in the middle of Rebecca's living room while the large man, painted as a living skeleton, barked orders, then so be it. If it meant saving her friends, then she would do as he asked.

"You will pay a price for what you ask," said the Baron. His voice was extremely deep.

"You cannot ask the spirits to suffer while you do not. You will take on their pain as they impose your will."

"I don't care. I will do what I need to do."

The Baron laughed, deep and full.

"You say that now, woman. We will see. Yes, we will see."

He drew a small bottle from his coat pocket.

"Drink this. It will bring the spirts to you. For a short time, you will have the gift of sight. You will see nothing of this world, only the world the spirits see. Remember, you can manipulate but not command them. Their faith in you must be strong. In their world, you will find the demon. There he cannot hide. If you live through this, you will earn the loyalty of the dead and become the queen they desire. But if you fail, a new queen they must choose."

"Glad you're so optimistic about my chances," said the nervous Ethel.

Again, came the deep, unnerving laugh.

"If I were a betting man, woman, I would not put a plug nickel on you," he said, still laughing. "Let's see how long you will survive."

Ethel took the small bottle and drank it as requested. Her head started to spin, and she felt like she was dropping down a deep, dark hole. She looked down at all the shapes and figures drawn upon her body. She could not only see them but felt them move over her body. It was the snakes that kept her attention. They seemed to slither across her small frame.

*

"What the fuck, Vinnie! You're driving like an old lady," said Franky from the back seat of Howard's Chevy Impala. "It will be dark in a couple of minutes, and we got another twenty miles for Christ's sake."

It was Benjamin, who was riding shotgun, who responded.

"Hold on, Franky. I know that we're all in a hurry to get to Brandy and Josette, but he is doing the best he can. These roads might be plowed, but they are slick as hell."

"I about lost it a couple times, already. We are not going to help them if we don't get there," added Vinnie, keeping his eyes on the road.

"I'm sorry," said Franky. He fell back into the seat. "I'm afraid if we don't get there soon, it will be too late."

"Better slower than in a ditch," said Benjamin.

"Yea, I know, I know," said Franky. He slapped the back seat and growled.

"FUCK!"

"Any idea how we kill this one? I mean, the priest is gone, and…" started Benjamin.

"I don't know. I guess we will need to figure that out when we get there," snapped Franky. "If we ever get there."

Franky knew this last remark was unwarranted and said it anyway. He was not angry at Vinnie, or Benjamin for that matter. He was growing increasingly anxious. It was true that they had no idea how to fight this thing. At least with Mary they had a plan. Even though it fell apart at the worst moment, it was a plan. When Franky saw the darkness coming out of the hole, he realized the full extent of powers the demon held sway over. He knew that, even if they faced the beast with all their guns, knives, and axes, God only knew the powers it would unleash to strike them all down.

"What about luring the bastard into some place, locking him in, and burning the place down?" offered Vinnie.

"Does that sound familiar to you, Franky," asked Benjamin.

"That's the same fucking plan we had with Banthom," said Franky.

"Well, it worked the first time. We did eventual light the fucker up," responded Benjamin.

Deep down, Franky knew this idea was nothing more than something to hold onto. They did not have the gas nor a location to trap him in. And there was nothing ensuring the damn thing would die in the flames anyway. Still, it was something.

"True," said Franky, "I guess it's something to build on."

*

Phillip suffered in excruciating pain, laying naked on the barn floor of the Brickman's Farm. His legs were disjointed at the hips and his arms disjointed at the shoulders. When the creature had emerged this time, he fled with an urgency that Phillip had not felt in him before. While the creature kept him aware, in its rush to get moving, it let Phillip know more than what it had intended. Phillip now knew that the beast that possessed Mary was back in Hell. He also knew the beast that controlled his body was now in fear of those that were capable of her demise.

These thoughts gave him some comfort, but only for a moment. The beast seemed to read his thoughts and emotions, the same as Phillip had read his. So, the beast, as he lumbered down the back field towards Parksville, let Phillip know his true intentions. He was going to make sure that Phillip saw the demise of his true love. He would watch helplessly as the creature tore Josette apart, making him watch as the beast ripped his unborn sons from her mutilated body.

Fear, the breath of which Phillip had never felt in his many adventures, engulfed him. In human form, he knew he would have collapsed to the floor, unable to deal with the reality of what was happening. In the creature's grasp, he could do nothing but watch as they rushed across barren, snow-covered corn fields.

*

By the time they had reached Phillip and Franky's house, Sam, Josette, and Brandy were exhausted. Sam knew that Josette's life was now in danger. She looked pale and her breathing was labored. The streets were empty as they made their way back into town. There were no kind strangers offering assistance, or random policemen patrolling to offer aid. They had to walk the entire way, and that may have been too much for the girl.

A woman in her condition didn't need to be anywhere but in bed, thought Sam, covering Josette with the blanket laid out on the back of the couch.

"Brandy, can you check the phones? We need an ambulance."

"Sure thing," said Brandy, walking into the kitchen. "She has preeclampsia."

"And she still agreed to partake in this little adventure?" questioned Sam, somewhat irritated.

"Yes. If you had a chance to save your wife, would you?" said a weakened Josette looking up at him.

Sam thought of Linda and what lengths he would go to.

"Yes, I guess I would. But you can do no more, my dear. Your life, and those of your two sons, now depend on you getting rest."

"Phones are still down," came Brandy's voice from the kitchen.

"Damn," said Sam. "We have got to get her to the hospital."

Light pirouetted across the far wall of the living room. Sam rushed to the large picture window to see a car pull into the driveway. From the back of the car, he saw Franky emerge and run towards the house. He was followed in short order by Benjamin.

"They are here!" yelled Sam to the others.

Brandy ran to the front door and swung it open. Walking over to meet them, Sam could see Franky was already on the front steps of the porch. Benjamin was close behind. Looking past them, Sam saw Vinnie bending over to retrieve something from the back seat.

Sam was just about to say his welcomes when he saw it. A large, dark figure ran out of the darkness. Vinnie stood holding the jacket he had just retrieved when the creature vaulted. Its gaping jaws landed squarely on the back of Vinnie's skull. Sam knew Vinnie had never seen it coming.

"Vinnie! My God, help Vinnie!" yelled Sam. It was too late. Vinnie's skull cracked. Sam could hear Vinnie's screaming from the doorway. The creature shook the man as if he were playing with a stuffed toy. By the time Franky and Benjamin fired their weapons, the creature had run away, leaving Vinnie's lifeless body bent and broken on the curb.

"Get your asses in here!" ordered Sam.

The two men stopped firing and looked at each other. With a nod, they made a mad dash for the door. Brandy slammed it behind them. The lock clicked.

"Shit!" shouted Benjamin. "I never even saw the fucking thing coming!"

Sam saw Josette remove her blanket and get up.

"Franky, Benjamin," she said weakly. Just as she was walking over to greet them the beast came crashed through the picture window. It landed on the living room floor, sending Josette flying backwards. The beast stood, looking around assessing his situation, then lunged toward Josette.

*

Since the moment she drank the potion, her home had become a conclave of lost spirits. They gathered around in multitudes. They appeared to be from every time period since the beginning of New Orleans itself. There were men, women, children, rich and slave. The Baron had guided her this far, but now, it was up to her. He had told her they would know her intentions. They only waited for her word. Still, Ethel was unsure.

"You can do this, momma," she heard a soft voice say. Looking down, she saw a little girl hanging onto her bare leg. It was her daughter, Marie. A tear ran down Ethel's cheek. She had always felt her presence and knew she was close at hand. Even Josette had pointed it out in the trailer in Tampa.

"You have the most beautiful spirit standing next to you," Josette had said to her that day. And it was true. She was still so beautiful.

"We will go to the new world together someday," spoke Marie's spirit. "For now, you must be strong. Tell them, tell them."

Ethel stared down at her, crying.

"Now, mommy. They must go now," the child urged.

"Go, my children," Ethel said at last with all the confidence she could muster. The house cleared and the spirts where gone, except for Marie, who stayed behind.

*

The barrage of gunfire within the house was not enough to keep the creature from landing directly on Josette. It raised its right claw for the fatal blow when the house filled with the spirits of the dead. Their worn and tattered bodies gathered around them. While the others looked confused at the creature's pause, Josette understood his hesitation immediately. She watched as they circled around him.

The creature let out a terrifying growl and tried unsuccessfully to throw them out of his way. Josette took advantage of the distraction and started to pull herself backwards across the floor. The creature saw her retreat and leapt towards her again, but the most incredible thing happened next. All the lights in the house went suddenly went out followed by the streetlights shining through the window. It was completely dark, except for a small glow illuminating in the middle of the room. The small speck of light grew. Josette watched as the spirits merged. One by one, they walked into the light, making it grow ever brighter.

*

Ethel screamed in pain as her body hovered off the floor with her arms spread wide. She was now consumed in the light streaming from her. The pain was beyond comparison. She could feel the spirits' inhumane suffering as their life forces joined. She could hear their tortured souls crying out.

"I can endure no more!" she screamed.

"But you must, woman. This is not a game. You are facing the forces of evil," laughed the Baron. "You knew there would be a price to pay. Stop now and you will fail. You and your friends will die."

Ethel searched for the comfort of her daughter's loving eyes, but she, too, was gone.

"The purer the spirit, the brighter the light," laughed the Baron.

*

Even though Brandy could not see the spirits themselves, she could clearly see the light growing in the middle of the room. Within seconds, the room was as bright as daylight. She didn't know why, but somehow, she felt Ethel's presence in the room. The beast had stopped attacking Josette. It backed away from the light, but the light was too quick. It overtook the beast. Its shrieks almost brought Brandy to her knees. The creature's head shrunk, and its fur fell off in clumps. What fell to the floor immediately evaporated.

"The sun! The light is having the same effect as the sun!" exclaimed Franky.

"Give me that!" said Brandy, grabbing the shotgun from Franky.

Phillip's face started to appear, first his nose and chin. Soon, it was Phillip's head atop the creature's shrinking torso.

Brandy lifted the gun. She had Phillip in her view.

"He has to die by the hand of someone who loves him!" she shouted.

"No! "screamed Josette. "Phillip! My God! Its Phillip!"

Brandy's finger paused on the trigger. Phillip looked over at her, his bright, blue, loving eyes begging her. Brandy tried with all her might, but she couldn't do it. The light started, at last, to fade.

A gunshot rang out. She turned to see Franky holding a pistol at the end of his outstretched hand. The house shook. A large, black cloud of smoke and flames swirled like a miniature tornado around the still-transforming Phillip. He screamed in pain, then the cloud was sucked downward through the floor. As the smoke cleared, Brandy saw that the creature was completely gone. In middle of the black, scorched wood lay the dead body of Phillip Parker. In the center of his forehead was the mark made by Franky's bullet.

"Oh my God! No, no!" screamed Josette. She attempted to get up and walk towards Phillip, but she collapsed and fell unconscious on the floor next to him.

*

Just as the bullet ripped through Phillip's head, Ethel hit the floor. She landed with a loud thud.

"Tell me, woman. What is it you see?" demanded the Baron.

Ethel opened her eyes. What she saw was not

what she'd expected. She was not back in Rebecca's modest home, but in Phillip Parker's house. She could see his dead body lying on the floor and Josette lying next to him. Sam and Brandy were rushing to her aid.

"I see the house. I see the dead body of my friend Phillip Parker," replied Ethel.

"You are stuck between worlds, the living and the dead. Your gift of sight will not last long. Is the creature dead?"

Ethel saw Franky, who stood in the same potion he was in when shooting Phillip. Benjamin walked over to him. Slowly, he lowered the man's arm and embraced Franky. Franky's eyes were red and swollen, tears flooding down his cheeks.

"No more, Franky. Your days of fighting these battles are over. You have suffered more than any man should."

"Yes," said Ethel, bawling as she sat up. "The spirits, they are all leaving."

"You survived this time, woman; they have done all you asked. I guess they did choose wisely," said the Baron, chuckling. "Who knew?"

"Are they safe now?" asked Ethel. Even though she could not see anything other than Phillip's house, she still felt the Baron's presence.

"For now, yes. But you and your nasty little group of friends have made some powerful enemies. I do not take sides in these battles. Yes, you won this one, but the war will still rage on."

Ethel's attention now moved to Brandy. She

sat on the floor next to Josette, patting her hand. She hadn't saved them all but, at least Brandy, Benjamin, and Franky were alive.

"What about Josette? Will she live? Will her kids survive?" Ethel asked, choking on her tears.

"You ask me questions I do not know the answer to, nor do I care," responded the Baron.

Ethel could feel his presence leave her, Phillip's house started to fade, and exhaustion overtake her. She closed her eyes and felt herself fall into a deep sleep.

AFTERWORD

Franky was soaked but didn't care. It was not the first time, nor would it be the last. If there was one thing he knew for sure, bath time came with its challenges. It had been three years since Phillip died, and it was the first time that any of the survivors felt like celebrating the holidays together. It just did not seem right without Phillip and Josette.

They had managed to keep the brain-dead Josette alive for an additional three weeks. Her boys were preemies and it was kind of touch-and-go for a while. But both boys were now healthy young boys, with a propensity to drown people during their baths.

Josette had taken care of everything down to the letter. The day after she passed, her attorney Brice Wentworth knocked at Franky's door. He gave Franky the mounds of paperwork Josette had drawn up in case she and Phillip had both passed. In it was clear instructions that Franky would be the Godfather of the first born, who was to be named Phillip. Benjamin would be the Godfather of the second, who would be named Kip. They would share joint custody with the boys, residing in the States.

This was all conditioned upon their acceptance of this responsibility, of course. If not, the boys would return to London and reside with Josette's mother. The men agreed to care for the boys, understanding that, when they got older, they would spend their summers in Ireland and the rest of their time with Franky. She made Benjamin the guardian of her estate, making sure that all her money would go to their sons.

"Stop that, boys," said Franky. Kip and Phillip splashed each other and giggled.

In some ways, he thought that Josette had gotten it wrong. The boys were not identical and Phillip was the shorter brunet. He looked so much like Josette that it sometimes took Franky's breath away. The similarities stretched beyond just looks. He often caught Phillip sitting and carrying on full conversations when no one else was in the room, almost like someone was playing with him who only he could see. Kip, on the other hand, was a tall blond. From the moment he was born, he seemed to study the world around him. Most of the time, he was quiet and focused hard on any project set before him.

So much like his dad, Franky thought.

And then, of course, there was little Vinnie. After everything was said and done, it was the loss of loved ones that brought Hazel and Franky even closer together. They were married just one year prior, and the adoption of Vinnie was fairly painless. Vinnie Lake was now officially his son, and he loved him with all his heart. Just last month he found out there was another Lake on the way. Their little family was growing by leaps and bounds. Hazel was pregnant again, only this time with a girl. Martha would be her name.

A Martha Lake, after all these years. The thought made Franky simultaneously joyful and melancholy.

"Ok, boys! Time to get out! You are getting water on Aunt Ethel's floor and she will have my hide,"

Franky snatched the boys up one by one out of the tub and dried them off with the infamous towel monster.

Ethel and Brandy had just moved into this house in the Garden District. Since Ethel could not come to them, they would celebrate the holidays in New Orleans. Both women were still in amazing health for their age, and neither one was letting any grass grow under their feet.

"Franky, Benjamin's here, and it looks like he has a ton of shit to bring in," came Hazel's voice from down the stairs.

Figures thought Franky. *We don't have enough room at home now for the crap he buys them.* The house in Parksville was sold and they moved into Hazel's place over a year ago. *By the looks of things, a bigger house may be in order.*

Franky patted drying little backs, butts, and feet, and his thoughts turned to Benjamin. *I hope he never drags you kids into his hunt for the last book.* While Franky had Hazel, and Brandy had Ethel, Benjamin did not have that one person he needed to help him deal with his loss. Mary had meant more to Benjamin than he had ever let on.

Benjamin dealt with his pain by throwing himself into research. Franky knew he was determined to find the last book and return it to the Church. Franky could only hope he would give up on this endeavor and enjoy his life. It would take some time.

"Sam, Linda, and the girls are on their way from the airport!" Hazel called up the stairs.

The End

Printed in the United States
By Bookmasters